The Riviera Conspiracy

By

Jill St. Anne

ISBN: 1-4033-2673-8 (e-book)
ISBN: 1-40332-674-6 (Paperback)
ISBN: 1-4033-2675-4 (Dustjacket)

Library of Congress Control Number: 2002091818

This book is printed on acid free paper.

Printed in the United States of America
Bloomington, IN

1st Books - rev. 07/24/02

Prologue

San Francisco, California
Labor Day Weekend

The massive steel hull of the ship shook violently, throwing Christina to her knees. Her face began to sweat from the blazing heat. Salty perspiration dripped into her eyes. Another blast launched her head first onto the metal deck. The fire was coming closer.

She shot up from bed and opened her eyes. Thank God it was only a nightmare. The tremor however was real; another aftershock from last week's earthquake. Her bed had stopped shaking, but she was still rattled from her reoccurring dream. She knew that the anti-ballistic missile chip was back where it belonged, but the fear that it almost fell into the wrong hands continued to grip her.

She climbed out of bed and scanned her room. Perfume bottles, artistically arranged on her dresser after the Richter Scale hit 6.5 a week ago, fell to the floor for the second time in six days. A few pictures tilted crookedly on the wall. Luckily, there appeared to be no serious damage.

She limped into the bathroom and splashed cold water onto her face. A bruised and battered portrait stared back at her in the mirror. The explosion last week had left her looking like hell. The deep cuts and scratches on her nose and cheekbones had turned into crusty purple scabs. Her normally piercing green eyes looked dull and lifeless. The painful burns on her slender hands had developed into swollen, tender blisters.

Her leg still ached, but she knew she would heal fast. At least she was safe. It was finally over.

After splashing more water on her face, she stepped back from the mirror and cracked the faintest smile. Or was it just beginning?

Chapter One

Three and one half months earlier

"NPR newstime is 5:29 a.m. Please stay tuned for local traffic and weather." The radio intrusively came to life.

Christina Caldwell reluctantly rolled over and whacked her alarm to silence it. Weather, she thought, a weather report was hardly necessary. The sound of the deep, comforting foghorn was enough to confirm that it would be another cold, damp, summer morning. She eased out of her heavenly bed and stumbled in the dark over to her closet.

From a heap of clothes, she pulled a pink turtleneck, a gray sweatshirt and a pair of black, spandex leggings. Even though it was mid-June, it was San Francisco, and the weather was almost never balmy. She guessed that it was still less than 50 degrees outside and probably misty. After pulling her shoulder length, strawberry blonde hair back into a thick ponytail, she was ready to hit the path from her Marina District condo to the Golden Gate Bridge and back.

The hypnotic sounds of the squawking sea gulls and the crashing waves enabled her to think clearly; the cold water sprayed against her face, arousing her senses and kicking her brain into gear. She breathed hard and deep, filling her lungs with the salty sea air. The final stretch back to her condo was coming up. If she pushed herself she would finish the six-mile loop in less than 35 minutes.

Each run reminded Christina how much she loved living here. She had moved to San Francisco from Los Angeles several years ago after attending a political fundraiser in San Francisco for Senator Richard Cartwright, a promising presidential candidate. The smog-free air and the cool weather lured her from L.A. to the Bay Area, just as the high powered job offer at the now-defunct, investment banking powerhouse of Drexel

Burnham Lambert had enticed her into moving to Los Angeles after business school back East.

After a ten minute cool-down walk to her condo and a hot shower, she emerged refreshed and energized. As she was wiping the steam off the mirror above the sink, she heard her doorbell ring. She put on her oval, titanium framed eyeglasses and peered around the open bathroom door. Rosa, her loyal and tireless housekeeper, had just walked into the front hallway.

"Christina—" Rosa's eyes opened wider as she glanced into the kitchen and then into her bedroom, "what happened here? A tornado touch down in the Marina District?"

"I know," Christina apologized, "it looks like an obstacle course, but I haven't had more than two seconds to deal with this all week."

Rosa picked up some wet towels off the floor. "You leave the mess to me. You're a busy young lady. If you spend all your time cleaning house, I have no job."

"I don't know what I'd do without you, Rosa. I'd probably be buried in here alive if you didn't dig me out once a week." Christina got down on her hands and knees and began crawling around the floor. "Have you seen my black pumps?"

"I tripped over them in the hallway." Rosa snapped a towel in Christina's direction. "Now, go dry your hair!"

"I don't have time!" Christina grabbed her hard leather briefcase, slipped into her shoes, and ran out the door. "Bye, Rosa!"

"Never time," Rosa said, shaking her head. "Always rush, rush."

Christina raced down the stairs to the garage. The fog was starting to burn away, so she lowered the convertible top on her Saab. She let the wind dry her hair as she drove the 20 minutes to her Montgomery Street office in the Financial District. She parked her car underground and stopped at the espresso bar where she ordered two nonfat lattes and two blueberry muffins.

Just before 8:00, Christina pushed through the heavy, mahogany doors and strode across the thick Persian carpets in the foyer of her office: the West Coast branch of a powerful New York investment bank. A client once joked that the last time he'd seen so many Oriental carpets there'd been a 'Going out of Business Sale' painted out front. Christina could live with the firm's pretentious-is-best decor, but she always felt a bit guilty walking into the reception area. The rain forest destruction required to panel the walls was enough to cause a full scale Greenpeace rally.

Walking toward her office, she smiled and said "good morning" to Julie, the twenty-year-old receptionist who sat behind a massive Louis IVX desk. Above her, English bronze letters spelled out KINGSTONE & COMPANY.

"The morning won't be good for long," Julie said, not looking up from her Glamour magazine. "Jacobs has been calling non-stop for you. I transferred him through to Margie."

Christina felt her muscles tighten. She never looked forward to calls from Andrew Jacobs, her supervisor in New York. He was probably harassing her about the status of the Symex financing. Unfortunately, she still hadn't secured Kingstone as the primary underwriter. At least not yet.

She clicked in her high heels down the long, marble corridor, otherwise known as the 'hall of fame', to the corporate finance division. Polished brass plaques, commemorating the billions of dollars raised by Kingstone for their clients, hung proudly on the walls.

"Hi Margie." She set the steaming latte and the gooey blueberry muffin on her assistant's desk. "I heard Jacobs has been hunting me down." Christina bought Margie breakfast every morning. It was the least she could do for the invaluable support Margie provided. She organized files, stayed late on nights before new client presentations and always went the extra mile when needed.

"Sounds like he's on the war path." Margie took the plastic cap off the latte and sipped some foam. "He said the Symex deal's gonna blow up in our face if we don't get the docs from Stinson today!"

"Great," she said sarcastically. "Ralph hasn't been returning my phone calls. Looks like I'll have to drive over to his office and hound him."

"I'm not worried," Margie wiped some white foam from her mouth. "You always manage to bring in the biz." She lifted a stack of paper from her desk and handed it to Christina. The ream of paper contained at least one hundred prospective client names, complete with their direct lines and a brief summary about each of the companies. "Sorry to have to do this to you first thing in the morning, but these are hot off the modem from New York."

"They're asking for a miracle. Right?" Christina picked up the heavy pile and started reading the attached memo. "What!? This is impossible!"

"Moses parted the Red Sea, didn't he?" Margie said.

"Very funny." Christina's bright and cheery mood suddenly transformed into one of panic. "How am I going to set up meetings with half of these companies by the end of the month?"

She headed into her office. Before crossing the threshold behind her, Margie shouted, "Brandy confirmed dinner tonight."

Christina turned around. "When you get a chance, will you please call Postrio and see when you can get us in? I better tell Susan that Brandy's free tonight." She had no time to play social secretary this morning, but Brandy Jensen was in a position to refer her employee's 401(k) program to Kingstone.

Christina turned on her heel, and walked briskly over to the office of Susan Anders, her best friend and the firm's high-technology analyst. They had been pals since their mid-twenties, working their way up through the ranks of various investment firms and sharing their personal trials and tribulations along the way.

Susan had long, naturally curly brown hair, a heart-shaped, pretty face and large, amber eyes. She had her African-American mother to thank for her beautiful skin: smooth and the color of light cocoa. Her lips seemed to stay a perfect shade of red, regardless of whether she was wearing lipstick or not. Actually, neither Susan nor Christina wore much make-up at all. They simply didn't have the time to worry about it.

Susan, of course, was on the phone and probably talking to a CEO or CFO of one of the hundreds of companies she followed. As was her habit, she was twisting her hair around a pencil when Christina entered her office. She held up her index finger and motioned for Christina to sit down amidst the stacks of prospectuses and research reports that were piled on the chair opposite her desk.

While Susan was talking, Christina sipped her coffee and began flipping through the pages of small companies that were potential candidates for another IPO or a private placement while simultaneously watching the Bloomberg monitor that sat on the side of Susan's desk. She couldn't afford to waste one minute waiting for Susan to get off the phone.

A familiar Nasdaq symbol flashed on the colored screen. "Yes!" Christina shook her clenched fists. "Comtech is up another two points today!"

Susan smiled at her from behind her cluttered desk and gave her a 'thumbs up'. They had taken that company public last June, and since then the stock had tripled. It was time to sell. Christina reached for the second phone on Susan's desk and punched the number to her favorite trader.

"Jack Murphy!" he barked.

"Jack—it's Christina. What are Comtech warrants going for today?"

"Good morning to you too, Christina," he said sarcastically. "I'm fine. How are you?"

"Sorry, Jack. I'm a little frenzied. Anyway, our hold back period will be over Friday and I want to unload my entire position."

Christina was referring to the underwriter warrants the firm gave her as a bonus for completing the deal under a time crunch that crippled everyone else on the team.

"23 and a quarter by 23 and three quarters," Jack rattled off.

"Great," Christina said, "put a sell order in at the market for Friday." She would have an extra hundred grand in her bank account by the end of the week.

"Done," he said. "Now, how 'bout givin' me a call when you're not ready to pull your hair out."

"Sure, maybe sometime next week. And thanks, Jack. I'll talk to you soon." Unfortunately, Jack wasn't quite her type. His idea of a fun time was sitting around on Saturdays and Sundays, watching whatever sporting event was on the tube. Christina would rather hop on her mountain bike and ride the dirt trails out to the ocean. She preferred to keep their relationship entirely professional.

"Finally!" Susan slammed down the phone. "Hi, Christina! What's up?"

"Well besides Comtech, I've got a small problem. If I don't get Ralph Stinson from Symex to sign on the dotted line today, our private placement will crater, along with my bonus."

Susan's concerned face looked up from one of her three computer screens. "Symex—the defense contractor." She frowned and put down her pen. "Bombs; missiles; how and *why* would we be involved with them?"

"Symex is spinning off a new division that manufactures microprocessors. I'm trying to get us to finance the new company."

"That sounds easy enough, but won't we need a special government clearance rating to get anywhere near them?"

"No—that's precisely the point. The new company will have nothing to do with the missile division."

"That's a relief." Susan pulled her hair into a bun on the top of her head and secured it with a pencil. A small row of silver rings, pierced to the cartilage above her turquoise studded earlobes, was now visible. "The liability on those defense deals usually outweighs the benefits."

Susan leaned forward onto her elbows and whispered. "So—what's this new chip they're making?"

"Sorry," Christina shook her head. "I signed a confidentiality agreement. But as soon as we iron out the details, you'll be the first to know."

"I better be." Christina stood up and started to walk to the door.

"Hey wait!" Susan shouted after her. "Can't you give me any details?"

Christina turned around. "Not yet, but from what I know so far, this new chip will rock the Valley."

Christina suddenly stopped herself from leaving Susan's office. "Shoot! I forgot! Brandy's free for dinner tonight and she wants you to join us."

"Thanks, but no thanks. I've been here since the crack of dawn crunching numbers, and I'm already exhausted." She closed her eyes and began rubbing her temples. "Sometimes I think I want to transfer over to client development."

"Not a good idea." Christina held up the pile of paper that she'd received that morning. "In addition to all these cold calls I have to make, which will of course *easily* result in face-to-face meetings, New York just pushed another $10 million quota down my throat. Believe me, the pressure where I sit is just as intense."

Susan played an imaginary violin.

Christina sat back down in front of Susan's desk and put her stack of papers down. "This dinner is really important," Christina pleaded. "I promise we won't talk business the entire night."

"Sorry, Christina, I wasn't planning on seeing clients today or going out after work." Susan kicked her leg up from behind the desk to reveal a rolled up khaki pant cuff and a hiking boot. "See, you look like a super model in that snazzy, pimento colored suit, and I'm dressed to lead an outward bound journey."

"Don't sweat it," Christina said. "You always look great—even after a week of camping with no running water!"

"Thanks, but I'm still in no mood to go out tonight."

"C'mon Susan." Christina begged. "The three of us have been trying to get together for months. It's a small miracle that our schedules are clear on the same night."

Just as Christina was ready to go for the close, Margie poked her head into the office. "Nine o'clock. That's the best I could do."

"Well?" Christina looked over to Susan.

Susan leaned over her desk and set her chin on her hand. "What restaurant?"

"Postrio."

Susan threw her hands in the air. "I'll do it for your sake." She called Brandy on the speakerphone.

"Brandy Jensen," answered a low, raspy voice.

"Hi Brandy. It's Susan and Christina, your two dates for tonight."

"Oh hi!" Recognizing them, her voice happily went up two octaves. "You got my message?

"Just a few minutes ago," Christina said, "and we have everything set up. Bix for drinks at 7:30, then dinner at Postrio."

"Great!" Brandy said, "I love Postrio. How did we get in on such short notice?"

"I left that to Christina," Susan said, "our resident A-list socialite."

Christina shook her head. "Don't give me too much credit. I couldn't get us in until nine."

"Perfect," Brandy said, "more time to catch up at Bix. I'll meet you there, and please make sure a double martini's waiting for me. My weekend was the worst! I'll tell you about it tonight."

"Great, we'll see you then."

Christina glanced down at her plastic, sport watch that she'd forgotten to take off after her run. "8:30!" she yelped. "I need to get my ass over to Stinson's office. Meet in my office at seven."

Chapter Two

By the end of the day, Susan's eyes burned from staring at her computer screen for the past twelve hours. She shut off her monitor and buzzed Christina. No answer. She decided to head over to her office anyway. After a hard day, Susan enjoyed relaxing in Christina's office, which had a spectacular view of Alcatraz Island.

She sat down in a comfortable, leather club chair, played one of her favorite CDs and popped the cork on a split of Veuve Clicquot she found in the stash that Christina kept in her bar fridge. She poured the bubbly champagne into a crystal champagne flute and watched sailboats glide across the Bay at dusk. The sensation of the effervescent liquid hitting her cheeks refreshed her skin and brought her back to life.

On the cherry wood counter, above the refrigerator, stood a silver framed picture of herself and Christina that was taken at a recent party on a client's yacht. She smiled as she remembered what a fantastic time they'd had that afternoon. In the picture, Christina looked tan and fit. Her green eyes sparkled like emeralds, and her blonde hair glistened in the sun. In addition to Christina looking carefree and happy, this was one particular photo Susan liked of herself. The camera captured her long, brown curly hair whipping in the wind. One hand held a bottle of Corona and her other arm was wrapped around the dark haired, hunky captain with the Pepsodent smile.

With her feet propped on the windowsill, she closed her weary eyes and thought that she could get used to this: a nice office, making sales calls by day and entertaining clients by night. On the other hand, she thought, she was in no mood for Brandy tonight. Susan realized that all the glitz and glamour, hand holding, and wining and dining that Christina endured would start to take its toll after a while. Christina was out almost every night with clients. No wonder she never dated. Susan also knew that there was no way she could deal with the weekly sales meetings, the relentless pressure to bring in more business, and the constant fear of being out of a job if she fell short on the amount of money she added to the firm's bottom line.

After pondering the differences between their jobs, the more comfortable she felt with hard facts and numbers, a cluttered office, and the faith the firm's clients placed on her to give accurate advice.

Her job, however, was not without its perils. Susan knew that her own career was on the line every time she offered her professional opinion. Her 'buy,' 'sell,' and 'hold' recommendations often caused giant gyrations in a company's stock price. One inaccurate 'sell' could cut a small company's market cap in half; an overzealous 'buy' could catapult a stock price to a new high, pushing the price-to-earnings ratio into a dangerous, overvalued range. If that wasn't enough pressure, there was always the individual investor to worry about. No one is right 100% of the time, and it was not uncommon for a stock price to go down the day after an analyst recommended it.

A loud rapping at the door and the sound of a man's voice calling Christina's name interrupted her thoughts. Startled, Susan turned around to face a man in his mid-forties. His mousy brown hair drooped lifelessly around his pasty face. He wore thick glasses surrounded by black, plastic frames and a wrinkled white shirt with a pair of brown polyester pants. At first glance she thought that something was wrong with Christina's computer and he was here to fix it.

"You're not Christina." He pushed up his glasses.

"No, I'm Susan." She stood up to shake his hand. "May I help you with anything?"

He didn't touch her extended hand. "Yeah. Make sure she gets this." He threw a large, manila envelope on Christina's desk and left without saying another word.

"Nice meeting you also," she mumbled.

11

Susan's first instinct was suspicion. She had no idea whom that man had been. For all she knew, he could've just dropped a letter bomb on the desk. The horrifying memory of the 101 California Street massacre was still vivid. She pinched the corner of envelope and held it to the overhead, fluorescent light. She saw the outline of a letter sized document and felt ridiculous for suspecting a mail bomb.

"Hi Susan." Christina had just entered her office and plopped her briefcase on the sofa. "Great Salsa music."

"Oh, hi Christina. And by the way, it's Samba. I can't believe you don't know the difference."

Christina poured herself a glass of champagne. She noticed the large envelope Susan was holding. "What's that?"

Susan handed it to Christina. "A guy who looked like a computer repair man just dropped this off for you."

"That must have been Ralph Stinson." Christina smiled and opened the envelope. "And this is our signed Letter of Intent and the corresponding documents." She pulled the document out and held it up victoriously in front of Susan. "Believe me, he's no computer repair man." She laughed as she thought of Ralph. "He's an MIT grad, an ex weapon's specialist for the Army and one of the top engineers at Symex Corporation."

"O.K., I'm impressed, but I have to tell you—he really gave me the creeps. I nearly called office security."

"Don't be ridiculous." Christina walked over to Margie's office in the next room, placed the file on her desk and wrote her a note asking her to make a copy of the entire file and lock the original in her credenza. "Ralph is harmless, but he does resemble the quintessential mad scientist. You should have seen his office. What a mess! Since he never showed for our appointment, I had to clear a space on his desk to place our contract. I'm shocked he actually noticed it. And even more shocked that he signed it!"

Christina finished her glass of champagne and punched the speed dial button to the New York office. She left a message for Jacobs that she had the deal signed, sealed and delivered.

"Let's get outta here." Susan heaved a huge leather bag over her shoulder.

"What's with the backpack?" Christina asked.

"Backpack! Christina, you're so out of it! This happens to be the latest trend handbags. Anyway, I wouldn't talk. You live out of that beat up briefcase of yours."

"Touché."

Chapter Three

Bix, located on a dark, obscure alley in the Financial District, was one of Christina's favorite spots to grab a drink and listen to jazz. The two-story restaurant gave them a sense of stepping into a 1930's supper club. Men and women attired in business clothing lined the long, polished mahogany bar. They gracefully sipped their drinks while exchanging empty pleasantries.

The ladies found a small table and flagged down a waiter. Christina ordered a straight-up martini for Brandy, a Cosmopolitan for herself and a beer for Susan. As the waiter turned away, Brandy burst into the restaurant. She was a vivacious real estate agent who had started her own firm five years ago, specializing in the sale of multi-million dollar homes. She had frosted blond hair and long red fingernails. She usually wore oversized sunglasses propped on her head, expensive costume earnings and a serious amount of makeup. The minute she walked in, heads turned. Despite her somewhat crass personality, she possessed a magnetic presence and loved the attention she received.

"Hi Christina, Hi Susan!" she yelled from across the room. "I hope my martini is waiting. Traffic was a bitch!"

She fell into the nearest chair and lit up a cigarette. "It's great to see you two." The white, tightly wrapped roll of tobacco dangled loosely from her crimson lips. "It's O.K. if I smoke isn't it? We're in a bar, right?"

Christina fanned away the smoke. "It's been illegal for several years now."

Brandy ignored what Christina had told her and took a long drag. "So—how's my portfolio doing?"

"What happened?" Susan laughed. "The statement bandit struck again in your neighborhood?"

"You know I never open those things!"

"Statement or no statement," Christina added, "it's still up over 35%."

"Fabulous! You two are the best. I'm so glad you yanked my savings out of that money market account."

Brandy, who earned exorbitant commissions selling Pacific Heights mansions, had met Christina three years ago while she was an account exec for the firm's private client services group. When Brandy realized that she needed some serious investment advice she asked a few people in her office whom they trusted enough to hand over a small fortune. Several had mentioned Christina's name, so Brandy gave her a modest amount to invest. After the sum doubled in two years, she turned everything over to her. With Susan's help, Christina created a diversified portfolio of biotech companies, semiconductor manufacturers and a few blue chips. Her advice was right on the mark, and since then Brandy hasn't stopped bragging about her hefty rate of return.

"So Brandy," Susan said, "tell us what happened this weekend that was such a downer."

"Oh yeah, I was trying to forget." Her martini arrived and she promptly drained half of it. "I was doing floor time one morning and this lady from St. Louis called. She told me that her husband got transferred out here, and that their five bedroom, stone Tudor, on a wooded acre, was on the market for five hundred grand. Her first visit to California was last weekend and let me tell you, she was horrified! At one point, the poor thing broke down in tears. I thought she was ready to pack her bags and fly back to Missouri."

She took another sip of her martini. "I mean, what would you do if the only place available in that price range was a two bedroom condo, with one car parking in a so-so part of town? Anyway, after an endless day of that scene, I got home and Maxwell informed me he wanted to start seeing other women."

"Brandy, that's awful," Christina said.

"Which? The lady from St. Louis or Maxwell?"

15

"I guess both, but I'm really sorry to hear about Max."

"Me too, but I'm due for a change of pace." Brandy took another drag from her cigarette and blew the smoke toward the ceiling. "I could use some fresh blood." She glanced toward the group of men leaning against the bar.

"How are you going to make that happen?" Susan asked.

"I don't know, maybe take a vacation or something."

"That's exactly what I need." Christina took off her glasses and rubbed her eyes. "I'm so burnt out. I have a feeling that if I don't take a break soon, I may never wake up one morning."

"Speaking of taking a break," Susan poured the remainder of her beer into a glass, "yesterday, I was talking to one of our analysts in New York who just got back from Europe. She had a fantastic time and told me she came back a new person."

Christina began to reminisce about the summers she'd traveled in Europe and the junior year in college that she spent at the Sorbonne in Paris.

"It sure is dreamy over there," Christina mused.

"Dreamy?" Susan asked. "Have you been staying up late watching Brady Bunch reruns?"

"You know what I mean." Christina laughed at herself, thinking how foolish she must have sounded. "It's so romantic over there. The food, the people, the history, and my personal favorite: those long afternoon siestas."

"What's your favorite country?" asked Brandy. "I've never been anywhere except Mexico."

"Definitely Italy!" Christina answered. "The food is fabulous, and the men to die for!"

"Men," Susan said, "that's a new concept. I can't remember the last time I had a relationship that lasted more than three dates."

"Ditto," Christina said. "Actually my record is two-and-a-half. I count lunches as half dates. Anyway, I almost made it to three-and-a-half."

"What happened?" Susan asked.

16

"When he asked me out to dinner for the next evening, I told him that I had a seven a.m. meeting in San Jose that morning. I knew that I would be wiped out by the time I got home. When I asked for a rain check, he said 'maybe.' Bottom line: he never asked me out again."

Susan raised her glass to her mouth and polished off her beer. "He sounds like he would have been too uptight for you anyway."

"Probably, but no matter who the guy is, it seems that whenever I start getting close enough to having a meaningful relationship, everything crashes around me." Christina sighed and crossed her arms. "I guess I'm better off single."

"How 'bout we move on to a more pleasant topic." Brandy stubbed out her cigarette. "Tell me more about Italy."

Christina smiled at Brandy. "First of all, everyone smokes. No one would think of giving you a hard time for lighting up in a restaurant."

"Sounds like a place I need to visit," Brandy said.

"Why don't we go over there together?" Christina suggested. "We'd have a great time!"

Susan and Brandy tilted their heads, contemplating Christina's proposal.

"Well, what do you think?" Christina asked.

Simultaneously, they raised their glasses to toast their European vacation. "Yes!"

Christina threw two twenties on the table, and waited for the valet to bring Brandy's black, new 740 iL BMW around. When they reached Postrio, the street in front of the restaurant seemed unusually crowded. Rows of cars, parked two deep, blocked the entrance.

"What's going on tonight?" Brandy asked the parking attendant.

"The owner's up from Spago cooking dinner for a private party. I heard it's for some group of hot-shot L.A. movie people."

As soon as they were seated, they ordered a bottle of champagne to celebrate their decision to hit Europe together and began perusing the menu. Brandy, looking around the restaurant, thought she recognized a friend of hers.

If anyone captured the image of the classic jet setter it was Robert Carmichael. The last Brandy had heard, he was involved in financing movies and was splitting his time between the Russian Hill penthouse she'd sold him a couple years ago in San Francisco and a beach house in Malibu. It had taken her six months to find him the perfect place, and during that time they'd become close friends. Unfortunately, Rob's work and social schedule prevented them from seeing much of each other. If he wasn't attending an extravagant charity ball, yachting through the Caribbean islands with friends, or chateau hopping around Europe, he was working on his next movie. Over the years, he would periodically send her a postcard from one exotic place or another.

"I think I see a friend of mine." Brandy stood up, waved her arms above her head and shouted Rob's name across five tables of diners.

Rob turned around, startled to hear his name. His eyes widened and then he broke into a smile. He excused himself from his table and walked over to where the women were sitting.

"My God, Brandy." Christina gawked at the tall, dark haired man approaching their table. "He's a dead ringer for a young Cary Grant!"

"He's also incredibly charming and rich," Brandy whispered.

"Brandy! How fabulous to see you!" He gave her the customary Hollywood air kiss on each cheek.

"Great to see you too." She forcefully patted the empty chair next to her. "Sit down for a moment."

She introduced Christina and Susan and poured him a glass of champagne into an empty water glass.

"So, Rob, how long have you been in San Francisco and why haven't you called me?"

Rob shook his head and smiled at the other two ladies. "She's never been one to beat around the bush." He turned to Brandy. "I just flew up yesterday."

"Business or pleasure?" Brandy asked.

"You know me, my business is my pleasure. But tonight I'm celebrating! We've just finalized the financing on a movie we're filming here."

"That exciting," Brandy said. "What's it about?"

"It's your typical shoot 'em up, action film, starring Brad Pitt and Sandra Bullock. We're all banking on a real hit. Anyway, what's new with you?"

"Knee deep in selling property. But tonight I'm taking a breather and having dinner with the girls. Actually," she batted her eyelashes, "we're mapping out a trip to Italy. Do you have any suggestions where we should go?"

"Everywhere in Italy is worth seeing, but I love the Ligurian Coast."

Brandy ducked to miss one of his swinging hands. Rob was always known for being overly animated.

"My favorite town is Forte dei Marmi—it means marble fortress. It's a fun beach town and I'm positive you'll love it. Also, if you go, I want you to try a restaurant called Il Castello. It's superb. I'm trying to entice the owners into opening one in Beverly Hills."

"Thanks for the tips," Brandy said. "So, how long will you be in town? We really need to catch up."

"I won't be back until we start production sometime in August."

"Perfect, call me then."

"Will do. I better get back to my table." He turned to Christina and Susan. "It was nice meeting you. Maybe in August

19

the four of us can get together. I'll give you a tour of the movie set."

"That would be great!" Christina said. Susan smiled and nodded in agreement.

When he was out of earshot, Susan said, "Forget Max. Why the hell aren't you dating Rob?"

"Well, as luck would have it," Brandy said, "I'm pretty certain that he prefers the company of men as opposed to women."

The three of them let out a slow, comical sigh, and then ordered their dinner and another bottle of champagne. They talked non-stop about their trip and after rearranging their respective schedules, they eventually agreed on their departure date—the Saturday before the July 4th weekend—less than two weeks away.

-\-\-

Christina's head was pounding when she stumbled into her condo just after midnight. She cursed herself for drinking so much on a work night.

She pulled out her cell phone to recharge the battery and noticed that she had a message.

"Christina—it's Ralph Stinson here. Call me when you get this message. I don't care how late."

He sounded agitated, so as much as she hated to make a business call, she pulled up his number on her phone and placed the call. He answered on the first ring.

"Ralph, it's Christina. I'm returning your call."

"Did you receive the documents I dropped off this evening?"

"Sure did. Thanks for personally delivering them." Christina kicked off her shoes and pulled off her jacket. "Is there anything else I can do for you?"

"Uh-yes," he stammered. "I need them back."

"What!" She nearly dropped the phone. "You can't rescind now! You signed. I have a binding, legal letter of intent."

"Don't be so anxious," he shot back. "I'm not backing out, I- uh- just need to look over a few of the pages."

Christina's heart returned to a normal pace. "No problem, I'll have Margie messenger over a copy tomorrow morning."

Ralph cleared his throat. "Actually, I need the exact file that I dropped off last night."

He was really pushing her now. "Ralph, you know I can't do that. Once I get an original signature, the documents must remain in our possession." She walked into her bedroom and started to get undressed. "Don't worry, you'll have a copy on your desk by the time you get to work."

"But, I—-"

"I'm sorry Ralph," she cut him off. "That's the best I can do. Call me at the office tomorrow afternoon if you need to discuss this any further. Now good night." Christina hung up the phone before he could respond. She was too tired to be polite.

Chapter Four

By six o'clock that evening, Christina had still not heard from Ralph. As far as she was concerned no news was good news. She felt relieved that Ralph was able to solve whatever minor emergency was troubling him.

Exhausted after a day of client appointments and agonizing over which accounts she could actually sign on, Christina walked into Susan's office. She felt spent and knew she looked haggard. Susan looked pretty frazzled herself. Her normally light brown complexion was flushed and her hair was pulled into a haphazard pile on top of her head. A chopstick, hopefully, Christina thought, not one that was used for today's lunch, pierced the mound of curls.

Christina slumped into the chair facing Susan's desk. "Are you about ready to sign off? I can't focus on valuations any longer. Plus, I spent the last half-hour fighting for our position on the left for the Symex deal. We're this close to getting it." She pinched her fingers together. "And I'm not going to settle for the right."

After a deal is completed, the three primary institutions that financed the transaction are listed on the offering documents from the top left to the bottom right, in the order of importance and the amount of money raised. The prestige factor of a prominent investment bank, such as Kingstone, drops off precipitously if it's seen on anything but top left.

"I know, I'm beat too, and my eyes are burning from looking at this screen. I'm trying to figure out how in the world Pharmlyn justifies its market cap of one point three billion. They have a negative cash flow and no earnings!" She squinted at the glowing green box and scrolled downward, using the mouse under her right hand. "Ah, here it is. They have a five year research contract with Johnson & Johnson, plus grant money from Merck."

"You're our high-tech analyst," Christina stood up and squinted to see the screen. "Why are you here at eight thirty sweatin' it out over a biotech issue?"

"For my personal portfolio. I heard they might be developing an oral drug for Type I diabetes."

"Anything I should know about?" Christina was never one to pass up a hot tip.

"I'll let you know tomorrow after I talk to my friend at Morgan Stanley." She pulled away from her computer. "Enough of this," she sighed, "let's iron out our itinerary."

"Just what I was thinking," Christina sat back down. "How about this?" She picked up a pen and pointed it in the air as she spoke. "We'll fly into Nice, and although it's in France, we'll be able to take the train down the coast and stop at places along the water."

"Which ones do you have in mind?" asked Susan.

"I think there's a train station at Santa Margharita Liguria, right in the heart of the Italian Riveria. We could stay for a couple nights, and from there we can visit Portofino. It's a quaint, little harbor you wouldn't want to miss. Then we could pack up and head down to Cinque Terre."

"So, you've been moonlighting as a travel agent?" Susan pulled the chopstick out of her hair and massaged her scalp.

"Remember, darling, I've been there. We could all benefit from my lousy mistakes and lucky finds."

"What about that town Brandy's Cary Grant mentioned?"

"Right, Forte dei Marmi. That's a little further south. We could make that our last stop."

Susan leaned back and propped her feet on her desk. "It sounds like we better make some hotel reservations."

"Personally, I think it'll be much more adventurous if we just wing it. We don't want to be locked into anything."

"I don't know, Christina. After all, it's peak tourist season."

"You're right, but we want to have fun, and not worry about missing a train, or a hotel check-in time."

"O.K." Susan closed down the window on her computer screen, "sounds like a plan. I'll make my plane reservations tomorrow."

Christina returned to her office and called her parents in Chicago. Her mom's cheerful voice answered.

"Hi Mom!"

"Hi, honey. So glad you called. Let me get your father. He'll pick up in the study."

Her mom shouted downstairs. "David, Christina's on the phone."

"What have you been doing, Mom?"

"Running non-stop, but loving it. I was just elected to the Art Institute's board of directors."

"Mom, that's great! Congratulations!"

"Hi sweetheart." Her dad's warm voice bellowed into the phone. "How's my girl?"

"I'm fine, thanks." Christina filled them in on her latest activities. "I just wanted to let you know that some girlfriends of mine and I are taking off for Europe next week."

She heard her mom sigh. "It seems like we just dropped you off at the airport when you were in college. Remember, honey, be careful on those trains."

"Connie," her dad interrupted, "she's thirty years old, and can take care of herself. But, if you run into trouble, sweetheart, you call us."

"Don't worry about me," Christina laughed as she started to say goodbye. "I'll call you when I get back. I love you."

Just before she hung up, her dad asked her: "Any chance you'll stop over at O'Hare?"

Oh no, she thought, here it comes. The usual 'how come we never see you anymore?'

"Sorry, Dad, not this time. I booked a direct flight."

She hated telling him that because she could tell that he really missed her.

"I wish you would take some of that vacation time and visit us." It hurt her to hear her dad with such disappointment in her voice. "Maybe over Thanksgiving?"

"That's a possibility, but I can't be too sure about anything these days."

"I understand," he said. "Have fun in Europe. Bye, sweetheart."

"Bye, honey," her mom added. "Be careful!"

A flood of nostalgia swept over her as she hung up the phone. Tears came to her eyes. Her parents had been devastated when she decided to leave the family nest and head for California. Her dad's dream had been for her to go to law school after Wharton, and then join his firm. He had hoped that one day she would take over his practice. She has never stopped feeling guilty, but she knew that they were proud of her.

Chapter Five

"What do you mean, you haven't started packing yet?!" Susan raised her voice into the phone. "We're leaving tomorrow, and it's nearly midnight!"

"I've been so busy trying to wrap things up at work," Christina said, "the last thing on my mind is what I'll be wearing for the next three weeks. Plus, Ralph Stinson kept me on the phone for over an hour. He wanted to know every last detail about our trip. When we were leaving, how he could reach me, et cetera."

"He sounds a bit uptight."

"He'll be fine. I just told him I'd check in periodically and let him know where we're staying."

"Well, since we haven't made <u>any</u> hotel reservations, I have a feeling that we'll be doing a lot of walking looking for those phantom rooms, so you better bring some good hiking shoes."

"Don't worry," she laughed, "I'll leave my black stilettos at home."

"Basically," Susan continued, "I'm keeping my wardrobe simple—lots of swimsuits, shorts, comfy skirts and more swimsuits!"

"We should bring at least one dressy outfit," Christina interjected, "in case we want to do something more glamorous than sit on the beach and hang out at sidewalk cafes."

"Yeah, you're right. I'll pack my new silk slipdress."

"Also, you're not going to like this, but I have to bring one of my files from work."

"No," Susan groaned.

"Yes," Christina answered. "The Symex account. We want it to close this quarter. Plus if I'm going to be in touch with Ralph, I'll need it."

"Are you worried you're not going to make your quota?"

26

"Not really. But, Ralph needs this deal as much as I do. From what I've heard, he's been passed over for promotion after promotion. He's making a lateral move over to the new company and he's hoping for a fresh start."

"Now you got me stressed," Susan said. "We're leaving tomorrow and I know nothing about this company. I'm gonna be three weeks behind the eight ball by the time we get back from Italy."

"Susan, calm down," Christina said. "I just firmed up all the details this afternoon. I've been swamped, and honestly, there's nothing you could've done about it today. We have ten hours to kill on the plane, so I thought we could talk about it then."

"Good idea. Now get packing!"

-/-/-

The ride to the airport took less than twenty minutes. The three women were so excited that they barely noticed the taxi stop at the United Airlines International terminal.

Christina checked her large duffle bag and turned to Susan. "I'll run ahead to the gate. If you don't mind, hang on to my carry-on. It'll be easier for me not to have to lug it."

"Sure, no problem." Susan took her bag while Christina dashed to the gate.

Susan noticed Brandy's two pieces of brass bound, leather Louis Vuitton luggage and wondered how the hell she was going to carry all that. "Brandy, you don't have any I.D. tags. I'll attach my card. O.K? This way all of our luggage will stay together."

"Sure—thanks for noticing."

While Christina was waiting in line at the ticket counter, Brandy and Susan cut in with her.

"Hi, you two," Christina said. "Why don't you go buy some magazines or something? I'll get our seat assignments."

When Christina returned from the ticket counter, she handed them their boarding passes in a first class envelope.

They jumped up when they were asked to board, as did the rest of the First Class passengers. A French family of four sat in front of them and a group of tired, Japanese men who appeared to be traveling with two German body builders unloaded behind them. The three women settled comfortably into their extra-wide leather seats and ordered their first drink: champagne mimosas.

As usual, the flight attendants in first class went overboard pampering the passengers. Two gourmet meals were served in between continuous rounds of drinks. In addition, two full-length feature films were shown. Brandy, who had taken a Valium was soon out like a light.

"Where's my carry-on, Susan?" asked Christina.

Susan slipped off her woven, leather sandals. "I checked it at the curb, with the rest of the luggage."

"You did? Oh my God! That's the bag with my files."

"Sorry about that, I must have misunderstood." She popped several large, dark green vitamins in her mouth and washed them down with her champagne and juice.

"Don't worry, it's not your fault." Christina shivered and wrapped a blanket around her shoulders. "Luckily I remember most of the important points."

"So, what do I need to know before I report to New York?"

"Basically, what you need to convey is that this microprocessor they've developed is a gold mine."

"What kind of chip are you talking about?"

"It's called the SMX Power 750. It's supposed to be more powerful than Intel's Pentium V. They want to start distribution this fall. We really need to move on this."

"The Pentium V? The sequel to the Pentium Pro?"

"Exactly. Can you imagine, a chip more powerful and less expensive than the Pentium V? Ralph told me that they have an entire warehouse ready to be shipped."

"Miss Caldwell, Miss Anders," the flight attendant interrupted. "May I pour you some more champagne?"

"I think I'll switch to water," Susan said.

"Miss Caldwell," the flight attendant asked, "what would you like?"

"I'll stick with mimosas. Thank you."

As the flight attendant walked away, Susan whispered to Christina. "I'm sure our investors would kill to hear that piece of news."

"You bet they would. I can hardly wait until you inform the 'Street.' I can't tell you how great it feels to have landed Symex. Besides clinching my sales goal for next quarter, the potential they have to topple Intel is right at their fingertips. After losing the Intel account five years ago, I'd say I'm ready for a little revenge."

Susan clinked her glass to Christina's. "Nothing like a healthy business rivalry!"

Chapter Six

"Time to start playing bumper cars," Christina said as they stepped into the terminal. "We're going to have to force our way through this crowd and find the baggage claim area."

They watched bag after bag shoot down the carousel, but did not spot theirs.

Christina leaned against a pole. "We've been waiting over an hour. I have this sinking feeling that our luggage is lost."

"Great. Now what do we do?" Brandy lit up her sixth cigarette since deplaning.

"I guess we'll have to file a report at the customer service counter," Susan said. "Last time I trust those sky caps!"

"I'm sure we have nothing to worry about." Christina pushed her hair bangs off her forehead. "The bags probably missed the first plane and were put on the next outbound flight to Nice. We'll have United deliver them to our hotel—when we find one, of course."

Christina noticed Brandy frantically searching her carry-on bag as they marched over to customer service.

"You guys aren't going to believe this." Brandy looked up from her purse. "I think I left all of my travelers checks in my suitcase."

"Don't worry, Brandy." Now two out of three of us, Christina thought, have misplaced something important. "I remembered to bring a couple hundred Francs."

"I have a thousand dollars in travelers checks," Susan said. "We can exchange some money once we get to the hotel."

"Ooh no," Brandy piped in. "I read my Frommers on the plane, and it said that changing money at the airport or the hotel is the same as asking to be robbed."

"Good 'ole Brandy," Susan chuckled. "I guess you never forgot those first lean years in real estate."

"You bet I didn't!"

"Listen, guys." Christina took off her glasses and rubbed her eyebrows. "Our bags aren't actually lost, just delayed." She tried to remain calm, but prayed that her file wasn't lost.

"Right." Susan added. "And remember, our business cards are plastered all over them. The airline should have no trouble spotting the luggage once we file a claim. Why don't we find the lost baggage counter and tell them we'll call them when we know which hotel we'll be staying at."

"At least that's finally over," Christina said as they walked outside the terminal. "Filling out those forms ranks right up there with filing my 1040's!" She hailed a cab and they piled into the first one that swerved over to the curb.

"L'Hotel Negresco, si'l vous plait," she told the driver.

About 15 minutes later, they arrived at the heart of the French Riviera. Their hotel, which occupied the corner of the block, was an elegant, white Belle Epoque building with a peach roof that was trimmed in what appeared to be green, tarnished copper.

The cab driver turned to Christina. *"Sept cent francs, s'il vous plait."*

From the back seat, Brandy poked Christina in the shoulder. "What did he say?"

"He said $100 American dollars, please. That's what!"

Christina reluctantly handed him the fare. "This must be the special rate you charge American women," she muttered. *No tip for this guy!*

They approached the man at the front desk and inquired about reserving three rooms. The desk clerk had slick, short black hair and a skinny black mustache that curled upwards on the ends. He pursed his thin lips together and slid his finger along his greased mustache. "Mesdames, we have been booked solid for six months. I am sorry, but I'm afraid there are no rooms available."

Susan gave Christina an 'I told you so look' and then let her forehead clunk onto the desk.

"There must be something," Christina pleaded.

The clerk let out a deep sigh. "Let me check." He fastidiously tapped the keyboard, searching for an available room. "Ah— here we are." He held up a well-manicured finger. "We have one room left. I'm afraid it's quite small for three people, but there is a sofa by the window." He looked up from his monitor and smiled. "And, I might add, it has a spectacular view of the ocean."

"We'll take it." Christina turned to Susan. "I'll sleep on the couch."

The women were thrilled to see their bright and sunny room. The view reminded Christina of the David Hockney paintings she had seen at a recent MOMA exhibit.

"Let's hit the beach!" Christina said. "It's a gorgeous, sunny day, and I'm not going to waste it in here."

Brandy pulled herself up from the bed. "All of our bathing suits are in our luggage."

A mischievous smile came across Susan's face. "It looks like we'll have to hit the hotel boutique and buy some authentic French bikinis."

They tried on several suits: one-pieces, thongs and strings, all of which left little to the imagination.

Brandy held up a bathing suit bottom that consisted of a piece of dental floss on the backside and a small triangle of material on the front. "Even if I did lose those last ten pounds, I wouldn't be caught dead in one of these!" She hung it back up and pointed to the rack of one-pieces. "I think that low-cut black tank is more my style. At least I won't have to starve myself for the rest of the trip."

Susan, the most voluptuous of the group, settled on a cream colored, macramé two-piece. She held it next to her body and looked in the mirror. "On second thought," she patted her hips and shook her head, "I'm not taking off my shorts unless I'm flat on my back!"

"I don't know why you're so self conscious, Susan," Christina said. "You've got great curves, plus a tiny waist. That's more than I can say!"

Christina, who had a thin, runners body, but not much of a chest, bought a fluorescent orange string bikini with a matching floral sarong, that she wrapped loosely around her waist.

Armed with towels, tanning lotion and magazines, the women ran across the busy Promenade des Anglais, dodging speeding cars and mopeds, and headed for the ocean.

"What's the deal with these boulders?" Brandy scooped up a tiny pile of pebbles.

"Oh, I forgot to tell you," Christina said. "You won't find many sandy beaches here. But the hotel beach club has lounge chairs that we can use."

They staked out a space and slathered their skin with banana and coconut smelling oil and watched the scantily clad people parade across the sand.

"I've never seen so many tanned, hard-bodies in one place," Christina said.

"And the women are topless!" remarked Brandy.

"When in Rome…". Susan whipped off her macramé top and tossed it in the air.

"Nice tattoo," Brandy said, noticing a small black marijuana leaf inked above Susan's right breast.

"Please, don't remind me." Susan covered the design with her hand. "It's an indelible souvenir of my wild and crazy days at Berkeley."

Brandy pulled out the Cosmo she'd bought at the airport and began flipping through the fashion ads. Christina started leafing through a narrow pamphlet.

"Christina! What are you doing?" Susan snatched the brochure from Christina's hand. "We're on vacation, girlfriend. Why are you reading all this technical garbage?"

"Remember I told you that our new client, Symex, is working on some top secret government project?"

"Yeah, you mentioned it."

"Well, I think something big's going down."

"Like what?"

"Before we actually landed the account, I started digging and discovered that they've been getting some serious money from DARPA and the B.M.D.O."

Susan groaned at the thought of being sucked into a work related conversation when she should be concentrating on people watching and achieving an even, base tan. She didn't, however, want to cut Christina off mid-thought. "I know what DARPA is, but what the hell is the B.M.D.O?"

Brandy shot up from her white, wooden lounge chair. "Hey, I don't know what DARPA is."

"The Defense Advanced Research Projects Agency."

Brandy huffed. "That does me a lot of good." She fell back onto her chair and resumed reading her magazine.

"It's a small division of the Army's R & D department," Christina explained. "And the B.M.D.O. is the Ballistic Missile Defense Organization. The Cold War may be over, but the race to perfect the ballistic missile sure as hell isn't. From what I could tell, I think it's one of those Black Projects I hear about from time to time."

"Black Project?" Susan pushed up her sunglasses and looked at Christina.

"You know, those top secret projects commissioned by the government. But because of the high level of security surrounding everyone involved, the general public is kept in the dark."

Brandy threw her Cosmo onto the sand. "I can't believe you guys! This is the last thing we should be focusing on. Look around us: Water. Beach. Men! That's why I'm here."

"Me too. But I admit, it is kind of scary," Susan said. "Especially if we really had to put that technology to use."

"Or someone used it against us." Christina applied another thick layer of lotion to her legs.

"So how do you know anything about this?" Susan asked.

"I picked those up at the company." She pointed at the brochures Susan was still holding. "Then I surfed the Net. It's amazing how much information is floating around in cyberspace. As far as where they're getting their funding, I spotted some financials sitting on Ralph's desk. Anyway, none of this is proprietary. All the top secret information is in the plans, which are probably stored on a DVD disk and are under lock and key at the company."

"I'm just glad we're not at war." Brandy rolled onto her stomach. "Now, if you will excuse me, I'm going to get back to my article on 'The 10 Best Ways to Please your Man in Bed'. From what I've read so far, I could give them a few suggestions!"

Several drinks, and four hours later, Christina noticed Brandy pressing the red skin on her arms, leaving white, oval prints. "I'm frying out here!" Brandy said. "How about if we go back to the hotel and get something to eat."

Back in their room, they looked at each other with sunburnt faces and weary eyes.

"We've all been awake for nearly 48 hours," Christina said, "and I'm not in the mood to party all night."

"I'm starving and want to go to sleep," Brandy whined.

"How 'bout we grab something quick on the street and call it an early night," Susan said.

They ran down the stairs instead of waiting for the antique elevator, and found a local boulangerie that was still open. They bought a baguette, some mineral water and a wedge of brie.

"So much for experiencing the gastronomical wonders of France!" Christina said.

Famished, they didn't care what they ate, and devoured every last morsel of cheese and the entire baguette the minute they hit the sidewalk. Feeding time at the San Diego zoo seemed sedate in comparison.

"Hey," Susan said, "let's stop and listen to this guy. This is my kind of music." She pointed to a Moroccan man, with long dreadlocks and a large, bright white smile, tapping a steel drum and singing reggae music in front of an outdoor cafe. Back in their fast paced world in San Francisco he would have been invisible.

After a few minutes, a young schoolboy, living above the cafe, ventured outside and started playing his harmonica. The spontaneous energy became contagious, and a small crowd formed. Soon after that, the trio began dancing and tossing coins in the drum case. Giddy from no sleep, they burst out laughing at themselves. They never would've let loose like this at home!

By 9:00 p.m., even though the sun was still shining low in the sky, they were exhausted. They waved 'goodbye' to their Moroccan friend, and headed back for the hotel where they collapsed into bed and fell asleep the instant their heads hit the pillows.

Christina slept like a rock and awoke to the bright sun streaming into their room. Because they were so tired from the night before, they had forgotten to close the shutters on their windows. She rubbed her eyes and wondered why it was so blasted hot.

She looked at her watch and was startled to see that it was 3:30 p.m.! They had slept all night and into the next afternoon. Her back ached from sleeping on the small love seat—hardly a sofa by American standards. She jumped up so quickly that she almost blacked out. She ran over to the double bed where Susan and Brandy were sleeping and shook the bed. "Wake up! Wake up! We're missing a great day!"

Susan pulled the sheet over her head.

Christina yanked it back down. "No time for sleeping. The beach is calling us!" She looked at Brandy and knew she wouldn't budge, even if her life depended on it.

Susan moaned and eased herself out of the bed. Still in her bathing suit and cutoffs from the night before, she threw on a t-shirt and walked down to the lobby with Christina.

"Mesdames!" the desk clerk shouted as they ran across the gigantic, gold Aubusson rug in the lobby. "Your bags were delivered this morning."

They waved to say 'thanks,' and kept running.

When they returned to the hotel that evening, they were thankful to see that the bellboy had delivered their luggage to their room. They decided to splurge that night and have dinner at the hotel dining room.

While the valet pressed their outfits, Christina picked up her small bag and looked for her papers. "This is strange," she frowned. "I can't find the file. I'm certain I put it in my carry-on bag, so we could review it on the plane." She reached for her larger suitcase and began digging through it. She spotted her file folder, but a sick feeling fell over her.

"Susan, I hate to say this, but I think someone's been through my luggage."

"Why would you think that?"

"Because I never would have put anything important in checked baggage. Plus, I knew we had planned to talk about this on the plane."

"Let's look on the bright side," Susan said. "At least you found it. How about if I take a look at it?"

"You're right, at least it's not lost." Christina threw the documents onto the bed.

Susan picked up the thick, heavy folder and gave it a quick perusal. The first red flag that caught her attention concerned Ralph Stinson. Why would a scientist move from the missile division to the mainstream market area of microprocessors? Christina mentioned that it was a lateral move, but from her experience, it was more like a demotion. The rest of the information was highly technical and to study it properly required too much concentration. "No offense, Christina, but I think I'm going to back-burner this until tomorrow."

Chapter Seven

After three days of traveling along the Ligurian seaside, their train rolled into Forte dei Marmi, and Christina understood why the town's name translated to 'marble fortress.' She saw wall-like slabs of cut marble and granite stacked along the tracks for miles. Looking out the window at the piles of marble, she also noticed white-capped mountains in the distance and wondered if that could possibly be snow.

The train came to a screeching halt. "O.K. troops, this is it," Christina said. "I checked the map, and we have at least five kilometers to the ocean. We better cab it into town."

"Perfect," Brandy said. "I'm tired of dragging these bags, and all I can think about is sinking into a hot bath."

Christina called several local cab companies, but after waiting for nearly an hour, she realized that not one of them was going to show up.

"It's siesta time," Christina said. "We better get used to the summer schedule; no one works between one and four. We'd have better luck finding a cable car. Let's forget the cab idea, and hit the road."

Both Brandy and Susan groaned at the thought of carrying their luggage one more step. Wearily, they picked up their suitcases and started walking. At least they were dressed casually and wore comfortable shoes, with the exception of Brandy who was sporting brand new black, leather slip-ons. Christina's outfit consisted of a white t-shirt with "Race for the Cure" printed on it, blue, nylon running shorts, and a pair of well worn Nikes. Susan wore a white, cotton halter-top, denim cutoffs and leather sandals. After 20 minutes of walking in 90-degree heat they were exhausted and stopped on the side of the road to rest.

"I can't go any further," Brandy whined. Small droplets of her Lancome foundation were dripping down her face. "I wish I could ditch this designer luggage." She stopped and lit up a cigarette. "I have huge blisters on my feet and these steamer trunks I'm dragging around weigh a ton. Besides, I'm not used to all this exercise. Biking, hiking—what's next: climbing the Matterhorn?"

"Listen, girlfriend." Susan swung her hip out to the side and pointed her finger at Brandy. "None of us want to take another step. I'm also in a ton of pain, so why don't we just stop bitching and hitch hike. I'm willing to try anything at this point."

They stood on the side of the road and stuck their thumbs out.

"Matchbox cars!" Brandy fumed as she watched the miniature cars whiz by. "There's no way they could pack in the three of us and six pieces of luggage."

Luckily, a farmer who was transporting a load of fresh melon in his pickup truck noticed them. He swiftly pulled over when he saw the three, American tourists carrying maps, bottles of water and piles of luggage.

Because the farmer had a shorthaired terrier with him, only one additional person could sit up front.

"Christina," Brandy said, "you speak the most Italian, so why don't you squeeze up front. We'll climb in back with our luggage."

Christina crawled in the front seat and patted the dog's head. "Hi, Scruffy."

She felt the back of the truck nearly collapse from the weight of the luggage and the two women. After a few seconds she heard Brandy's high-pitched voice. "It smells in here!"

She heard Susan say: "Live with it. What do you expect? This fruit has been rotting in the sun all day."

"Yuck!" Brandy's voice again. "One of these melons just smashed underneath me. My shorts are soaked!"

Christina laughed to herself. The driver, unaware of what was going on in the back of his truck, rumbled toward town.

Over the noise of the engine without a muffler, Christina tried to communicate that they would like to be dropped in the center of town. *"Centro, per favore, centro."*

The driver stopped abruptly in the middle of a busy intersection. Irate Italians popped their heads out of their car windows, yelling, shaking fists and honking horns.

Susan quickly threw their luggage to the curb.

"Brandy, jump!" Susan yelled.

Christina shouted *"grazie"* to the driver and leapt out the door.

The farmer sped away, and the women saw him wave 'goodbye' in his rearview mirror. They sat down on the curb amidst their pile of luggage and contemplated their next move. While they were relaxing, they enjoyed watching the parade of Italians pass by on foot and bicycle. After a few minutes of watching this *passagiatta*, Christina noticed that Susan had a puzzled look on her face.

"What's bothering you, Susan?"

"I thought that this was supposed to be a beach town."

"It is; the ocean's just a few blocks away."

"I know, but why is everyone so dressed up?"

Christina looked out to the street and noticed that she was right! Women, with perfectly slicked-back hair, wearing black, skin-tight dresses, layers and layers of shiny jewelry, black pumps and carrying large gold-lame purses, peddled by on their bicycles. She wondered who would dress like that to ride a bike? The men appeared no less casual. They strutted by in their white linen shirts, freshly pressed khakis and shiny brown loafers. Their hair was also perfectly coifed and their eyes hidden by the latest style of designer sunglasses. She even noticed a few of them wearing silk scarves, neatly folded into the collar of their unbuttoned shirts.

"What's going on here?" Christina said. "This sure ain't Santa Cruz!"

They looked at themselves and started laughing after realizing that Forte dei Marmi was such a tony place.

"We must look like such fools!" Susan laughed. "These locals look like they just finished a photo shoot for Italian <u>Vogue</u>!"

"I should've known that if Robert Carmicheal recommended this town," Brandy said, "it would've been the style center of the coast!"

"I'd love to sit here and watch this fashion parade all day," Christina said, "but we need to find a hotel."

They lifted themselves off the sidewalk and looked behind them. A light pink, Mediterranean style hotel not too far away caught their eye. Flower boxes, dripping with scarlet geraniums hung under the windows, which were encased by faded, green shutters. The hotel displayed an ornate, celestial sign of stars, a moon and the sun. It was called *Hotel della Luna et delli Stelli.* Hotel of the Moon and Stars.

"I guess the farmer figured this was the place for us," Christina said. "Let's check it out."

"I say if we don't see cockroaches on the floor, we're staying!" Brandy said.

They dragged their bags across the sidewalk to the hotel. A slight, skinny Italian lady, with the name 'Donatella' sewn onto her light blue uniform, saw them struggling and rushed out of the hotel to help them.

"Prego, prego, i bagagli, prego!" She held out her hands and took one of Christina's bags.

"Thank you," Christina said. "I'm O.K. My bag is almost bigger than you are."

"Not to worry, a boy help me."

She ran back to the hotel and returned with a young red-haired man. He loaded the luggage onto a cart and wheeled it into the lobby. Donatella scurried back to the front desk to check them in.

The hotel lobby, expansive and airy, contained a large atrium filled with fully-grown potted palms and ferns. A tumbling waterfall, cascading adjacent to the plants, created an earthy aroma of a tropical rainforest. The floors, which were covered with softly colored rose and gray marble, looked as though they had just been polished. Christina stopped and marveled at the thirty-foot ceilings adorned with ancient frescoes, and the walls, lined with gilded mirrors and white marble statues.

While Donatella checked them in, a young, sultry looking man with chin length, wavy, black hair and large, almond shaped brown eyes walked over to the front desk.

Christina poked Susan in the side and discreetly pointed at him. She whispered: "I first noticed him in the library, glaring at us when we stumbled into the hotel."

The man walked behind the desk and took the women's passports from Donatella. He opened each one of them, analyzed the pictures, and then stared at the women, individually, for several seconds.

"Who is this Euro-snob?" Brandy whispered to Christina. "And why is he scrutinizing our passports?"

He gave the passports back to Donatella and said something in Italian to her. He returned to the library without saying another word.

Donatella sensed that the girls were bewildered. "That was Franco; he would like you to have rooms 31, 32, and 33."

"Sure, sounds great to me," Brandy said, "I'm ready to collapse."

"Who is he?" Susan asked as they rode the elevator to the third floor.

"I don't know," Christina said. "Probably the manager—or maybe the concierge."

Once in their room, Brandy stared in awe at their suite, which was situated on the top floor in the corner facing the ocean. "I guess the weak-and-helpless act we played in the lobby paid off for us."

Each bedroom had its own private bathroom and a large skylight in the bedroom. The three bedrooms shared a luxuriously furnished sitting room.

"What a great place!" Christina sank into a white, over-stuffed couch that sat in front of a massive granite fireplace. She pulled a floating gardenia from a crystal bowl and brought it to her nose. She ran her fingers along the smooth marble coffee table. "I hate to bring this up, but did anyone ask how long this room is available? I can't believe that during such a busy time, this fabulous suite just happens to be vacant!"

Susan began rummaging through the bar refrigerator. "Who cares! It's ours until they kick us out!"

Christina sat down in one of the chairs, reached for the phone and asked the hotel operator to connect her to the AT&T international operator. She called George Stinson at the office and left him a message with her contact information in Forte dei Marmi.

"Okay," she said as she hung up the phone, "I did what I had to do. Let's go downstairs and look around!"

Susan and Christina freshened up and walked downstairs while Brandy soaked her blistered feet in a hot tub of water.

Before they left, Brandy called out from the bathroom. "Hey, wait! Try getting us some reservations for tonight. Maybe that Castello place Rob mentioned."

"We'll do our best," Christina said. "Hopefully, the concierge can help us."

When she reached the lobby downstairs, no one was at the front desk. They ventured into the library, which smelled like old leather and cigar smoke. In front of the rows of antique, leather bound books, Christina saw Franco at a library table, sipping an espresso and shuffling through some papers. She pulled up a club chair and sat next to him. The appealing, subtle fragrance of musk floated in the air.

"So, you're Franco?" She smiled and extended her hand. "Christina Cald— I mean 'Hi, I'm Christina'." She almost kicked herself for reverting back to her business persona.

His warm hand encompassed hers. "Yes, I'm Franco. Nice to meet you."

"Thanks for the room upgrade. That was sure a nice surprise."

"It was my pleasure," he purred in a delicious Italian accent.

"I hate to impose on you again, but I was wondering if you could do us another favor?" She figured that being the concierge he probably knew all the hot spots. "Have you heard of the restaurant, Il Castello?"

"Ah," he let out a deep sigh. "Yes, of course."

"A friend of ours suggested we go there for dinner. And I was wondering if it's not to late to get a reservation for tonight."

"I could arrange that," he said, "but the three of you should not go to Il Castello together."

"Why not?"

"It is the most romantic and expensive restaurant on the coast." He spoke in a poetic manner that made each word sound like music. "You need to go there with a man you are in love with—or with a man who is in love with you."

"Thanks for the warning," Christina said, thinking how sexy everything he said sounded. "So, where do you suggest?"

"There's a little restaurant on the beach, called La Barca, and I think it would be more fun for the three of you. I would try that tonight."

"Thanks, Franco. It was a pleasure meeting you." She smiled warmly and walked away.

The three were starving, as usual, and wasted no time walking over to the trattoria. The aroma of roasting garlic and rosemary nearly knocked them over as they walked through the heavy oak doors. Large ship nets, made from thick ropes hung on the walls. The maitre'd was unexpectedly friendly and sat them at a table by a floor-to-ceiling window that opened onto the sand. The minute they sat down, their waiter brought them a bottle of Barbaresco, saying that Franco, from the Hotel della Luna had sent it over.

"How thoughtful," Christina said, as the waiter began pouring them all a glass of the deep, rich, red wine. "Franco is sure making certain that we're well taken care of."

Chapter Eight

The sweet smell of freshly baking bread wafting through the open window from the kitchen downstairs enticed the girls into awakening earlier than they would have liked the following morning.

"How about if I run out and get some Italian newspapers and the European *Wall St. Journal*?" Christina asked.

"The *Wall St. Journal*?" Brandy said. "No thanks! Pick me up one of those slick fashion bibles I keep seeing at all the kiosks."

"Sure, no problem. See you in a few minutes!"

Eventually they walked over to the beach to spend the afternoon baking in the sun. Because the summer heat was so intense, they had to limit themselves to a two-hour sizzle.

After taking relief back at the hotel, they ordered a pitcher of ice-cold lemonade. "Are you two up for hitting some of the boutiques?" Susan asked.

"I sure am," Brandy said. "I got some great tips from *La Moda*."

"I don't want to sound like a bookworm," Christina said, "but I really should brush up on my Italian."

Susan and Brandy didn't give it a second thought and headed out for their fashion expedition. Christina gathered her Italian books and began exploring the hotel grounds in search of a cool, quiet place to study.

She opened a door on the far side of the lobby that led to an outside area within the walls of the hotel. The courtyard at this time of day was enchanting. Magenta bougainvillea clung to the crumbling stone walls, a marble fountain gurgled in the corner, and mature grapevines, hanging from a pergola, shaded the area over a small, wooden garden bench. She found her sanctuary and knew she would be comfortable there for hours.

Reading her Italian lessons out loud must have attracted the attention of Franco, because after a few minutes, he walked outside to the courtyard and asked her if she needed help with her studies. She thought that it was very sweet of him to take the time and invited him to sit down on the bench.

His seductive Italian accent made it nearly impossible for her to concentrate; in fact, she probably would have been better off without his assistance, but she was flattered by his attention. She couldn't help but stare at his smooth brown skin and his large almond-shaped eyes framed by silky, dark lashes.

Christina closed her Italian book. "*Che hai fatto sta sera?*"

She fumbled through asking him what he'd done this afternoon. She wanted to know and understand him better, but that was all she could pull from her vast repertoire of Italian phrases and vocabulary words.

"Very good, Christina. You're learning fast."

"Nooo." Playfully, she pounded her book. "Answer in Italian. It's the only way I'll learn."

"Very well then: *Io ho dipinto il mio studio dietro il gardino.*"

With his response flowing like an operetta, he explained to her that he spent the morning painting in his studio behind the courtyard. Christina noticed that he was very pensive and could see why he would immerse himself into something as creative as painting.

"May I see some of your paintings?" Christina asked. She had already given up on attempting a meaningful conversation in a language she didn't fully understand. "I love art. I practically grew up at the Art Institute of Chicago."

"You're kind to express your interest," he said softly, "but I rarely show my artwork to anyone. I fear that other people would not understand the true meaning of what I paint." He looked down at the cobblestone floor for a few seconds and then turned to face her. He smiled slightly and pointed at her nose. "You look like a clown."

Christina giggled and covered her burnt nose. "I over did it our first day on the beach."

"I think it is *carina.*"

"What's that mean?"

"The nearest translation would be 'funny, yet cute'." He shifted closer to her. She stared at his lips, which were smooth and moist. Suddenly, her lips felt dry and colorless. She wanted to apply some lip-gloss but knew it would be awkward if reached for her Strawberry Lip Smacker. "So, Christina," he said, "what do you and your friends have planned for the evening?"

"No plans whatsoever." She pushed her hair behind her ear and let her sandal dangle loosely from her foot.

"There's a nightclub on the water that I think you would enjoy. If you like, I will drive the three of you."

"Sure, that sounds like fun. What time do you get off work?"

His luscious lips smiled slightly. "I'll meet you downstairs in the lobby at ten." He softly touched her face, brushed her bangs away from her forehead, and whispered, "Ciao, dolcina," in her ear.

She felt a wave of warmth pass through her body from this unexpected gesture of affection. Sitting in the courtyard, unable to study any longer, she watched Franco walk away from the bench and disappear into the long shadows of the late afternoon sun.

Chapter Nine

Susan and Brandy were living it up at the beach. The Hotel della Luna owned a private strip of sand that they had developed into a beach club. In addition to private cabanas, tennis courts and jacuzzis, there was an outdoor restaurant. Each afternoon, around 4:00 p.m., the guests gathered on the terrace to enjoy a late lunch of freshly cooked antipasto dishes that were deliciously prepared with locally grown ingredients.

Christina knew of this daily ritual and did not want to miss it. As she approached the outside dining area, she could hear Brandy's voice booming from the far end of the deck.

"Hi!" Christina said, "It looks like you two are soaking up the Italian way of life!" Susan and Brandy were surrounded by at least six handsome men.

Their table was covered with half-full glasses of red wine, bottles of San Pelligrino and a wicker basket of bread sticks. "We've been invited to go to this night club, 'La Campania', tonight with Franco and some of his friends," Christina said.

One of the men, who had short dark hair, bright blue eyes, and a deep brown tan, interrupted her. "La Campania is the most popular club on the coast. You will never get in tonight. Annabella, Italy's most famous pop star, is performing. The show has been sold out for months."

"It's sounding more fun than I thought!" Christina reached for a bread stick and started munching.

"We might as well try, what do we have to lose?" Brandy poured herself another glass of wine.

"Franco told us to meet him downstairs in the lobby around ten. Let's get something to eat." She was practically drooling over the marinated calamari and grilled vegetables she spotted at the next table. "I have a feeling we're going to be out late tonight."

Back at the hotel, they showered off the layers of sand and suntan oil and primped for their big night out. The combination of their hairdryers blowing full force, the curling irons heating and the CD player blasting blew a fuse and knocked off the electricity to their suite.

"Party's over!" Christina searched in the dark for the one dressy outfit she'd brought: an apple green, sleeveless mini-dress. She opted to wear her contacts tonight instead of glasses. Instead of letting her hair dry naturally, she turned the ends under with Brandy's curling iron. Brandy wore a sequined bustier with a tight black leather skirt. When the fuse blew she still had hot rollers in her hair and was touching up her red nails. Susan looked fabulous in an ankle length, gold silk, slip dress. Several silver bracelets, formed like a Slinky, wrapped around her wrist. She straightened her curly hair with a hot styling iron and secured her masterpiece with hairspray.

"We might as well get downstairs and wait for Franco." Christina dabbed on some lipgloss.

In the library, a young Italian man stood up to greet them. He had tousled, thick brown hair, a black goatee and a tan so dark it look like he'd smeared shoe polish on his face. "You must be the three American girls. My name is Stephano." His accent sounded like a combination of British and Italian. "I'm a friend of Franco's. And you must be Christina." He looked at her approvingly. "Who are your lovely friends?"

Christina barely had time to introduce Susan and Brandy before Stephano pressed himself between the two of them, locked his arms into theirs, and escorted them down the stairway to the bar.

"Who is this joker?" Christina heard Brandy say to Susan. "He sure has a lot of confidence!"

While they were waiting for Franco, Stephano poured them each a glass of wine. His shiny, gold Rolex dangled from his wrist.

Christina took a sip of wine, and while keeping an eye on the stairs she noticed Franco descending the massive, marble staircase into the lobby. Her heart skipped a beat. He wore a pale yellow linen shirt that accentuated his chestnut-colored skin and ecru, pleated pants and woven brown leather loafers with no socks. His black hair was still wet from his shower.

"Is everyone ready?" He slinked as graceful as a cat down the stairs.

The group walked outside behind the hotel and squeezed into a well-traveled Volkswagen Jetta. They followed the coast down about a mile to 'La Campania.' The club, built on stilts to let the ocean water flow underneath, was packed with people. The outside balconies spilled over with patrons who couldn't find a place to sit indoors, and the parking lot was inaccessible due to the crowd of hundreds standing on the pavement. Franco left the car on the side of the road. The five of them got out and started pushing their way through the screaming fans of "Annabella."

"There is no way in hell we'll get into this place," Susan shouted to Christina.

As they approached the entrance, the men who were guarding the front door noticed Franco and his friends. The bouncers left their posts and helped the group break through the crowd. Once in the club, a man in a white dinner jacket escorted them to a corner table, next to the stage, that was covered with a white linen cloth. The music was so loud that they could barely hear themselves talk.

Susan leaned over and shouted to Christina. "I guess this is one of the perks of working in such a nice hotel."

Without being asked, waiters brought over platters of food and placed three bottles of champagne into ice-filled silver buckets. Franco held out a chair for Christina, and then sat down next to her. He poured her a glass of champagne and looked into her eyes.

"Your eyes are exquisite." He leaned closer to her. "They match your dress perfectly."

"Thank you," she smiled slightly.

"So," he purred. "Did you notice the stars shining through the skylight above your bed?"

He put his warm hand on the soft skin of her thigh and whispered in her ear. "I thought you would find it romantic."

Blood rushed to her cheeks. She took a sip of champagne and was surprised how wonderful and delicate it tasted. It reminded her of Dom Perignon, but she didn't think that it was likely that Franco would allow the waiters to freely pour such quantities of this expensive champagne. When Franco turned his head to talk with the waiters, she pulled the bottle up from the bucket. The glass was indeed a dark, olive green, and the familiar antique gold Dom Perignon label, peeked out from the ice.

"This sure is nice." Christina turned to Susan and nudged her. "Why do you think we're getting such royal treatment?"

"What do you think?" Susan said, "Franco obviously has a huge crush on you! Enjoy it while it lasts!!"

After Susan finished her clarification, a man with long, wavy blonde hair, wearing jeans and cowboy boots, approached their table and asked Brandy to dance. Without hesitation, she jumped up. Christina and Franco were so enthralled in conversation, that they didn't even notice Susan and Stephano had also hit the dance floor.

Christina listened attentively as Franco discussed his artwork. He was also kind enough to suggest a number of historic sights and local haunts that they might visit while in Italy. He told her that while he'd lived in Tuscany all his life, he tried to spend as much time near the water as possible.

Christina shifted in her chair so that she faced Franco directly. "Franco," she said. "I have a silly question for you."

"No question is too silly for a clown." He smiled and lightly tapped her nose.

Christina laughed. "Since you've lived here all your life, maybe you could tell me why there's still snow on the mountain tops in the middle of the summer?"

He looked puzzled and then smiled. "Christina, my dear. That's not snow. That's marble. White, Italian Carrara marble."

"Marble! Now I understand." She sipped her champagne. "Are the statues in the lobby made from the same marble?"

"Indeed."

She began to wonder if it were his hypnotic eyes or the champagne that made her feel so dizzy. She yearned to know more about him. Did he have brothers and sisters? What did he do when the hotel shut down in the winter?

"Franco," she asked, "I was wondering…"

He put his warm hand on hers. "I must go now," he whispered, "Stephano will make certain that you and your friends get home safely."

He touched the tip of her nails and then moved his fingers under her palm. He lifted her hand to his lips and gently kissed the back of her hand. Before Christina could say anything, he brought his fingers to her lips and walked away from the table. She could not even utter the words, 'good night.' Why did he have such a numbing effect on her? Never in her life had she had the sensation of melting as the result of a man touching her hand.

Susan and Brandy returned from the dance floor to find Christina sitting motionless, staring into her champagne glass.

"What's come over her?" asked Brandy.

"I've never seen Christina like this," Susan said. "She's probably tired. Or maybe it's the champagne."

Christina looked up from her glass. "Have fun dancing?"

"We had a great time—Stephano is hilarious!" Susan devoured a cracker covered with caviar. "He didn't want to stop dancing!"

"Where's Franco?" asked Brandy.

"He had to go back to the hotel. I guess Stephano will take us home." Christina scanned the room, looking for him. "Where is he?"

Susan waved her hand toward the bar area. "He ran into some friends and he's buying them a drink."

Christina looked in the direction of the bar. Stephano was talking with a young Japanese man. He looked vaguely familiar, but she couldn't place where she'd seen him before. She also noticed two young men sitting near Stephano and his friend. They both had shaved blonde hair and wore black t-shirts, black jeans and sunglasses. Their biceps bulged under their shirt.

"What goons," she said to Susan. "Who would wear dark glasses at night?"

The Japanese man handed Stephano a white envelope. Stephano shook his hand and walked back to the table. He brought his drink with him.

"Who was that?" Susan asked him.

"That was Seike Yamashuta, a friend of mine from Japan. He's only here for a few more days, then he's flying back to the States."

"Which city?" Christina asked.

"San Francisco." He finished his drink, which looked and smelled like whisky on the rocks.

"That's where we're from." Susan smiled.

"Yes, I know." Stephano patted Susan's shoulder. "Franco told me."

"What does Seike do?" asked Christina.

"He's trying to start a business in Silicon Valley. I'll invite him to breakfast tomorrow at the hotel so you can meet him."

"Fine with us," Susan said. "Maybe we could help him out. We work with a lot people in the Valley."

"He would appreciate that," Stephano said. "He's been trying to make it on his own for several years now. He used to work for his father, but they had their differences."

"What kind of business is Seike's father in?" Christina asked.

"Electronics," Stephano twirled his gold watch. "Mr. Yamashuta owns one of the largest conglomerates in Japan. He's extremely powerful, and Seike only wishes he could be as successful one day. Unfortunately, he's not quite as smart. He got into trouble when he was in college back in the States. His father cut off his allowance and forced him to move back to Japan."

"He sounds like a real winner," Christina said. "By the way, who are those two thugs with him?"

"Seike made some enemies in his drug dealing days and feels that he needs 'protection'."

Christina nearly choked on her champagne. "Drug dealing days?"

"He only did that after his dad fired him." Stephano shrugged. "He's clean now. But he keeps those two neo-Nazi's around to help him out of messy situations."

"Lovely." Christina put her glass on the table.

Chapter Ten

They got home safely, with Stephano driving the Jetta, and fell asleep at 5:00 a.m. They would have slept until noon, if it had not been for the breakfast meeting that Stephano had arranged with Seike. Christina wasn't overly enthusiastic about getting out of bed to talk business, but Susan had taken a liking to Stephano, and she didn't want to let him down. When they got to the breakfast room, they saw Stephano, Seike, and his two 'friends' sitting at a table in the corner, smoking cigarettes and drinking coffee. When Stephano saw them enter the room, he immediately stood up and held out his arms.

"How can you girls look so beautiful after such a late night?" he asked. Seike and his pair of protection remained sitting down.

"Good morning, Stephano." Susan gave him a polite kiss on the cheek. "Is this your friend, Seike?"

"Yes, it is." He gestured toward Seike. "Seike, I would like you to meet my friends from California."

Seike's eyes were hidden by long, stringy, black bangs. He barely looked up from his coffee and didn't say a word. He lit a cigarette with a shaky hand and grunted "good morning." He turned to Stephano. "We need to get going, we have some unfinished business back in Frisco."

"That's strange," Susan leaned over and whispered to Christina, "I thought he wanted to discuss some business he was starting."

Christina was thinking the same thing, but didn't really care that he was leaving. He gave her the creeps, and she wasn't in the mood to talk about work.

Stephano escorted his friends to the door, shook their hands and then returned to the table. "I apologize," he said, "they behaved very rudely."

"How do you know these men?" Christina asked, hoping Stephano would not profess to be their dearest friend.

"Seike's father is a very important client of my family's business. We supply the marble for the interior of the many office buildings included in the Yamushuta empire. They also own some luxury hotels. We supply the marble for the bathrooms and the floors."

"So, you're in the marble business?" Christina frowned and took off her glasses.

"Right," he answered, "but I also have my pilot's license. I assist my father and brother with our business affairs, but my real passion is flying."

"How do you know Franco?" She chewed the stem of her glasses.

"Our families have worked together for years." He held his hand at his knees. "We have been best friends since we were little boys."

Christina was just about to ask him in what capacity they actually worked together, when Franco entered the breakfast room.

"Good morning ladies," he said as he sauntered over to the table. He wore a navy blue, double-breasted suit, a crisp white shirt with a red, patterned tie. He carried a slim, burgundy leather briefcase. He looked much older this morning than when Christina had first met him. "I trust Stephano got you home safely last night?"

"We feel like we just got home," Christina said. "But we sure had fun. Thanks for inviting us."

"It was nothing." He set his briefcase on the table.

"How about if we go to the beach?" Stephano asked.

"Sounds great!" Brandy said, "Are you two up for it?"

Susan jumped up from the table, but Christina said she would walk over later, after she'd studied her Italian for a few hours.

With everyone gone from the table, Franco sat down next to Christina. His aura seemed to envelop her. "Would you like some help with your studies?"

"Why, yes, thank you Franco." She crossed her legs and rested her elbows on the table. "But aren't you busy this afternoon?"

"Not particularly," he said. "In the summer, I get up early to work, and generally leave the afternoons free to paint. Besides, how often am I honored with the pleasure of helping an attractive, intelligent young lady learn my language?"

She found it impossible to resist Franco's overwhelming charm and was not accustomed to this deluge of compliments.

Franco got out of his chair first, extended his hand to hers, and led her out to the courtyard. Once again, she could feel herself melting at his slightest touch.

As they walked outside to the shaded enclave, she paused to ask Franco about a painting that she had been admiring since she arrived at the hotel. Above the mantle on the fireplace hung an enormous portrait framed in gilded gold. The picture was of a distinguished, aristocratic looking woman, with a long, elegant neck and thick raven colored hair pulled tightly away from her noble face. Her dark brown eyes, almost black, peered out into the room, as though they were alive and aware of her surroundings. The magnificent jewelry she wore was impossible to ignore. An exquisite pair of diamond and ruby earrings hung delicately from her ears. A brilliant diamond, surrounded by rubies, and set in platinum, clung loosely to the ring finger of her gracefully folded hands.

"Ah, yes," Franco sighed. "This is a picture of my great-grandmother, painted within months of her marriage."

"What a powerful looking woman. She must have commanded a great deal of respect."

"So I have heard." Franco turned toward the portrait and stared at it for several seconds. "She died before I was born, but I have learned throughout the years that she was truly the matriarch of our family."

Christina noticed the resemblance between her and Franco. The eyes, especially, were identical: dark, warm and penetrating.

They studied for over an hour. Franco closed the book after completing several chapters. "I think we have done enough for one day." He inched closer to her. "What are your plans for this evening?"

Christina eased the book back from him. Her fingers touched his for a split second. He moved his face closer to hers. "I don't have any plans," she whispered.

"No plans?" He brought a finger to the corner of her lips, ran it along her cheekbone and then to the edge of her eye. His mouth was inches from hers. "How come such a beautiful woman never has any plans?"

She was stunned by his closeness. She could hardly speak. "We're playing every day by ear."

"By ear?" He cocked his head and touched his ear. "I'm sorry I don't quite understand."

Christina thought how cute it was that he took her literally. "I'm sorry," she laughed, "that's an American expression."

"Ah, I see." He settled back into the bench and put his briefcase on his lap. "Very well then, we will have dinner together. I shall take you to Il Castello."

Butterflies fluttered in her stomach and her skin tingled. She clasped the book firmly. "That would be delightful. Thank you, Franco. What time shall I be ready?"

"I'll meet you downstairs at nine o'clock." He took off her glasses, looked into her eyes, and kissed her lightly on the cheek. "Until tonight."

Christina remained paralyzed in the courtyard for several seconds. What kind of spell was he casting upon her, and why was she so incredibly attracted to him? She didn't even know his last name—in fact she hardly knew anything about him.

Her thoughts were broken by one of terror.

"Oh my God!" she said out loud. "I need to go shopping!!"

She picked up her book, and ran out of the hotel to the beach to find Susan and Brandy.

She found them under an umbrella, asleep on their chaise lounges.

"Brandy! Susan!" she cried out, "You've got to help me!!"

Startled by her pleas for help, they instantly awoke from their nap.

"What's wrong?" Susan jolted up from her chair. "Are you all right?"

"Yes—I'm sorry," Christina said. "Franco asked me to dinner tonight and I didn't bring anything to wear!"

"Wait a minute—back up," Brandy said, "Franco asked you out? How did this come about?"

"It's not important. I'm desperate!"

"What restaurant is he taking you to?" Susan asked.

"Il Castello."

"You're kidding!"

"Let's go!" Brandy said, "Susan and I know where all the best stores are."

Unquestionably, Italy was one of the best places in the world to buy the latest fashions. Most of Christina's favorite designers were Italian: Versace, Krizia, Gucci, Giorgio Armani and Valentino. Because Forte dei Marmi was such a stylish resort town, dozens of these fashionable boutiques lined the streets.

The women bounced from one boutique to the next, watching Christina try on various outfits. She was looking for something classy, elegant and definitely sexy. After spending hours at several stores, they finally found their way to the most exclusive couturier: Valentino.

They hadn't yet ventured into this obvious, yet most expensive choice of shops for fear of what they might find. Many years ago, while in Paris, Christina had attended a Valentino fashion show and had been in love with his clothes ever since. Although Valentino was prohibitively expensive in the United States, she knew that she would be fooling herself if she thought she would find a bargain in Forte dei Marmi. Her skin prickled as she grasped the large, gold "V" that served as a door handle, and entered the boutique.

Brandy began scouring the neatly arranged clothing racks before an elegantly dressed Italian woman had time to greet them at the door. She looked at them in their beach clothes and turned up her nose. She seemed to assume that they were only casual browsers. Fortunately, Christina's Italian was proficient enough to explain to her what she needed, and assured her they were serious buyers.

After trying on several outfits, all different styles and colors, Christina kept coming back to a simple black, short, sleeveless dress. The hemline fell halfway up her thigh, and subtle, black lace graced the plunging neckline. She had found what she was looking for—all for only $2500 American dollars!

"There's no way I have any right to buy this," Christina said to Susan and Brandy. "The price is outrageous—it's as much as my mortgage payment!"

"Christina—listen to me," Brandy said forcefully. "This is a classic; you'll be able to wear this for the rest of your life."

Christina did not look reassured, so Brandy kept trying. "This dress is truly one-of-kind. No one in California, and probably not even in New York, will own this same dress. Also, it epitomizes who you are: classy, elegant and sexy. Take my advice, buy it!"

"I'm feeling delirious. I think I need to sit down." Christina slumped into the velvet chair in the dressing room and remembered why Brandy made so much money selling houses.

"O.K., you're right. Let's buy it and get out of here before I change my mind."

Feeling a bit full of themselves, they sauntered out the door.

Susan asked, "Can I carry your bag? I want to see what it feels like to stroll down the street, knowing I own a Valentino."

"Sure, be my guest," Christina said. "I'm too weak to carry it anyway."

When they got back to their room, they popped open a bottle of champagne and began to get dressed for the evening. Susan and Brandy had been invited to a party on Stephano's yacht, so they were also in a festive mood. Christina waited until she heard the clock chime a quarter past the hour before she left to meet Franco. She didn't want to seem overly anxious.

"Don't wait up!" She flashed a big grin and walked out the door.

Franco, who was talking to Donatella in the hotel lobby, fell silent when he saw her at the top of the staircase. She could tell that he was pleased, because he could not stop smiling. He looked incredibly handsome and regal tonight. He wore a blue blazer, embellished by some form of crest, and neatly pressed, tan cotton trousers.

"Christina, you look so beautiful. What happened to my American girl in her shorts and ponytail?"

"I trust that should be taken as a compliment." She almost tripped down the last stair, nearly destroying the graceful image she was trying to project.

"Of course. You're ravishing! Wait out front. I'll pull up the car."

She was startled to see a sleek, white, Mercedes convertible stop in front of the hotel. Franco slid out from behind the wheel and opened the passenger side door for her.

"New car?" she asked.

"No, not at all, this has always been my car. But I keep it at home—the Jetta is used for any of the staff members who need a car to run errands for the hotel."

"I see," she answered, somewhat bewildered. She settled comfortably into the soft leather seats, savored the fragrant night air and let the ocean breeze blow her hair freely in the wind as they drove down the coast. She felt no need to talk. Instead, she rested her head against the neck rest and gazed at the bright, full moon and the twinkling stars.

Chapter Eleven

The approach to Il Castello was along a small dirt road, lined by fruit and nut orchards. They drove about one mile up the windy road, before Christina began to notice the white restaurant, a renaissance-era palazzo, illuminated against the midnight-blue sky. It sat majestically on a hilltop overlooking the surrounding valley. Two enormous marble posts flanked an ornate iron gate that opened automatically as they entered. Franco pulled into the property beyond the gate and stopped the car. Two men in white dinner jackets simultaneously opened their doors and escorted them up the stairs.

The maitre'd showed Franco and Christina to a quiet, candle-lit table. Franco pulled out Christina's chair and sat down across from her. His skin glowed in the soft light of the candles. The reflections of the flame in his dark brown eyes made her wish that she were sitting next to him.

"This restaurant is lovely, Franco." Again, she noticed the emblem on his jacket. It appeared to have the letter 'G' on it, surrounded by grapevines, and the profile of an ancient warrior. "May I ask what that insignia is on your jacket?"

"Yes, of course." He looked down and pointed to the embroidery on his lapel "This is my family crest. The 'G' stands for my last name—Garibaldi."

"Does the crest have any significance?" The hovering waiters poured some champagne and brought out a platter of grilled portobello mushrooms and a plate of carpaccio, which smothered in capers, olive oil and Parmesan cheese.

"Well, it used to mean a great deal." Franco twirled his fork against the thin pink meat and placed it to her lips. "Try some. It's delicious."

She formed her lips over the fork and slowly sucked the meat. It was so supple; she didn't even need to chew it.

"Many generations ago my great-great grandfather was a revolutionist. He took part in the famous *Risorgimento*—the movement to unify Italy."

Christina's eyes widened. "I remember reading about that in my high school history class."

"It's nice to hear that such an important piece of Italian history has not been forgotten by the American text books." Franco finished his glass of champagne. The waiters immediately replenished it. "Since that time, his descendants— my ancestors—acquired much of the land here in Tuscany. In fact this palazzo," he glanced around the restaurant, "where we are dining tonight, was at one time, the home of my great grandparents."

Christina raised her eyebrows and tilted her head.

He laughed at her expression. "But now," he said, "we are all working people, just like the rest of the Italians."

For some reason she didn't believe that he was just plain working folk like 'the rest of the Italians'. "So, now you're in the hotel business?"

"Well, not exactly." The waiter poured them each a glass of Gavi de Gavi, a rich, red wine from the Piedmont region. "A century ago, before Forte dei Marmi was the resort town that it is now, the Hotel della Luna was my family's summer villa. We recently converted it to a hotel. I manage it for my father in the summer. It's more like a vacation from my real job."

"So what is your 'real' job?" Christina sliced a piece of the grilled mushroom and took a bite. It melted in her mouth and tasted like a tender, sirloin steak.

"We have been in the marble business for generations. My family once owned most of the mountains in this region, and we still own the rights to the natural resources. We excavate the abundance of marble and granite found in the mountainside, then we cut it and sell it around the world."

"So you and Stephano work together?" She took a sip of the robust, red wine.

"Yes, somewhat." Franco placed his fork and knife down on the plate. "Our company primarily supplies large slabs of marble and granite for the outside of buildings, whereas Stephano's company handles more of the detailed work."

"You seem so young to be running a worldwide business operation."

"Thank you for thinking that, but I am actually 36 years old." He reached across the table and lightly touched Christina's fingertips.

Christina eased her hand forward so that their fingers were intertwined. "Please tell me more about the marble business. All my clients are high-tech. I would love to hear more about something that doesn't involve silicon."

He continued talking about his company and told her that his most prestigious project to date had just been completed last spring. "I spent nearly an entire year with the Sultan of Brunei," he said. "We collaborated with his designers and architects and supplied the marble and granite for his family's compound."

"It must have been spectacular!"

He gripped her hand more tightly and brought it to his lips. "Now Christina, I appreciate you listening to tales about my business affairs—but, please, tell me more about yourself. All I know is that you have this wonderful sweet quality about you, one that I cannot describe properly in English. Also, it's obvious you are a very intelligent and driven young woman."

His string of adulations was interrupted by the noticeable presence of the waiters standing near their table. Franco and Christina had been talking incessantly for over an hour, and hadn't yet ordered their main course. Franco spoke to the waiters in Italian, and turned his attention back to Christina.

"I'm flattered by your compliments. I don't quite know what to say."

"There it is again!" he said. "You're smile is captivating— I've never met someone who smiles as much and as beautifully as you."

In response to questions from Franco, she began talking about her childhood in the suburbs of Chicago, her travels, her education, her current job, and her interest in art and outdoor sports. She, too, loved the water and had always been drawn to the ocean.

After a while, she began to feel ridiculous talking about herself. She looked down at her wineglass and thought that this man could not be for real. She had never before felt a more intense attraction to anyone. The respect and adoration Franco had for her was something she had only dreamed she would discover one day. How ironic, she thought, that she had to travel halfway around the world to find him.

Franco released his hand from hers and touched her cheek. "While you're here, I would like to take you to one of our marble quarries. It's quite amazing to see the stone in the raw form, before it is transformed into something as smooth as your skin."

She felt herself blush. She turned away and gazed out the window at the orchards, glowing in the moonlight, on the hillside his family once owned. Regaining her composure, she looked at him and said calmly, "Thank you, I would enjoy that a great deal."

The waiters continued to bring more wine, angel hair pasta with a light pesto sauce and a sea bass dish so sumptuous she could have sworn it was soaked in butter. After their dinner Christina knew that she was completely infatuated. Franco was everything she could ask for: sensuous, handsome, successful and intelligent. She could feel passion building and could hardly wait to leave the restaurant. She hoped that Franco was thinking the same thing.

But she knew she had to be careful. Every past relationship that had gotten this far either fizzled or ended up hurting her.

She felt Franco's warm hand start to caress the soft skin of her leg under the table. He leaned across the table, and whispered: "My darling, let us now leave Il Castello."

Christina lowered her eyelids and smiled. She lifted the napkin from her lap, folded it once, then twice, and placed it over her plate. She tried to maintain her composure, yet her heart raced in anticipation.

As they descended the marble steps, Christina felt Franco's assured hand on the small of her back. Shivers shot up her spine. The engine in Franco's white convertible purred as it waited for them. Christina slid onto the cool leather seat and crossed her legs. Franco tipped the valet and glided in behind the wheel. He turned his head and stared at Christina for several seconds. She met his penetrating gaze but quickly averted her eyes. He turned away and thrust the car into first gear. Christina's head snapped back as they fled the restaurant. They sped down the windy road and with each gear change, her heart seemed to beat harder. Her hair flew in the wind, the cool breeze massaging her scalp. The city lights, flickering on the hillside below, were like a thousand candles lit just for them.

When they reached the ocean, Christina felt the tires sink into the sand before the car came to a rolling stop. The headlights beamed across the dark ocean—a rumpled mass of black satin sheets, trimmed in soft white silk. The waves lapping against the beach sounded like slow, rhythmic breathing. Christina instinctively slipped out of her black, sling back sandals. Franco got out of the car and walked over to the passenger side. Christina reached for her door handle, but Franco shook his head. He opened the door and held out his hand. Franco's warm hand firmly gripped Christina's as he led her to the water's edge. The hypnotic, undulating waves drew them to the ocean like a magnet. The sand was cool and soft under her feet. 10 paces, 20 paces. She squeezed his hand. A private beach, a full moon, a million stars. What more could one ask for?

Franco broke their stride and pulled her to him. His eyes, as dark as the Mediterranean night, bore through Christina. She realized that she had been nervous all evening to return his gaze,

68

for fear of revealing her inner feelings. But now, all Christina wanted to do was to let this night unfold and succumb to all that Franco's eyes promised. He brought his hands to her face then his mouth to hers. He continued to kiss her hard, but his hands were curious; exploring first her ribcage, just below her breasts, then her hips and upper thighs. Electricity surged through her body. Franco's caresses increased in firmness and speed as he reached behind her and felt the top of her thighs at the edge of her panties. He did not linger there long, however. Christina's flesh singed as his hands discovered the smooth, pale skin that the sun never saw. Franco broke from Christina's mouth to soak in the vision of her face basked in moonlight. He dropped to his knees and began kissing her thighs. He slowly worked his way under the hem of her dress. His warm mouth on her legs sent tingles throughout her entire body. He pulled Christina down to him where he slipped her dress over her head in one, seamless motion. He removed his blazer and spread it onto the sand. The silk lining of his jacket felt soft and luxurious against Christina's back. With Franco now at her side, she could have stayed there forever. Christina unbuttoned his shirt while he caressed and cupped her breasts. His warm breath tickled her ear as he whispered her name. She found his belt buckle and released it. Franco gently rolled on top of her. Christina held her breath and first felt his luscious lashes on her cheeks, then his magnificent mouth finally on hers. They kissed hard and passionately for several minutes. Christina could feel Franco's eagerness on top of her. She could no longer wait to feel him inside her. He expertly pulled her panties off and then slid his fingers inside her warm and inviting body. He explored for several minutes, while lightly kissing her neck. He teased her by rubbing against her. She could not last another second. When he finally entered her, she felt a year's worth of tension flood from her body. While she closed her eyes and savored the pleasure her body continued to tremble. After Franco relented to his desire, he cradled her in his arms. Enveloped in Franco's existence seemed to make

Jill St. Anne

Christina's world a safe, beautiful place. She rested her head on the sand and looked up at the black velvet sky and the luminescent pearl surrounded by millions of glittering diamonds.

Chapter Twelve

The three women had designated the breakfast room at the Hotel della Luna as the place to share their adventures from the night before. By the time Christina got down to the dining room Brandy and Susan had already devoured a basket of bread and finished the entire pot of coffee and steamed milk.

"Thanks for waiting." Christina held up the empty breadbasket. She spotted a waiter and ordered some more coffee and rolls.

"We were starving!" Susan said. "We spent the whole night drinking and dancing on Stephano's yacht. All they had to eat was caviar and crackers."

"I'm sure you two gobbled that right up," Christina said. The waiter poured her a steaming cup of coffee and hot milk.

"Not really," Brandy answered, "we're actually getting sick of caviar. Can you believe it?!? In fact, I think I'm bloated." She pressed the pink flesh on her cheeks.

"Well—," Susan said, "tell us about your date with Franco! We've been dying to hear!"

Reluctant to reveal *everything* that had happened, Christina took a sip of coffee and pushed her hair behind her ears. "We had an enchanting evening. The restaurant was magical, and the time we spent talking and getting to know each other was incredible. I should also add that the chemistry between us is dangerous. To sum it up, I've completely fallen for him."

"How could that possibly happen?" Susan smiled.

"Where should I start?" Christina slathered her roll with strawberry jam. "Besides the fact that he's incredibly handsome, emotionally and physically sensuous, artistic, a wealthy businessman and a descendent of Florentine nobility. He also thinks I'm great."

"What did you just say?" Brandy set down her coffee cup.

"He thinks I'm great!" Christina repeated.

71

"No, not that part!" Brandy said, "I'm talking about the 'wealthy businessman and Florentine nobility.' He's just a kid!"

"No, he isn't," Christina replied. "He's actually 36 years old."

"Why is he working at a hotel?" Brandy asked.

"It's not his full time job." Christina snapped to his defense. "The hotel used to be his family's summer home. Franco manages it in the summer to help his dad."

"How did his family get so rich running a hotel three months a year?" Brandy stuffed another piece of roll in her mouth.

"They acquired their fortune by building a successful marble and granite business. He and his father now run it."

"I want to hear more about that 'dangerous chemistry' between the two of you," Susan snickered.

"I'll leave that up to your imagination." Christina winked at Susan. "Now, tell me more about the party on Stephano's yacht."

Susan shifted to the front of her chair and began waving a knife covered in jam in the air. "First of all, Stephano had originally planned the party for Seike and his friends, but as we know, they unexpectedly left this morning. Because he had already invited at least 30 people, he decided to go ahead with the party anyway."

She set her knife down and licked residual jelly off her fingers. "He sure has some gorgeous friends! He's also quite the man about town."

"You mean playboy." Brandy looked up from her coffee cup.

"I guess you could say that," Susan added, "but I think he's just a typical young guy with lots of money. I can tell he's in his element on his yacht, surrounded by beautiful women and lots of champagne."

"And drugs," Brandy added.

"I didn't see any," Susan responded.

"How could you have missed Stephano and those three bottled blondes snorting coke on the deck?"

"If they're coke heads, that's their problem, not mine." Susan flipped her hair. "Anyway, Stephano has invited us to jaunt over to Sardinia. We plan to set sail this afternoon. Can you join us?"

"I would love to go," Christina said, "But I don't think Franco could get away from the hotel. Besides, he's taking me to see his marble quarries."

"You would rather visit a stone pit than spend a few days on a luscious Mediterranean island?" Brandy questioned her as she lit up a cigarette.

"I know," Christina pushed up her glasses, "it may seem ridiculous, but we won't be in Italy much longer, and I want to spend as much time with him as possible."

Susan came to her defense. "I guess if I were completely head-over-heels with a scrumptious Italian man, I would stick around. Especially if that 'chemistry' is as dangerous as you say it is! Anyway, I'll give you Stephano's mobile phone number, just in case you need to reach us."

Yawning, Christina said, "I'm going back upstairs and taking a nap. If I'm asleep when you leave, have a fabulous time and be careful!"

-

Christina slept until 5:00 p.m., and probably would have kept sleeping, if the telephone ringing hadn't awakened her. It was Franco calling to see if she wanted to go over to the quarry with him before it got too dark.

"Of course I want to go," she said. "I'll be down in a few minutes." She rolled out of bed and put on a short, brightly colored sundress that showed off her golden brown tan. By the time she got downstairs, Franco was already waiting for her in the car. A wicker picnic basket was nestled in the back seat, filled with fresh baguettes, freshly cut flowers, fruit and candles. A bottle of wine was chilling in a silver ice bucket.

They sped off in Franco's convertible and wound their way up to the top of the mountain. As they got closer to the peaks, it became apparent to Christina that the mountains were indeed not covered with snow but with rugged marble. Centuries of erosion had carved dark gray streaks into the jagged edges of the stone.

When they arrived at the quarry, droves of sweaty male workers were leaving for the day. Flat bed trucks, filled with slabs of marble rumbled down the mountain. Clouds of gray dust filled the air. Large, metal machinery, used to excavate the marble, lay idle. Franco suggested that Christina wait in the car while he discussed some business with the foreman. After the workers left, Franco gave Christina a tour throughout the quarry. In spite of it being the hottest time of day, the caverns were as cold as a snow cave. As they walked deeper into the mountain where the stone excavation took place, Christina shivered. Franco put his muscular arm around her and pulled her hard and close to him. He placed his warm mouth on hers and kissed her passionately. She melted into his body and immediately forgot how cold she was.

"Let's go back outside," he murmured. "We don't want to miss the sunset."

The warm sunlight beating down on the mountainside was a welcome feeling. Franco walked back to the car and pulled out his lavishly prepared picnic basket. They found a flat part on the mountain that overlooked the sea and placed the basket on a white and red-checkered blanket that he'd pulled from his trunk. A bottle of Pouilly Fume, which had been chilling in the back seat, was now sweating. Franco poured them each a glass and dropped a bright, red strawberry into the wine. They clinked their glasses and took a sip of the cold drink. Franco removed one of the strawberries and brought it to Christina's lips. She took a bite of the ripe, succulent fruit. Christina fed him her strawberry as Franco gave her a piece of sweet melon wrapped in thinly sliced, salty proscuitto. Christina took a bite, and then he kissed her. His lips tasted as luscious as an entire basket of strawberries and felt as smooth as the melon. Franco unwrapped the silver and blue foil from a *Bacio de Perugina* and placed it on her tongue. The creamy, hazelnut flavored chocolate was rich and delicious. It melted in her mouth. She felt his lips on hers and then his tongue began exploring her mouth. They devoured each other and fell onto the blanket. Franco began stroking the top of her leg and then inched his way under her dress. Waves of pleasure began to rock her body. Franco removed his shirt and brought his warm chest down to hers. Christina kneaded her hands into the thick muscles on his back. Her skin was moist and hot. From the silver bucket by their side, she removed an ice cube, rolled it down Franco's chest and then brought it to her neck. Franco wrapped his mouth around the ice cube and guided it down her decollatage. It melted when it hit the hot flesh between her breasts. Franco licked the liquid from her skin in slow, rhythmic strokes. He reached into the ice bucket and removed the chilled bottle of wine. He set it on Christina's thighs and slid it down to her calves. The ice-cold bottle cooled off her sizzling skin. He slowly pulled the bottle along her legs toward her stomach. He teased her by letting it linger between her legs before he rolled it onto her belly. Her skin glistened like the wet, green glass. Where the cold bottle had traced her legs, his warm hands were now rolling her panties down to her feet. Christina kicked them off while he hastily removed his pants. He lowered himself back down to her and entered her quickly. Christina looked up at his face and savored the visual feast. Such a young, smooth visage; yet representing generations of strength and power. The taste of strawberries, chocolate, wine, and best of all Franco, lingered on her lips.

They continued to eat, drink and talk for hours while they watched the glowing orange ball set gently into the sea. At dusk, Franco lit the candles and they held each other in their arms until the moon rose high in the sky.

Chapter Thirteen

After spending the night in Christina's hotel suite, Franco ordered a hot breakfast, which they ate in bed, making Christina feel lazy and decadent. While Franco was in the shower, Christina ran out to the open-air market to buy some fresh flowers and her newspapers. At the kiosk, she noticed the headline of the European *Wall St. Journal*. She paused and drew in her breath. **"Two Symex Employees Shot in Silicon Valley Burglary."** Her hands shook as she opened the paper. She stood in the middle of the bustling market and read.

The article read that last night, three truckloads of microchips had been taken from the plant at Symex where they were packed and ready to be shipped to their distributor the next morning. In addition, proprietary designs had also been stolen. The night watchman was still in intensive care. The software designer had been released from the hospital the following morning. Regarding the theft of the proprietary designs, the company would not comment.

"Oh my God!" Christina said to no one who was listening. "This is terrible!"

She felt sick to her stomach. The stolen designs could have easily been the ones she was reading about on the beach. If this were the case, the missing designs would be far more harmful than a billion-dollar chip robbery.

Christina sprinted back to the hotel to find Franco waiting for her in bed and under the covers.

"Where have you been, my darling?"

"I went out to buy flowers," she panted, "only to find that something horrible has happened to one of my clients."

"Calm down, Christina," Franco sat up. "I can not understand a word you are saying."

"I'll explain everything later, but right now I need to reach Susan." Her heart was pounding. "What did I do with Stephano's mobile phone number?"

She frantically dug through her purse and found the scrap of paper with the number scratched on it. She phoned over to Sardinia and got through within seconds.

"*Pronto?*" Stephano answered.

"Stephano, it's Christina. Is Susan available?"

"Yes, she's right here."

"Hey—what's up?" Susan shouted into the phone. "It's great over here. I'm perched on the end of Stephano's yacht, soaking in the morning sun. Are you two going to make it? We're having a blast!"

Christina lightly stomped her foot. "No, we're not. Now, Susan, listen to me. There has been a terrible robbery at Symex. Two people were shot and a ton of chips were stolen. Also some proprietary designs were taken. I just read about it in the European *Wall St. Journal*, which means the news is at least a day old."

Susan's voice became lower and more somber. "Do they know who's responsible?"

"There are always leaks in the Valley, so it could've been anyone. But the chips aren't the main issue here. I think those designs that were stolen were the ones Ralph Stinson was working on before he transferred to the subsidiary."

"Ralph Stinson? The guy I met in your office?"

"Right."

"Are those designs the ones you were talking about on the beach in Nice?" Susan asked.

"Could be. If they get into the wrong hands, Symex is going to be in deep trouble."

"Not only Symex, but since they're a defense contractor, the Department of Defense is also in deep shit! I'll ask Stephano to power his yacht back to the mainland."

"Thanks Susan. We're going to have a huge investor relations problem on our hands."

Christina hung up. Her mind was racing. She thought that she should start looking through the folder Ralph Stinson had given her before she left. Maybe there was something in the "Competition" section of the prospectus that would give her some insight as to who might have known anything about what was going on inside Symex. She would later cross reference employees who'd recently left Symex for one of the competitors. As she pulled the file from her luggage, she remembered how she had originally thought she had put it in her carry-on bag. When she found it in her larger suitcase, she thought nothing of it at the time, but given all that had transpired, she felt as though this may not have been an innocent mix-up.

Could someone have deliberately taken the file and put it back in the wrong suitcase?

It began to make sense to her. She and Susan had been talking in the first-class cabin. They'd been discussing the Symex coup loudly enough for anyone who was listening to hear what they were saying. Anyone who was interested in high technology would have been able to realize that they were carrying some valuable information in their suitcases. What an idiotic move that was, Christina thought.

Christina crawled back into bed with Franco, where he was reading the newspaper. She explained, as well as she could, what her thoughts were. As she continued to look through the folder, she came across a manila file with "Confidential" stamped on it in red ink and the words Military Division written underneath.

She did not remember Ralph mentioning this to her. As far as she knew, the microprocessing division had nothing to do with military applications.

As a result of reading the "Confidential" file she discovered that the proprietary information Symex had developed for the U.S. Government incorporated neural networks. She understood enough to grasp that these were a form of a computing architecture that performs high level processing, using a large number of simple processing elements. She remembered from one of her physics classes that these elements were known as neurons. The component Symex was developing performed the hit-to-kill interception on a missile: essentially the brains of the lethal weapon. She deduced that this would be helpful to instantaneously track an enemy's Theater Ballistic Missile.

This clearly had nothing to do with the new chip Symex manufactured. But Ralph, being the absent minded professor he sometimes appears to be, must have accidentally included this in the file he had given her before she left for Europe.

She also discovered that 100% of the company's contracts were with the U.S. Air Force, U.S. Navy and the U.S. Army, who had commissioned them to provide technology for various military applications. She also read, from the internal memos in the file, that potential uses of this technology included guidance systems for ground-to-air missiles and interceptors, air-to-air missiles, and "threat warning" devices. If the enemy got control of this technology during wartime, the United States Armed Forces could be crippled instantly and thousands of American soldiers and Allies would be killed in the process. She thought of the possible uses and shuddered.

Christina took a deep breath and put down the file. What was this all about? And who could have been interested? She poured herself a cup of coffee.

Something about the missing luggage was haunting her, and she could not quite place what it was. It was driving her crazy.

Suddenly, what had been bothering her jumped to the front of her brain. She put her cup down so hard that the coffee sloshed over the rim.

Franco looked up from his newspaper. "What is it, darling?"

"When I first met Stephano's friend, Seike, I thought I had seen him before, but I couldn't place it." She jumped out of bed

79

to get a pencil. "I think Seike was on our plane from San Francisco to Nice!"

"That would make sense," Franco said. "Stephano told me that he had been in the Bay Area with some associates of his, trying to put together some business deal. In fact, I remember Stephano telling me they we're trying to firm something up in France. I'm sure it fell through—all of his endeavors eventually do."

"I need to find out for sure if he was on our plane." Christina tapped her pencil against her lips. "I know that the airlines won't give me a list of passengers, but I remember exactly where he would've been sitting."

She sat for a moment and then picked up the phone. "Let's see if this works." She punched the 800 number for United Airlines.

"Hello, my name is Christina Caldwell." She made her voice sound high and squeaky. "I was on flight 619 from San Francisco to Nice on July 1st. I was sitting in the second row, and Mr. Seike Yamashuta was sitting directly behind me."

She took a deep breath and continued. "Well anyway," she began to speak more rapidly, "he must have placed his notebook under my seat and I accidentally took it with me when we deplaned. I know that you can't give me his address, but if he calls, will you please let him know that I'll mail it to the United Airline ticket office in San Francisco?"

"Let's see." The operator tapped away on the keyboard. "Yes, he was on that flight, but he hasn't called yet."

"Thank you!" She hung up the phone and jumped on the bed. "I knew it! I knew there was something weird about that guy!" She sat cross-legged next to Franco. "What do you know about him?"

Franco set down his paper. "Well, besides understanding that he's an ex-drug dealer and a failure at business, I really do not know much about him. I've made a conscious effort to not get involved with anything he has to offer. As far as I can tell,

Stephano only befriended him because Seike's father is such a valued client. But Seike's all talk. At first Stephano was probably impressed with Seike's grandiose plans, but none of them have ever materialized." Franco shook his head. "He's always talking about hitting it big."

"I just hope that this wasn't the way he planned to do it," Christina said. "We have to call the police. They should arrest him!"

"Christina, Christina." Franco put his arm around her shoulder. "My sweet little detective. You have no proof whatsoever that he committed this crime. All you know for sure is that he sat behind you on the airplane."

Christina pouted. "I know, you're right. But it all makes sense." She pounded the pillow. "Everything fits—our luggage being stolen, him not wanting to talk to us, and then his returning to San Francisco sooner than expected."

"Yes, it does seem logical," Franco stroked her hair. "But how are you going to convince the authorities of this? I agree with you, you should talk to the police, and then hopefully they will locate Seike and question him. But until they have some concrete evidence they will not be able to arrest him."

She chewed the tip of her pencil. "The only thing that doesn't make sense is that the heist took place on Friday and we had breakfast with Seike Saturday morning. How could he have pulled it off?"

"Seike doesn't work alone."

Christina nodded. "He probably flew back early to wrap things up."

Franco pulled her closer to him. "Right. Now will you stop worrying?"

Christina brought the blanket up to her chin and paused before speaking. "Oh, Franco, I'm sorry, but I'm afraid we may have to cut our trip short. This is a serious problem and I have a feeling that we may be able to help the authorities." She turned her head to look at him. "I just wish I didn't have to leave you so soon."

"Don't worry, my darling," Franco looked affectionately into her eyes. "We'll see each other again. I do business all over the world. It's nothing for me to fly to San Francisco. And besides, what makes you think I would let you slip out of my life so easily?"

She felt better and crawled back under the covers with him where they snuggled under the soft blankets until they heard voices in the sitting room.

-

Susan, Brandy and Stephano had departed Sardinia as soon as Christina told them what had happened. Their bronze tans were the only brightness they had brought back with them from the island.

Brandy began unpacking her case of toiletries. "So much for me finding the man of my dreams!"

"There's no reason you have to fly back with us." Susan said to Brandy. "Why don't you stay a few more days?"

Brandy put her hand on her hip. "To tell 'ya the truth, I think I'm better off at home. I can't understand a word anybody's saying." She slung a towel over her shoulder and stomped off to the bathroom.

While Brandy was in the shower, Christina and Susan sat down on the couch in the living room.

"You really think that acquaintance of Stephano's could have masterminded this?" Susan asked.

"Yes, I do," Christina said as she curled her feet under her. "But I don't think they were close friends." She explained what Franco knew about Seike and his relationship with Stephano.

Franco approached Susan and Christina and sat down on the marble coffee table. He rested his forearms on his knees and clasped his hands together. "Stephano and I have been talking and we have an idea that may help you." He looked directly at Christina. "From what I understand, your plane tickets have you leaving from Nice. By train, it will take you at least one full day to get there. You'll probably have to stay over night and then endure a grueling eleven hour flight to San Francisco."

Christina frowned. "What do you have in mind?"

Franco sat up straighter. "I failed to mention this to you, Christina, but Garibaldi Marble owns a jet."

Christina crossed her legs and looked at Susan. "So far, I'm liking the sound of this."

Franco stood up when Stephano entered the room. "I have a business meeting in Toronto early next week, but it couldn't hurt to go over a few days earlier. The only problem is that of my co-pilot. He's occupied with my father for the next couple of days." He patted Stephano's shoulder. "But fortunately, Stephano would be happy to fill in."

Stephano chuckled and stroked his beard. "I could use a few more hours in a Gulfstream."

Franco continued. "We could fly you from here to Toronto, and from Toronto, you could take a commercial flight to San Francisco." He took Christina's hands. "What do you think?"

Christina jumped up and kissed him. "That would be fantastic! When do we leave?"

"We should leave first thing tomorrow morning." Franco cupped her face in his hands. "I'll call the pilot and ask him to prepare the jet for a trans-Atlantic flight."

"Oh, Franco." She hugged his waist and clung to his warm body for several seconds. "Thank you so much."

"My pleasure, dolcina." He kissed her on the top of her head. "My only regret is that I wanted to finish something I'm working on for you. It looks like I'll have to ship it to you later." He paused and stepped away from her. "Also, I must go to my parents' house this afternoon."

"That sounds nice," Christina looked up at him. "Do you see them every weekend?"

He looked down at the floor for a moment. "No, but every month, my family and another old Tuscan family get together for an afternoon dinner. It's not a formal affair, but my parents insist I attend."

Stephano interrupted them. "Remember, the jet's in Pisa, 20 minutes from here. So we need to leave here by 7:00 a.m."

"I better tell Brandy." She walked into the next room, but paused when she heard Stephano say, "Why didn't you tell her the real reason you're forced to meet with your family every month."

She saw Franco turn around and start to walk out the door. "Because it's not important."

Christina took a step back into the room so she could watch.

Stephano grabbed his elbow. "What do you mean it's not important? Your parents have been trying to get you and Alessandra together since you were born! And you have to admit, it would be a sure way to firm up those quarries you've been negotiating." He patted his ample stomach. "Plus, she's a fabulous cook!"

Christina's heart sank. *Could his parents really be serious?* She knew how important his family and the family business was to him. But was it important enough to marry someone?

Christina approached Franco and Stephano. "Listen you two." She forced a smile. "I'm going to have to kick you out of here so we can shower and get the dreaded packing out of the way."

Franco clutched her hand and looked her straight in the eyes. She could tell that he sensed something was wrong. "Christina, I'll be back at six. We'll spend the rest of the evening together."

"Sure, Franco," she smiled feebly. "Take your time."

She hoped she sounded confident and not concerned. But she knew she never could pull off a good poker face.

Chapter Fourteen

Christina and Franco spent a quiet evening together at the beach, walking for hours, hand in hand. The ocean breeze was warm and the smell of the salt water reminded Christina of the time they'd made love on the beach.

"How was your dinner?" She hoped he would truthfully tell her about the afternoon at home.

"Stressful, and worrisome." Franco took Christina's hand and led her along the shore.

"What do you mean?" Christina unbuckled her sandals. The warm water lapped at her feet.

"My parents will not give up." He stopped walking and looked out toward the setting sun. "They want me to marry an old fashioned Italian girl who stays home cooking all day and taking care of babies."

"That's not what you want?" Christina smiled sarcastically. "For some reason, I can't picture you with ten screaming bambinos running around the house."

"I would like to have some children, but not now."

"That's exactly how I feel." She squeezed his hand. "Maybe after I start my own investment firm, I'll settle down and have a family."

Franco picked her up and carried her out into the surf. "Does getting married fall into your sequence of events?"

She giggled and squirmed as she tried to regain her footing.

"Well, does it?" He pretended to let her drop into the water.

"Of course!"

"That's what I wanted to hear." Still holding her in his arms, he kissed her while the water swirled around his feet. He pulled away and smiled. "How come whenever I kiss you, I taste strawberry *sorbetto*?"

"I'll tell you when I'm planted firmly on the sand."

85

Franco carried her back toward the beach and set her down onto the sand. Christina smoothed her sundress.

"I got hooked on Bonne Bell Strawberry Lip Smacker when I was a kid." Christina laughed. "I guess some things we never outgrow."

"Like my love to paint." Franco picked up her sandals and carried them for her. He wrapped his arm around her shoulders. "Except that I started with crayons and upgraded to oils."

Christina lightly elbowed him in his side. "Okay, you made your point."

"My point is simply that you are *carina*."

They continued walking along the beach for several minutes in silence. His arm around her shoulder, hers around his waist.

"Franco," Christina asked, "just how much pressure are your parents putting on you to marry this girl?"

"A tremendous amount. They've made it very clear that my position with Garibaldi Marble is not secure unless I marry this woman."

Christina stopped walking. "I can't believe that still happens!"

"It sure does. But, I have to be honest with you, Christina. The family business means a great deal to me. It has been a part of the Garibaldi heritage for generations." Franco pushed his hair away from his face. He took a deep breath and exhaled slowly. "Alessandra's father is an old man, and he is not well. He told my father that if I marry Alessandra, the two companies would merge after his death."

"My God," Christina looked directly into his eyes. "That is an enormous amount of pressure."

"Yes. But what they don't understand is that I'm not going to be forced to marry someone I love only as a sister. There is no passion between Alessandra and me."

He turned to Christina and pulled her closer. He put his hand under her loose sundress and on her warm back. "Unlike us." He kissed the white skin that her skimpy bikini top shielded from

86

the sun and looked into her eyes. "What we have between us is what a marriage should be about."

Her entire body tingled. He made her feel wonderful and only hoped that his attraction to her would prevail over his business interests.

"You have added such fire to my life." He nibbled her neck and caressed her back. "I cannot commit to marriage without these flames of passion."

Christina wished that she could voice her thoughts as poetically as he always did. "I can't remember the last time I felt like I was on top of the world. Being with you has changed my outlook on life. I'm no longer going to make work a priority."

He pulled away from her. "That's a strong statement, Christina. I only wish I could speak with such conviction."

She wondered what it would be like to marry a foreigner. Where would they live? Where would their children go to school? America or Europe?

She shook her head to rid her mind of those ridiculous thoughts. She wasn't even in the running! She didn't cook much; she hated staying at home all day; and she wasn't Italian! That's three strikes. Not to mention she wouldn't have a prayer with those parents of his.

Trying not to dwell on Franco's betrothal, she pulled him toward the water. He swept her in his arms and carried her into the crashing waves. A forceful surge of water nearly knocked them over. They ran back to the shore and fell onto the dry sand. The sun had just set and the beach was void of people. Wisps of gray clouds brushed the deep rose sky. Franco rolled onto Christina and pinned her wrists with his strong hands above her head. Christina squirmed in the sand as he brought his mouth down to hers. He tasted her strawberry flavored lips and smiled. His tongue found hers and they savored the heavenly moment when nothing else mattered. Franco released his mouth from hers and slid down to her feet. He began to kiss her red lacquered toes and her slender ankles. His lips wandered up her endless legs. He pushed her sundress over her waist as he tickled her belly button with his tongue. With his head on her stomach, she stroked his thick, wavy hair. The sun had sunk into the sea by now, and the sky was dark gray, but the air was hot and full of moisture. Small beads of perspiration formed between Christina's breasts. She slipped her dress over her head and tossed it in the sand. She felt free and exhilarated. Franco inched upward. His mouth met hers. Christina dug her fingers into his muscular back and then began releasing each of the five buttons on his jeans. He crawled out of his pants. The contrast of his soft, silk boxer shorts and his hard body was too much for her. He slid her panties down her leg as she ripped his shorts off. He pressed himself against her and their bodies became one. He never took his eyes away from hers. He brought his hands to her cheeks and cradled her face. He opened his mouth, about to say something, but instead he closed his eyes and wrapped his arms around her. He held her so tightly and so completely. Even without words from Franco, Christina knew what he had wanted to say. Yet she wondered if he would ever verbalize it.

The warm and balmy breeze lulled them to sleep.

Christina awakened the moment the gold ring of sun had peaked above the horizon, changing the gray of dawn to a purple, pink and orange glow. She rolled over and watched Franco as he slept. He was peacefully still. In the midst of the black stubble on his chin, Christina noticed a light red scar where hair could no longer grow. She kissed her fingers and brought them to his chin, where she gently touched the pink line. She wanted to awaken Franco and tell him that she wished she could watch every sunrise with him for the rest of her life, but she took a deep breath, trying to stave off tears. She had to force herself to stay in the moment and not get carried away with unrealistic expectations and emotions. She had been down this road before and didn't want to go through the heartache and disappointment again. She closed her eyes and thought that despite what might happen in their future, she would have last night and this morning as a memory forever. She knew that she would always hold a special place in her heart for him, as she would in his. That had to be enough—for now.

-

After brushing the sand out of their hair, they briskly walked back to the hotel as the sleepy town of Forte dei Marmi was waking up. The humid air was already warm. Merchants hosed off the sidewalks in front of their shops. The familiar aroma of freshly baking bread wafted onto the street. Christina and Franco would have liked to stop for a quick breakfast at one of the local *panettaries,* but they knew the others would be expecting them.

By the time they made it to the hotel, Susan and Brandy were in the lobby waiting for the car. Susan was talking on Stephano's mobile phone. Brandy was brushing on mascara.

Susan looked up when she saw Christina and covered the receiver. "I've been talking to Ralph for the past half hour. The guard's still in the hospital and they have no idea who's responsible for the robbery. On top of this, their stock has dropped 50%!"

Christina took the phone from Susan. "Hi Ralph, it's Christina. We'll be back in 24 hours and we'll get right on your investor and public relations problem. Now, let me ask you this. Did those designs that were stolen have anything to do with the military division?"

"Yes." The connection was garbled, but Christina noted concern in his voice. "This is extremely urgent. Susan said you might have some ideas?"

"Maybe," Christina said. "In the meantime, could you please make sure we're put in contact with whomever is in charge of the investigation?"

"Well, yes of course," Ralph said. "But frankly, I'm amazed that you would know more over in Europe than we would here."

"I'll explain when we get back."

"We'll need all the help we can get. But I'm afraid the investigation has left the realm of the local police department. The theft of valuable microprocessors is one thing, but stealing top-secret plans for missile defense applications is another problem alltogether. In addition to answering a few fundamental questions with the local police department, both you and Susan will have to talk to the FBI."

"That's fine. Whatever we can do." The pit in Christina's stomach grew even bigger. She snapped the phone shut as their limousine pulled to the curb. Christina ran upstairs to get her luggage, while the chauffeur started loading the rest of the bags into the trunk.

When they arrived at the private airfield, Stephano told everyone to wait in the car while he and the pilot conducted the pre-flight inspection. After nearly one-half hour, Stephano returned, and told them that they were ready to fly.

Franco's plane was far more luxurious than Christina had imagined it would be. She felt as though she stepped into a marble showroom. Every counter top was covered with marble or granite. She should have expected no less, considering marble was their business. They sat in what felt like a comfortable living room, as opposed to an airplane passenger compartment. A wide screen T.V., stereo system and fully stocked bar flanked the front of the plane, and six leather chairs and a leather sofa sat to the rear.

The trip literally flew by in less than eight hours. Franco explained to her that this particular model of the Gulfstream flies at 54,000 feet, cutting the flight time down from a commercial airline by almost 25%. Christina napped, watched some videos and discussed with Susan how to handle the investor relations problem that they may have been responsible for by inadvertently leaking some information. Franco mostly talked on the telephone, worked on his laptop computer and helped the women make their travel arrangements to San Francisco.

During the course of the flight, Christina finally got the nerve to ask him something she'd been wondering about for the past week.

She snuggled closer to him. "So Franco, why did you, an astute business man, give the three of us such a fabulous suite and hardly charge us for it?"

"I'm afraid I lost my head for business when I saw the three of you fall out of that melon truck, laugh uncontrollably on the curb and then drag all that luggage of yours across the street. It was wonderful to see such a light-hearted attitude."

"That's sweet of you to say, Franco. But still, you went way overboard. We never expected such hospitality."

"Well, I must admit, I was attracted to you the minute I saw you—those gorgeous legs were hard to miss. But I didn't fall completely for you until I started helping you with your Italian lessons. It was then when I saw your sweet, innocent and playful side. You may be a serious business woman at work, but there is so much more." He stroked her hair, kissed her head, and whispered, "Grazie, bella."

"No, thank you, Franco," she nuzzled closer to him. "I've had a wonderful trip, and you've inspired me to make some serious changes in my life."

"I am glad to hear that," he said. "Now dolcina, I regret that you were not able to see the painting I have been working on for you. It's almost finished, so I will send it to California on a container ship."

She loved it when he called her 'dolcina'. It roughly translated to 'sweet thing' or 'sweetness' in Italian. It made her feel good about herself that he thought of her that way—not for her success, her accomplishments or her appearance.

"Is it *that* big?" she asked.

He laughed at her reaction. "No, of course not. Garibaldi Marble sends container ships of marble nearly every month to the Port of Oakland. From there we ship the marble throughout the West Coast and up to Vancouver. It will be no problem to enclose a private shipment."

"I can hardly wait!"

He kissed her forehead. "In order to avoid problems with the customs officials, I will call you when I have an idea when it will arrive. Also, I'll make sure you get a visitor's pass. The port is enormous. It's not every day a young woman walks onto the docking area and picks up a package."

"I'm familiar with the port," she said. "I see it all the time when I drive over the Bay Bridge."

"Good, so you won't get lost."

Stephano emerged from the cockpit to tell them that they were starting their descent. They would be in landing in Toronto in 20 minutes.

Chapter Fifteen

Franco had arranged for his limousine to take them directly from the private airfield to the international terminal. On the way to the gate they discussed with Stephano how he could help them locate Seike. He gave them Seike's numbers in Tokyo, but they all assumed he was still lurking in the Bay Area.

Because their connection between flights was tight, there was little time for long, emotional good-byes.

They slumped into the limo. Christina turned to Susan.

"I've been so focused on dealing with this investor relations disaster that I nearly forgot I may never see Franco again."

"You'll see him again," Susan said. "I'm sure he'll arrange to get over to San Francisco one way or another." She looked out the window. An Air Canada, jumbo jet roared above them. "I hope he brings Stephano with him. We really hit it off."

"I'm glad that worked out for you," Christina smiled. "But I have to admit, I am surprised you'd be interested in such a cosmopolitan playboy!"

"A little variety here and there sure can't hurt!"

Brandy reached for one of the glass decanters that were arranged in the side compartment of the limo. She poured some vodka into a glass of ice and took a big swig. She held up her glass. "Here's to your Italian stallions." She gulped down the rest of her drink. "I guess I'll have to stick to home-bred American men."

The reality of the ending of their dream vacation finally sunk in as their plane lifted off the runway, enroute to San Francisco.

"What a whirlwind," Christina mused as she stared out the plane window. Square, brown houses, green clumps of trees and long rectangular streets slowly diminished in size. "I can't believe everything that happened in just two short weeks. I had a fabulous vacation, met the man of my dreams, and then it all ended in disaster. Especially for Symex."

"Don't forget the national security of the United States." Susan added.

"I just hope that Seike is not smart enough to understand the full ramifications of those designs."

"Me too," Brandy said, "especially after hearing all that war and missile stuff you were talking about in Nice. I never thought what could happen if the enemy were in control."

Christina released the air phone from the seat in front of her and punched Ralph Stinson's direct line.

"Hi Ralph. It's Christina. We're landing on time. Do you want us to meet you anywhere?"

"That's not necessary," he said. "I've arranged for the FBI to meet you at the airport as soon as you land. You'll be driven directly to their Northern California Headquarters. This predicament is far worse than I had originally thought. I'll let the FBI fill you in. This line is not protected."

A pang of guilt swept over Christina.

"We'll cooperate in any way possible," she said. "We'll do anything we can."

"Thanks Christina." Ralph's voice disappeared into the crackle of the airwaves.

Christina pushed the phone back into its holder and turned to Susan. She bit her lip. "Susan, I feel so responsible."

-

When the plane touched down at San Francisco International Airport, the flight attendant told them that a government car was waiting for them on the tarmac. They were escorted down a side staircase at the front of the plane. Two FBI agents, dressed in what seemed to be their standard attire of dark suits and sunglasses, waited for them.

"Good afternoon, ladies," the taller one said, flipping open his badge, "please get in quickly. Your bags will be here in a few minutes."

The luxury of not having to hassle with the airport terminal was soon overcome by anxiety. The agent in the passenger seat began to bombard them with questions.

"So, ladies," he turned his head around to face them in the back seat. He had a bushy brown mustache and a mole on his left cheek. "Mr. Ralph Stinson, of Symex, mentioned that you might have discovered something we should know about." He pushed his sunglasses onto his head. "What is this?"

Christina explained that she thought Seike Yamashuta, who had been sitting behind them on the plane to Nice, may have overheard them talking about Symex. It was possible he'd stolen their luggage, with the confidential file in it.

"See-kay." He looked up from his notes. "Do you know how that's spelled?"

"No, I don't, but his last name is spelled like it sounds."

He scribbled on a pad. "Thank you, we'll call this into headquarters and run a report on him."

He thumbed through a folder. "We've begun a thorough background check on each of you. From what we've discovered so far, it looks as if Ms. Jensen will not be essential to our investigation. So we'll be happy to give you door-to-door service to your house." He looked down at his folder. "I see you live in Pacific Heights."

"That's right," Brandy said. "And I can hardly wait to get home."

Two airport officials walked toward the car carrying their luggage. When the trunk was slammed shut, the driver started the ignition.

As the car sped off the tarmac, the man with the mole began speaking again. "Now, for you two." He pointed a stubby finger at Susan and then at Christina. "We're taking you to our office for some further questioning. A special agent from the Foreign

Counter Intelligence division in D.C. flew in yesterday to oversee this investigation. You're meeting with him in an hour. Also an Airforce General and a technology advisor from DARPA will be on call to answer any questions pertaining to the Symex project."

Christina began to feel queasy. She knew that this was serious, *but a special agent from the Foreign Counter Intelligence division? An Airforce General? An advisor from DARPA?* She was in way over her head.

As the car pulled into Brandy's driveway, the agents admonished her not to leave town without notifying them or not to discuss this case with anyone. Christina wished they could all hop out of the car with her. Brandy gave them both a hug good-bye and told them to call her tomorrow.

Christina heard the agent in the passenger seat make a phone call and spell Seike's name. He held for a while and then jotted some notes on his pad of paper. Other than that one call, the ride to the headquarters was uncomfortably quiet. Even a yawn or a whisper would have cut the tension like a razor slicing a taut guitar string.

When they reached the gray, stark office building on Golden Gate Avenue, in San Francisco's Civic Center, the two women were ushered to a sparsely furnished office. Special Agent Peters, the man in charge of the investigation, sat in his windowless office, behind a plain metal desk, puffing a cigar. His head was shaved completely bald. Heavy, brown eyebrows, speckled with gray, called attention to his dark eyes. The FBI agent handed him the report that had been taken in the car.

"Sit down ladies," Peters said gruffly. "I just need a few minutes to scan this." He leaned back in his chair and began to read.

Susan and Christina settled into a pair of stiff metal chairs and waited. He nodded several times and scribbled a few notes.

He finished reading and put the report on his desk. "All right now," he sighed. "You think a character by the name of Seike Yamashuta is involved?"

"Yes," Christina nodded.

"The agents who picked you up did some preliminary research. All they discovered were a few drug trafficking charges."

"Yes, but—" Christina jumped to the front of her chair.

Peters held up his hand. "Please, let's start from the beginning. Tell me how you think this all happened."

Christina took a deep breath. "I knew very little about the defense work Symex was doing," she told him. "As an investment firm, we're only involved in the semiconductor aspect of the business. All we know is that they had just completed manufacturing a chip that is supposed to be less expensive and more powerful than Intel's Pentium Pro. These chips, as we are all aware of now, were the ones that were stolen. The reason Susan and I were discussing the company on the plane was because we both needed to further research the technical aspect of the business; for example what differentiates the SMX PC 750 from the Pentium V."

Susan interrupted. "I just learned about our new client the night before we left for Europe." Christina noticed that she had purple shadows under her eyes. "Because I'm the analyst, I knew that I would have to present Symex to my associates in New York at our quarterly meeting in October. A logical place to discuss this project was on the plane, considering that we were sitting next to each other for eleven hours. Because the chip aspect of the business was the only one we would be representing, that's all we discussed during the flight."

"Right." Christina looked at Susan and then at Agent Peters. "Seike must have heard what we were discussing, and given the monetary value of high powered chips, we think he took our luggage to search for more information about the company." She leaned back in her chair. "Have we provided you with enough information to warrant an arrest for Seike?"

"No, you have not." He ran his large hands over his slick head. "We have enough information to bring him in for questioning, but unfortunately, we have no idea where he is, and it sounds like you don't either. Am I correct?"

Christina nodded. "What about the telephone number in Tokyo? Did you try that?" She was beginning to feel nauseous. Her skin felt clammy. She wasn't sure if it was from the travel, the lack of sleep or the circumstances surrounding the heist.

"The agents who picked you up at the airport tried that number, but it's been disconnected. And according to the Japanese phone company it's been inoperative for months."

"Now," he puffed his cigar, "let me tell you where we're at. All current employees, including those who have worked for the company within the past ten years, are presently being investigated. The most urgent problem, that of the missing designs, needs to be attacked immediately. The robbery of the chips is a financial setback for Symex, but not nearly as catastrophic as the missing ballistic missile plans. What they have been working on is very serious. If these designs got into the wrong hands, the security of every American citizen and our allies would be placed in peril."

"How did they know to take the designs?" Christina asked.

"I'm sure they didn't have any idea what they were," Agent Peters tapped his cigar. A pile of ashes fell into a metal tray. "The engineer who was shot told us that the perpetrators came in, popped him and went directly to the securitized building. The set of disks that contain the designs were in a case marked BHAAD1. The perps probably had the sense to realize that whatever was in that case must be rather important."

"Bad One?" Susan asked. "That sounds like the name of a rap group."

"No, Miss Anders." Agent Peters did not seem to appreciate her sense of humor. "BHAAD1 is not a rap group. It's an acronym that stands for Ballistic High Altitude Area Defense. We only hope that whoever stole those designs does not understand the full ramifications of the project. The BHAAD system is the only core theater missile defense system which, when completed, will be capable of engaging the full spectrum of theater class ballistic missile threats."

"Sorry to interrupt, Agent Peters," Susan said, "but you're speaking a foreign language."

What Agent Peters was talking about began to gel in Christina's brain. She recalled the "Confidential" file she'd read while in Italy.

"Let me simplify." Peters leaned back and put his hands behind his head. "This is serious stuff. The BHAAD system will provide us with the capability we need to defend ourselves against ballistic missiles that carry lethal hit-to-kill interceptors. These missiles will also fly at higher levels and have longer ranges. I say *will provide* because they haven't been manufactured yet. The designs are only the first step.

"Whoever stole the designs has the power to manufacture missiles of their own and sell them to whomever will buy. And trust me, there are plenty of buyers out there. The reason this technology is such a breakthrough is because our current form of defense, such as the PATRIOT Advanced Capability, cannot perform on the same level as BHAAD."

"You mean the Patriot missiles from the Gulf War? The ones that were supposed to blow the SCUDS out of the sky?" Christina asked.

"Yes." He puffed his cigar.

"We get the picture now. Thanks for clearing that up," Susan said.

Peters continued. "China is neck and neck with us in the race to develop a long range, ballistic missile. Our intelligence officers spotted one on the Wuzhai Missile and Space Test Center. It's called the Dong Feng-31."

The women stared at him with blank faces. Wuzhai and Dong Feng were words that meant nothing to them.

Peters leaned his bulky chest forward and spoke in a lower voice. "This missile has a 5000 mile range and carries multiple warheads. It has the power to wipe out the entire West Coast."

Christina clutched her stomach. She felt the blood drain from her face. A wave of nausea swept her body.

"Now do you understand the serious nature of this investigation?"

The women nodded.

Peters settled back in his chair. "Our main concern is that whoever masterminded this robbery could take the Symex designs to any country or any terrorist group engaged in warfare or one which is in the process of remilitarizing."

He held up his finger. "The only bright side to this robbery so far is that the designs are worthless without a small encryption chip that must be inserted in a specially formatted computer in order to decipher the plans on the diskette."

He took another hefty puff on his cigar and continued talking. "As far as we know, we don't think that particular chip was taken. We confirmed that the master is still in the safe at Symex. However, a rough prototype, even with a few bugs in it, would provide enough information to crack the code. The lock on the safe was changed as soon as we were made aware of the robbery, and FBI agents have since guarded it around the clock. When we changed the locks, we asked the company to confirm the number of prototypes that were manufactured. Several were in the safe with the master, but we need to make sure that there aren't any others floating around somewhere. Currently, not even the president of the company can get into the safe without being accompanied by a high-level FBI agent."

He stubbed out his cigar. "Our objective here is to find whoever has these plans before they realize how valuable they really are." He sat back in his chair and crossed his arms. "That's why we brought you in for questioning. We appreciate your lead regarding Mr. Yamashuta."

Agent Peters got up from his chair. "All right ladies, you're finished—for now. I'll have a car take you back to your homes. But, I'm warning you," he pointed at them as they stood up, "be careful, and do not mention this investigation to anyone. No one is to be trusted until this matter is completely resolved."

They were half way out the door when Agent Peters called out to them.

"Miss Caldwell—I forgot to ask you about the file you received from Ralph Stinson. Do you have it with you?"

Christina turned around. "Well, yes."

"I'll need to keep that as evidence."

"Sure, I'll go out to the car and get it."

He escorted her out to the parking lot where she dug through her suitcase. She found it buried under her dirty clothes. She hoped she remembered everything she needed to know, and then handed it over to Agent Peters.

They somberly got into the unmarked government car and Christina reflected upon the past few weeks. She thought how strange it was that their vacation to the Italian Riviera would end with them being driven home by a Federal Agent. As the car rolled away from the dreary building of the FBI Headquarters, the mystical, romantic interlude that had taken place between her and Franco, just days before, faded into a distant memory.

Chapter Sixteen

Christina was relieved to finally be in the comfort of her own home and could hardly wait to sink into her feather bed. She was exhausted and fell asleep immediately, without even checking her messages. Luckily, tomorrow was Friday. She would try to sleep in. Later, she would go to her office and attempt to make a dent in her mail.

Because of jet lag, she awoke at 3:30 a.m. It was still too dark to go running, so she listened to her messages. There were several from her friends and family, all wanting to hear about her trip.

To her astonishment, she heard a message from someone at Senator Cartwright's office in Washington D.C. She replayed it to make sure she was hearing it correctly. The Senator's secretary asked that she call his office. There was a reception in his honor being held in San Francisco, and the Senator would like for her to be his guest.

Why would Senator Cartwright be calling her, she thought? She remembered meeting him at the fund-raiser she'd attended several years ago, but the event was so crowded that she'd barely had a chance to exchange more than a few words. He was an extremely influential, handsome politician from California who was politically savvy enough to have the support of both Silicon Valley in the North as well as the entertainment community in the South. Because of his immense popularity he was considered to be a leading presidential contender. Still in his early forties, and after his divorce last year, he was one of the most eligible bachelors in the country. By now, it was still only 7:00 a.m. in Washington D.C. She made a mental note to call in a few hours.

She continued listening to her messages. There was no word from Franco. She wondered why he hadn't called to see if she made it home safely. She thought she had come to the end of her tape when she heard some static. An unrecognizable voice crackled from her machine.

"Return what's not yours!" the voice hissed. "It's not worth losing your life!"

The hairs on her arms and neck stood up. She played the message again. Could this be from Seike? The voice sounded mechanically altered, so she could not determine whom it was. One threatening message was not going to scare her. But, she saved it so she could play it for the authorities later.

The sun was finally coming up. She really needed to go running; it would be her first good run in nearly three weeks and she was looking forward to the exercise and fresh air. Her route along the Marina Green, the Saint Francis Yacht Club and out to the Golden Gate Bridge reminded Christina that in spite of her travels to fun, exciting places all over the world, it was great to be home. As far as she was concerned, she lived in the best place on Earth.

While she was jogging, she thought about Senator Cartwright. Why would he call *her*, out-of-the-blue, and request that she accompany him to a party in his honor? Was he interested in her socially or did this have something to do with her Silicon Valley connections? She picked up her pace. And why hadn't Franco called?!?

-/-/-

Christina was not the only one awake early that morning.

Given all the cutting edge research that takes place in Silicon Valley, San Francisco is the perfect base from which to conduct surveillance activities regarding the technological progress of industrialized nations.

The Chinese Consulate, a large white building in the Cathedral Hill section of town, with windows trimmed in light blue paint and iron bars covering the heavy glass, was bustling with activity this morning. Upstairs in the parlor room, the

Consul was hosting a breakfast meeting to discuss trade practices and the MFN status, while downstairs in a room completely segregated from the main house, an entirely different type of business was taking place. The basement, which looked more like the command center for NASA, was humming with the sound of computers and powerful surveillance equipment. A young aide, looking at a flashing computer screen, took off the earphones he was wearing, and reached for one of the many telephones that sat on the table next to him. Late last night an anonymous caller had phoned regarding the sale of some valuable information. Instructions had been left to call back at precisely 9:00 a.m.

The phone answered on the first ring. The aide asked the caller to identify himself. Of course he did not, but he explained that he had something he knew would be of interest to the Chinese government. The caller requested that someone meet him in the bar at Tadich Grill on California Street at 2:00 p.m. The aide agreed only a split second before the phone went dead.

-/-/-

Christina walked up the wooden stairs to her apartment after her run and reached for the phone to call Senator Cartwright. She was nervous, while at the same time excited, as she called his office.

"Senator Cartwright's office," his secretary answered.

"Hello, this is Christina Caldwell calling for Senator Cartwright." She pulled off her running shoes.

"Good morning, Miss Caldwell, I'll put you right through. The Senator has been expecting your call."

"Christina, thank you for returning my phone call." His voice sounded smooth and friendly. "How was your trip?"

"It was fabulous," she answered, thinking what an understatement that was. "How did you know I was traveling?"

"I called your office, and they told me you were in Europe. Did my secretary tell you about the reception at the Sheraton Palace next week?"

"Yes, I heard something to that effect on my answering machine. Thank you for inviting me, but I have to be honest with you, Senator,"

"Please, call me Richard," he interjected.

"O.K., Richard," she took her phone and walked over to the kitchen, "we hardly know each other, and I am not quite certain why you called me." She cradled the phone between her neck and shoulder while she ground some coffee beans and put a kettle of water on the stove.

"I know more about you than you think. I noticed you at my fundraiser a couple years ago, but because you were always surrounded by a such a large group of men, I had trouble getting over to you."

Hardly, she thought. As she remembered it, the situation had been entirely reversed. However, she appreciated the flattery and his sense of humor.

"I asked a few people who you were, and made a point of trying to get together with you at some point in the future."

"That was three years ago!" The kettle began to whistle. She poured the hot water into her French, glass and metal coffee maker that she'd owned since her days at the Sorbonne. "It's nice to hear you don't jump into things quickly."

He laughed at her remark, and Christina was beginning to feel more comfortable talking with him.

"You may have heard that I've been going through some personal problems," he sighed into the receiver, "in addition to being extremely busy here in D.C."

"Yes, I heard a little about your divorce." Christina was not all *Wall Street Journal* and *Investors Business Daily*. She would occasionally pick up a *People* magazine, or at least read one when she was getting her hair cut. Apparently, his wife had been having an affair with an actor in Hollywood. She plunged the metal coffee filter against the coffee grounds. "So, tell me more about this party at the Sheraton Palace."

"I thought we could talk about that and catch up on what you've been doing, when I'm back in San Francisco. I'll be in town this Thursday, and I was hoping we could get together for dinner."

She was not prepared for this invitation. "Uh…" she said flailing.

"It would give me such pleasure," the Senator pressed her. Why don't you make reservations at a place of your choice?"

Christina wondered if this would betray Franco. But, after all, she wasn't going to sleep with him—just have dinner.

"Where are you staying?" she asked.

"At the Fairmont on Nob Hill."

"I'll make reservations nearby. How does 8:00 sound?"

"Sound's perfect! I look forward to seeing you again."

"Likewise," Christina said.

They both said good-bye. Christina sat stunned in her chair, still sweating from her run.

After he hung up, Senator Cartwright leaned over his desk and pressed the intercom button on his phone to summon his secretary.

"Yes Senator?" she answered.

"Call Saunders and let him know I have a meeting with Caldwell Thursday night."

He then leaned back in his leather chair, put his feet on the antique desk that had been used by Everett Dirksen during his long tenure as the Illinois Senior Senator, and smiled.

-/-/-

It was nearly 7:00 a.m. Christina stepped into the shower and began to lather a rich, herbal shampoo through her hair. She heard the telephone ring. Her answering machine clicked on and she heard Franco's delicious accent. She ran out of the shower, grabbed a towel, and picked up the phone.

"Franco!"

"Did you make it home safely, my darling?"

She sat down on her sofa. "It's great to hear your voice. Thank you again for flying us back to the States. It sure made things easier for us."

"I'd do it again in a minute. How did your meeting go with the police department?"

"Yesterday was the FBI," she said. "We still have the police to look forward to this morning."

She remembered that Agent Peters told her not to talk about this with anyone. While she felt it was safe to talk to Franco about it, she still thought she should be careful. For all she knew, her phone could be bugged.

"I would be careful, Christina. You must remember, Seike can be quite dangerous. Please leave the investigating to the authorities. You have enough to worry about."

"But I feel so responsible. If we hadn't been discussing the company on the plane, this entire debacle would've been avoided."

"Why don't you come visit me in Toronto until this settles down? I'm already missing you and I'm concerned for your safety."

"That's so sweet of you, Franco," Christina said, realizing that he actually cared for her. She wondered if she should tell him about the Senator's call. "I miss you too. I can't tell you how upset I was when I listened to my messages and didn't get one from you."

"I'm sorry, dolcina. My secretary rearranged my meetings. From the minute I arrived, I have been locked in conference rooms and on job sites. But after tomorrow, my schedule should lighten up."

"I wish I could come to Toronto, Franco. But I've been gone for over two weeks. I have a ton of work waiting for me. Could you take a small detour to San Francisco before returning to Italy?"

"I will do my best. But I may have to fly from here to Hong Kong. Maybe I could stopover on Thursday. How does that sound?"

Christina was silent. How was she going to handle the conflict she had Thursday night with Senator Cartwright? Honesty was always the best policy, and she was not going to waiver from that now. "Thursday would be perfect," she said. "I can hardly wait to see you. But, unfortunately, I have a dinner engagement for a few hours Thursday night."

"A dinner date?" The tone of Franco's voice changed. It was darker, more somber.

Christina felt somewhat guilty. "For some reason this senator from California, Richard Cartwright, called and invited me to dinner."

"Senator Cartwright?" Franco sounded astonished.

"You've heard of him?"

"Christina, he's an infamous ladies man."

She was beginning to feel worse. "I'm sure it's just business."

"Christina, be realistic," Franco protested. "Even though there may be a slight business undertone, he is most certainly interested in you personally."

"He's really well connected in The Valley. I think I should listen to what he has to say."

"How can you be so naive?"

"Franco, that jealous Italian streak is showing. Haven't you ever had dinner with a woman marble distributor or architect?"

"Well yes, but…"

"So you see," Christina interrupted, "it happens all the time. How about this: If you're able to make it Thursday night, you can pick me up at the restaurant after dinner and we'll drive back to my apartment together."

"That sounds reasonable. I'll call you later in the week to let you know if I will be able to clear my schedule by Thursday. I must go now. Ciao darling."

Christina was glad to hear that he was acting so mature and felt better about being honest with him. After she hung up, she called Susan to wake her and to see if she wanted to drive into the office together. Her machine answered.

"Susan… wake up," she shouted into the machine. "It's Christina."

Susan finally picked up the phone, sounding groggy. "I'm too tired to go to work this morning."

"We should at least make an appearance and go through our mail. We have no idea what other bombshells may have dropped while we were away. Also, remember we still have to stop in at the police department this morning."

"Oh—that's right." She yawned into the phone. "Pick me up in half an hour."

-

The meeting at the San Francisco Police Department was far less intimidating than the one at the FBI. In fact, the department was such a zoo that they started nearly an hour late. Susan and Christina sat on worn, wooden chairs in the waiting area, where they watched a disparate group of prostitutes, protesters, and homeless people parade through the corridor.

Christina and Susan were both dressed casually. Christina in faded Levi's and a white, long sleeve linen blouse. Her blond hair was pushed away from her face with a tortoise shell headband. She could still feel the sand in her sandals. Susan wore a long, flimsy skirt, a jeans jacket and cowboy boots. Her brown curly hair hung loosely around her face. Finally, Sergeant O'Reilly pushed his way through the glass doors. He was a rotund man, with a round face decorated with many red, broken blood vessels on his nose and cheeks.

"Sorry to keep you waiting. The mayor's trying to clean up the streets by arresting the homeless and making us deal with the problem." He wiped his forehead with the back of his hand. "Why don't you follow me back to my office."

They sat down in two tattered leather chairs opposite his cluttered desk. Pictures of his wife and children sat buried in stacks of paper. Wood framed awards, honoring his years of service, hung on the walls.

"How 'bout some coffee?" From a pot, permanently stained with coffee, he poured a cup for himself.

"No thanks," they said politely. Christina wondered if Susan was also thinking about the rich, Italian espresso that they had been accustomed to drinking for the past two weeks.

"Yup." He began digging through his piles of papers as he looked for his report. "I've been on the force nearly thirty years, and it's only been recently where we've had problems with stolen micro-chips. What's it going to be ten years from now—people stealing the vaccine to the AIDS virus to sell on the black market?"

He found the report he had been looking for, brushed off some crumbs, leftover from a half-eaten sandwich that sat on the side of his desk. "Ah, here it is. So you think a Japanese guy—Seike Yamashuta—is behind this?"

"We're not certain," answered Christina, "but we have reason to believe that he may be involved."

She told him the story she'd had relayed to Agent Peters. At the end of her recount, she pulled a small cassette tape from her purse. "I also brought you a tape from my message machine. Someone left me a threatening message, and I think it may have been Seike. I was hoping you could have it analyzed for me."

"Sure, let me have it." He extended his pudgy hand across the desk. "You've answered everything I need to know for now. I'll get back to you if I have any more questions—and I'll let you know what turns up with the tape."

The two women got up from behind the desk and shook his rough hand goodbye. He handed them his business card. "Here, take this. It has my beeper number on it. Call me if you run into trouble."

"Thanks." They slipped his card into their wallets.

"What a character!" Susan said after they were out of earshot. "Did you see that jelly doughnut smashed between his papers?"

"Yeah," Christina smiled, "but I really liked him. He reminded me of my old high school principal."

They finally made it to their office and found nearly a foot of mail on each of their desks. Christina briefly went through her correspondence, which included over 200 e-mail messages. At 2:30 she eventually walked into Susan's office.

Susan stood by the side of her desk with a stack of mail. She threw a few letters onto her desk and the rest into her waste paper basket.

"I can't believe all this junk mail!" Susan said. "Have you heard from Franco?"

"Yesterday." Christina pulled an L.L. Bean catalogue out of the garbage can. "He's probably swamped with meetings." She flipped through the catalogue and threw it back into the trash. "I thought we should give Ralph a call."

"Better now than never," Susan said.

"Hi Ralph," they said together on speaker. "Any news yet?"

"Unfortunately, nothing. How did everything go at the FBI?"

"Frightening." Christina sat down. "We also just got back from the police department. And last night, when I was going through my messages, I think I got one from someone who's trying to scare me off his trail. I gave the tape to the police to analyze the voice pattern."

"It sounds like you'd better be careful. Let the authorities handle this."

Christina readjusted her headband, pulling her hair tighter off her face. "It's impossible for me to sit still, especially knowing

111

that those designs may be in the process of being sold to the highest bidder as we speak. By the way, do you know if the stolen chips have hit the market yet?"

"As far as we know, they haven't surfaced. Anyway, we must do something about this stock price. Our investors are screaming and demanding that we do something to push it back up."

"We're working on a press release, but let me tell you, it's hard to make this sound any different than it is."

"Good point." She heard Ralph breathe into the phone. "By the way, do you still have the file I gave you last month?"

"No, in fact I was just going to ask you to get me another copy. Agent Peters took it from me yesterday."

"He *did?*"

"Yes, I thought he needed it for evidence or something." She began to worry. "Should I not have given it to him?"

There was a silence. "Ralph?" Christina said. "Are you still there?"

"Uh—yes, I mean no, it's not a problem. I'll give Peters a call to make sure everything is in order, and I'll have another copy messengered over to you this afternoon."

"Thanks, Ralph, we'll talk to you later."

Margie beeped through as they were hanging up.

"Mr. Jacobs is on line two for you, Christina."

Christina looked at Susan. A cold chill swept through her body. All she needed was heat from Jacobs.

"Yes Mr. Jacobs." Her hand shook as she picked up the receiver. "This is Christina."

"What's this I hear about you being involved in this Symex problem?" His voice was loud and gruff.

"We're not involved, we just think we may know who is responsible." She tried to keep her voice from quivering.

"I don't like the sound of this. If Symex finds out that you, in any way, could have jeopardized their financial condition, you'll be looking for another job."

"Don't worry, sir, everything will be fine." She could barely eke out the words.

Things were far from fine.

-/-/-

While Christina ate a sandwich at her desk, the last of the business lunch crowd was finally clearing out of Tadich's and returning to work. Tadich Grill, known as the best fish joint in town, opened during the Gold Rush of 1849, and has been an institution ever since. It's still the only place where one still can sneak a puff from a cigar in the bar area, and the three martini lunch has not sprinted into the sunset along side the health craze.

At the end of the restaurant, in a dark, shadowy area, two men, one Asian, one Caucasian, were seated at a small table, hunched over and whispering with their heads close together. This was their first contact since the phone message left at the Chinese consulate. The waiter approached their table and asked them if they would like something to drink. The two did not appreciate the interruption. One put up his hand, gesturing to leave them alone. Curious, the waiter continued to watch them. He saw the Caucasian man give the other man a single sheet of paper. After the young Chinese aide looked at it, he nodded his head. The other gentlemen, the one who initiated the meeting, swiftly left the restaurant. Sitting alone at the table, the Chinese man ordered a drink and walked over to the pay phone. After hanging up, he walked outside into the bright sun. He covered his eyes with black sunglasses, slipped into his souped-up, low riding Honda and sped away.

They had a deal.

Chapter Seventeen

By Thursday morning, Christina had finally regained her momentum at work, and was able to concentrate on something other than the Symex fiasco, and the fact that she had not heard from Franco. She was just about to call Ralph Stinson when Margie buzzed through saying that Senator Cartwright was on the line.

"Thanks, Margie." Christina felt a bit nervous. "I'll take it."

She picked up the receiver. "Hello Richard. Are you already at the Fairmont?"

"I am, and I have to run into the next room for a meeting in a few minutes. Are we still on for dinner tonight?"

"Yes, I made reservations at Venticello. It's just a few blocks from the hotel."

"Why don't you meet me in the lobby at 7:45, and then we can walk over to the restaurant together."

"Sounds great. I'll see you then."

She wished she had heard from Franco. She missed him and was clinging to the hope that he would meet her after dinner. Because she didn't know where he was staying in Toronto, she was unable to reach him. She thought it was strange that he hadn't called and wondered if he was angry about the dinner meeting with the Senator. She felt horrible, thinking that she may have jeopardized her relationship with Franco by agreeing to have dinner with Richard. She assuaged her fears by telling herself that they were only having dinner. Just in case he called while she was out to lunch, she would tell Margie she would be at Venticello this evening.

It was after 1:00 p.m., and her stomach began growling. She called Susan to see if she wanted to take a quick walk outside and grab some lunch. The fog had burned off nicely, leaving a warm and sunny afternoon in its wake.

114

They made their way over to the Embarcadero, a paved walkway along the Bay. Christina was oblivious to the people eating lunch on the iron benches and the homeless asking for spare change. Thoughts of Franco and her dinner tonight with the Senator preoccupied her mind. *Why hadn't Franco called?* Maybe he would surprise her and show up at Venticello in a long, white limousine with a dozen red roses and a bottle of champagne. She caught herself daydreaming, and thought that she had better stop fantasizing and check back into reality.

Christina stopped walking and gazed out at the water. A seagull landed on the railing a few feet away. She watched it flutter its wings before flying away. She turned to Susan. "Do you honestly think Franco would not call me just because I'm having a dinner meeting with Richard?"

"Christina, please get real! Richard Cartwright is one of the most eligible bachelors in the world. I'm sure Franco has heard of him."

Christina changed the subject. "What's going on with Ralph? I haven't talked to him in a few days."

"Me either," Susan said. "I thought maybe you've been staying in touch. I hope they're not going to fire him for hiring us."

"I doubt that." Christina was still staring blankly at the Bay. The sound of a freighter horn startled her. Small yellow tugboats began pushing a huge cargo ship out to the Pacific Ocean. She looked at her watch. "We better high tail it back to the office. We've been out here nearly a half hour."

Christina had decided to work late at the office, run some errands, and then meet the Senator at the Fairmont. She'd purposely worn an elegant, navy Armani suit, with a colorful Hermes scarf and pearl earrings, suitable for office and evening. She hoped the suit would convey the sense of business that she wanted to maintain with Senator Cartwright.

Still no call from Franco. She wondered if she had alienated the one man with whom she'd thought she could have a future.

Since the Fairmont on Nob Hill was just a short cable car ride from her office, she left her car parked in the lot beneath her office building. She had an ulterior motive: hopefully, Franco would show up at the restaurant to drive her home. Underneath her simple suit, she wore a silk, black, lacy merry widow and silk stockings. She could hardly wait to feel his warm hands slide her stockings down her leg and caress the rest of her body.

The fog had rolled back in. Christina shivered as she clung to the outside rail of the cable car. She couldn't tell if she was trembling from the cold weather, or because she was nervous at the thought of seeing the Senator again. She was running a bit late and hoped she would have some time to slip into the powder room to comb her wind blown hair.

No such luck. As she walked into the opulent lobby of the hotel, which recently received a makeover from its toned down bordello image of earlier years, she saw Senator Cartwright sitting in a maroon velvet chair by the entryway. He looked older and more distinguished than when she'd last seen him three years ago. His hair was nearly completely gray, but his face was still angular and chiseled. She could see why he was the object of so many women's attentions.

"Hello, Christina." He stood up from his chair, towering over her with his broad shoulders and 6'4" frame. "It's nice to see you again. You're even more stunning than I remember."

"Thank you, Richard. It's nice to see you again, also." She realized she was going to need to be careful and not let the evening stray from the intended purpose of 'catching up.' He had only gotten more handsome with age.

They walked together from the Fairmont along Sacramento Street, passing the Pacific Union Club and Grace Cathedral. They talked about innocuous subjects such as the history of Nob Hill and the barons of industry, Stanford, Huntington, Hopkins and Crocker, known as the "Big Four", who'd built the city.

Stanford had founded a university, Crocker a bank and a shopping galleria, and Huntington and Hopkins each had a hotel that bore his name atop Nob Hill.

Heads turned as they waited for their table at Venticello, a quaint, rustic Italian restaurant. Christina had not considered that she would be in the presence of one of the most recognizable men in California. Because the restaurant was so small, none of the tables were private. The Senator, of course, did not mind: after all, he would be running for president one day.

"Christina," he said softly, "if this makes you uncomfortable, we could go somewhere else. How does a four course meal back at the hotel sound?"

"No, thank you. I'm fine." She clutched her briefcase firmly. "Let's stay here."

They were shown to their small table covered with a red and white checkered tablecloth. A single candle flickered in the center of the table. Richard held her chair and ordered them a bottle of Barolo. After they had sat down, Christina began to feel a bit more at ease. She swept her hair behind her ear and crossed her legs under the table.

"So, what's keeping the Chairperson of the Senate Armed Services Committee busy these days?"

He sighed and shook his head. "It's been a tough ride. I'm working on passing a bill to raise funds to speed up the development of our theater missile defense arsenal. Those damn Democrats—oh, excuse me, I assumed you're a Republican."

"Don't worry." She dipped a piece of fresh focaccia bread into some extra virgin olive oil. "I guess you could call me a liberal Republican."

"Anyway, the Democrats are fighting me every step of the way. We've been trying to kill the Anti-Ballistic Missile Treaty, and they've been putting up roadblocks."

"Are you afraid that a foreign power such as North Korea, China, Iran or Iraq could easily launch an attack and we, under the guidelines of the Anti-Ballistic Missile Treaty, would be left crippled and unable to defend ourselves?"

"Yes, exactly!" He reached over to pour Christina some more wine. She covered her glass with her hand.

"I agree with you." She finished her glass of water. "We don't know which terrorist group or rogue nation is ready to attack us or our allies."

"Christina." He put down his glass of wine and looked into her eyes. "I must say that I'm rather impressed that you're concerned with this issue, and for that matter, know the least bit about it. This is precisely why I've invited you to accompany me to this fundraiser. I need to have someone like you by my side: A woman who can hold her own talking with anyone from the pampered wife of a corporate CEO, to the Chief Financial Officer of a major Silicon Valley company, to a physicist from Stanford. They're all supporters of mine and will be out in force next Tuesday."

"I'm honored that you would ask me." She adjusted her glasses. But let me tell you, the last fundraiser that I attended was not what I thought it would be."

Richard frowned. "What happened?"

"It's kind of funny actually." She smiled and took off her glasses. "I was under the impression that for a thousand dollars a plate, the food would be fabulous. My date thought the same, except that he starved himself all day. For that kind of money, he assumed the dinner would be an all you can eat buffet." She took a sip of water. "Boy, were we disappointed. Three ham and cheese casserole dishes greeted us on the buffet table. And can you believe it— they were still in the aluminum foil pans! The only other choice was rubber chicken, which was sloshing around in puddles of some unidentifiable cream sauce. Needless to say, we didn't eat much. Guess where we ended up?"

Richard's eyes were smiling. "Please," he swirled his wine in the large, round goblet, "indulge me."

118

"A drive-thru McDonald's window. We bought two Quarter Pounders and two vanilla shakes."

Richard laughed. "I think that experience is more typical than one would think. The food is always atrocious." He leaned across the table. "But what do you think? It couldn't hurt your business development efforts to attend."

"Sure, I'll go." She winked at him. "I just won't expect much."

He held up his glass. "Here's to an evening of plastered smiles, plastic hors d'oeuvres, and pomp and circumstance."

A waiter stopped by and poured Richard another glass of wine. Christina was still nursing her first. "Now, Christina," Richard said, "tell me what you have been working on these past few years."

"You could say that I'm buried in a small crisis at the moment."

"Oh?" His brows arched. "What kind of crisis?"

"I really can't talk about it. The matter is confidential. When everything gets resolved, I'll tell you about it."

He held up his glass and said, "Promise?"

She clinked his glass to his. "Promise."

The Senator was less intimidating than Christina had initially thought. She was glad that she accepted his dinner invitation and was looking forward to the reception next week. Discreetly, she glanced out the window, wondering if Franco would ever materialize. He had not. Instead of dwelling on it, she looked back at Richard and decided to enjoy the rest of this evening. It was far more pleasant than she had anticipated.

They walked outside into the cold, foggy night. Bells from the cable cars were heard clanking in the distance. She looked around for Franco.

"Would you like to walk back to the hotel with me and catch a cab?" he asked.

"No thank you." She shivered and wrapped her scarf more tightly around her neck. "I'll catch the cable car on California

Street and ride it down to my office." She wanted to linger a little longer, just in case Franco showed up.

He extended his hand in a business like fashion. "Well then, I guess this is where we say 'good night'." He shook her hand. Then, unexpectedly, he kissed her lightly on the cheek. "Thank you for joining me tonight," he said softly.

"Thank you for asking," she said. Luckily it was dark outside, and he did not notice her blushing. "Please call me next week and give me the details about the party. And, thank you again for dinner."

Christina watched the Senator turn around and walk back to the hotel. He sure is handsome, she thought. Franco, however, was the man she was yearning to be with. After Richard crossed the street, she reached into her purse and pulled out her small, StarTac flip phone. She called her house to check her messages, just in case Franco had left one. She heard a strange beeping signal. This was odd, she thought. She wondered what was wrong. Maybe it was a busy signal and someone was leaving her a message, although it didn't sound like a traditional busy signal. She would be home soon enough, and would pick up her messages at that time.

Chapter Eighteen

The monotonous, high-pitched beeping of her telephone was the first sound she heard as she pushed her front door open. She flicked on the light. She felt every nerve on her spine shoot up her back.

She was accosted by the sight of overturned furniture, drawers pulled out from the dresser and broken lamps. Her phone had been knocked off the hook. This time Seike had gone too far. Hearing no strange noises, and presuming that whomever had done this was no longer lurking in her apartment, she crept toward her living room. Nothing seemed to be missing. Her skin prickled. She tried to call the police, but couldn't get a dial tone. Whomever had been here had clipped the phone line. They had taken the tape from her answering machine. She remembered Sergeant O'Reilly's card. She beeped him and then placed a call to Susan from her cell phone. She didn't want to stay in her apartment alone tonight. Susan told her that of course she was welcome to sleep on the couch.

The police got to her apartment in less than ten minutes.

Christina breathed a sigh of relief as she saw the familiar face of Sergeant O'Reilly. "Thank god you got the call and came over." She wanted to give his teddy-bear frame a big hug.

"Me too, young lady." After a quick glance around the apartment, he instructed the younger officer to start dusting for prints. "What do you think happened here?" He pulled out a small note pad from his shirt pocket.

"At first I thought I got robbed, but I haven't noticed anything missing."

"Let's have a look." He started surveying the apartment. He lumbered into her living room where he noticed a broken window. He poked his head out the window, which stood two stories above a small garden. "Yup—this wasn't a random break-in. Someone deliberately climbed up this tree here and broke

121

into your apartment. It would have been much easier to hit one of them lower units."

"And look over there," he said as Christina walked over to the window. "Your next door neighbor has all the lights off and the window is wide open!"

"What's the motive here?" Christina asked.

"We can't answer that yet. Let's keep looking." He lumbered into her kitchen. "Yup—see this." Her refrigerator door had been left wide open. All of her spices had been pulled from the cabinets and dumped onto the floor. "They were most certainly looking for something."

"What would they be looking for?" Christina shook her head.

"Listen, sister, I've seen this a million times before. They were looking for something that was valuable to them. I think it has something to do with that computer account you're working on. I know it's probably a great piece of business, and all that, but I'd remove myself from it as much as possible. If the same people who were responsible for heisting the chips did this, they're not afraid to use a gun. Remember, we still have one guy in the hospital. Anyway, I'd think about it. You're a young gal— you don't want them to screw up the rest of your life—or even lose it."

He closed up his notebook and shoved it back in his shirt pocket. "Stay in touch, and if anything turns up missin', give me a call."

"Thanks Sergeant." She stood by the door and saw them out.

Just before he left, he turned around. "Oh, I forgot to tell you. That tape you gave me—we couldn't pinpoint exactly whose voice it was, but we're certain of one thing: it wasn't an Asian. If anything, it's someone from the South."

"This whole thing is becoming more bizarre by the minute." She leaned her back against the wall in the front hallway and slowly slid down to the floor. Contemplating everything that happened, she remained in a crouched position for several minutes, her elbows on her knees and her chin cupped in the palms of her hands.

It was nearly midnight by the time she got to Susan's apartment. Susan answered the door with a pint of Häagan-Daz in her hand. The pungent aroma of freshly smoked marijuana hung in the air. It was not uncommon for Susan to take a few tokes from a joint, in the privacy of her own home, when she was overly anxious. "I've been eating since you called! I'm so nervous. How are you?"

"I hope you have another pint for me." Christina dropped her duffel bag onto the floor. "All this chaos has made me hungry!" She regretted that she had been so enthralled in conversation with the Senator that she'd barely touched the osso buco that had been so carefully prepared for them.

"The police want me to resign the Symex account." Christina rifled through the freezer for some ice cream. "Of course, I would never consider doing such a thing. I worked for over a year trying to bring it in. I don't get it—I'm basically just a salesperson without access to privileged company information. Why would I be a threat to anyone?"

"I don't know, Christina." Susan licked her spoon. "This recent maneuver to scare you off has scared *me*! The account is in the door; someone else in the firm could take over from here. It seems that whomever took those chips is afraid that you may lead the police to them. And, it's probably true!" She scraped the last bit of ice cream from the container. "The more you know about the company, the more the FBI wants to know, and the more they know, the more Seike—or whomever—wants to cut you out of the loop. It's not worth getting your throat slit!"

Susan was beginning to sound frantic. She waved her spoon in the air. "I hate to say this, but I think you should get out while you still can. Why don't you tell Ralph tomorrow that you want to resign the account."

"I'll think about it." She pulled a cotton t-shirt from her duffle. "I still don't understand why anyone would be after me, but let me tell you—it really pisses me off that they broke into my apartment." She began rummaging through her duffle, looking for her toothbrush. "It makes me want to dig even deeper." She found her toothbrush and held it in the air, like she'd just won a trophy. "But don't worry, I'll get to the bottom of this!"

"Oh great. The last thing I wanted to do was put a fire under you." Susan pulled out a sheet, a pillow and a wool blanket she used on camping trips from the closet. She threw them onto her brown, leather couch. "Before we go to sleep, you **must** tell me about your dinner. Also, wasn't Franco supposed to have flown in from Toronto to see you? What happened to him?"

"I don't know, and I think it's rude that he didn't even call to tell me that he wasn't going to make it. Since I didn't know which hotel he was staying at, I called and left a message with his office in Italy, but he never called me back. Maybe he got tied up and will call when he gets back to Italy."

"Or, maybe he's more upset than you thought he would be about your 'date' with the Senator. You don't think he could have trashed your apartment in a jealous rage do you?"

"Susan! Don't be ridiculous!!" Christina spread out the sheet on the couch. "I must admit, though, that I did feel like a fool, standing there freezing on the street corner, hoping Franco would show up to drive me home." She pulled her hair into a ponytail. "It would've been nice to not have to walk into that war zone alone. What if they were still in there? You know, the more I think about it, it's a pretty frightening thought that someone is trying so hard to shut me up."

"I agree, and I'm glad you're finally coming to your senses."

Christina fell onto the couch and was about to set her head on the pillow.

Susan grabbed the pillow out from under her. Sooo— how was dinner?"

"Much better than I expected." Christina pulled the blanket up to her chin. "He's actually a pretty decent guy and I'm looking forward to the reception next week."

"You mentioned something about that to me yesterday. How can I get a ticket?"

"I'll see if Richard can comp you one."

"Are you kidding? That would be great. What time is it?"

"I don't know yet. Richard is supposed to call me early next week to give me more details. But I have a feeling that he may be calling me sooner."

"What does that mean?!?" Susan threw the pillow at Christina.

Christina ducked. "I'm not quite sure. Let's just call it women's intuition. Anyway, I need to crash. What time are you setting the alarm for?

"7:00."

"Good. That's sleeping in for me."

-

The piercing shrill of the telephone startled Christina out of a deep sleep. She shot up from the couch, forgetting where she was for a moment, and looked around the room for the phone. She heard the message machine click on with Susan's voice screeching from the speaker: "Christina, it's me. Pick up if you're awake."

She finally located the phone. "What happened? Why didn't you wake me up?"

"I tried," Susan said, "but you were dead to the world. You really needed the sleep. Take your time coming in."

"Don't worry, I will." She stretched her arms toward the ceiling. "My back is killing me. I really appreciate the hospitality, but I think I'm going to have to see a chiropractor."

"Sorry about that. Come to think of it, some of the men I've thrown on the couch have said the same thing. Anyway, the coffee should still be hot."

"Thanks, I'm going to need a strong caffeine jolt this morning."

"So, what are you going to do about Symex?"

Christina massaged the back of her neck. "I'll give Ralph a call when I get in. Can you please transfer me to Margie? Thanks for the wake-up call. See you soon."

The phone clicked. A few bars of classical music played in her ear.

"Hi Margie. By any chance did Franco call last night and leave a message with you?"

"Sorry none from him."

"Thanks," she said morosely, "I'll be in an hour."

Before she hung up Margie caught her. "Wait, Christina! You had a few other calls. Do you want to hear them?"

"Fire away."

"Jacobs from New York—he wanted to know what's going on with Symex; Senator Cartwright—he said call him at the Fairmont: also Brandy called—she said it was nothing important."

Christina hung up the phone and dialed the Fairmont. She knew Richard wouldn't wait until next week to call.

The front desk operator said that he wasn't in his room, but would she like to leave a message? Christina left her name and number.

"Hold one moment, please," the operator said. Within five seconds the operator connected her directly to his room.

"Hello Christina." It was Richard. "We're meeting in my suite this morning, but I told the front desk to put you through. I called last night to see if you got home safely, but your phone was out of order."

"You don't know the half of it," she said. "My place was broken into last night."

126

"Are you O.K?" He sounded genuinely concerned.

"I'm a little shaken, but I'm sure I'll get over it."

"I should have escorted you home. Any respectable gentleman would not have let a young lady go home alone. I promise, it won't happen again."

"Please, Richard, don't worry about it. This wasn't your fault. I've been living alone for nearly 10 years and have made it home safely every night except this one. The police think it has something to do with the account I'm working on."

"Is that one you won't tell me anything about?" he asked.

"How'd you guess? Anyway, I know you're in the middle of a meeting. I'll let you go. We can talk later."

"Are you sure you're all right?" he asked.

"Not really." For the first time she admitted that she was a little scared.

Chapter Nineteen

When Christina finally made it into work, she found Susan in her office struggling over a spreadsheet on her computer. Susan looked up from the monitor when she saw Christina walk into her office.

"Hey—how are you feeling?" Susan asked.

"I'm O.K." Christina set her briefcase on the chair. "Thanks for letting me sleep in."

"Listen Christina, I don't think you should go back to your apartment. For some reason, someone is trying to scare you and I think you should lay low for a while. You're more than welcome to stay at my place for as long as you need to."

"Thanks, Susan. I really appreciate the offer, but I know my neck and back couldn't take another night on your couch." She rubbed the top of her shoulders. "I think I'll check into a hotel this weekend, and probably stay through the week."

"Which one?"

"Probably the Sheraton Palace. It's within walking distance of the office, and since I have that party there Tuesday night, I wouldn't have to worry about drinking and driving."

"You've got a point there." Susan focused on her computer and gripped her mouse. "Now get outta here. I really need to get back to this spreadsheet. I have to e-mail this to New York before five o'clock their time."

"I better get going also. I have a million phone calls to return. Come say good bye before you leave."

She worked quietly in her office for a few hours, relishing the few hours she was preoccupied enough to not think about the threatening message and the break-in. Late morning, Margie beeped through and told her that Senator Cartwright was on the line.

She picked up her phone. "Hi Richard, how are you?"

"I'm fine, how are **you** doing?"

"I guess I'm fine, but whomever broke into my apartment last night has succeeded in scaring me into not going back there for a while." She organized a stack of files and pushed them to the side of her desk.

"That's probably a good idea. Are you going to continue staying at your girlfriend's?"

"She offered to let me stay there as long as I like, but I think I am going to check into the Sheraton Palace."

"Christina, please don't take this the wrong way, but I don't think you should stay alone. Why don't you stay here at the Fairmont? There are two empty rooms that open up to the suite area we have been using for our meetings. It's completely separate from my room— with it's own lock and phone line."

Christina took off her glasses and bit the stem. "Thanks for the offer, but I wouldn't feel right about doing that."

"Really, you shouldn't stay by yourself. The security on this floor is more than you would ever get at the Sheraton. Many foreign dignitaries stay here, and the hotel is accustomed to providing the type of protection you need. We can even have you check in under an assumed name."

Christina swiveled her chair around to look out toward the Bay. A giant cargo ship, stacked with brightly colored containers, inched toward Alcatraz. She thought about what Richard had said and figured that maybe he was right. She liked the idea of the added security, and besides, the hotel was just up the hill from her office.

She swiveled back around. "All right, you sold me. Are you sure it's still empty?"

"Positive. I'll call the front desk and make sure they prepare it for your arrival. I need to return to Washington today, but I'll be back Sunday night. Think of it this way, at least I'll be on the same floor, just in case anything should happen."

"Thanks, Richard. I appreciate your help." At the door, Susan gestured wildly for Christina to get off the phone. "I better sign off. Maybe I'll see you Sunday. Thanks again."

"Christina," Susan said as Christina hung up the phone, "I just got off the phone with Stephano. Franco's at the Four Seasons."

"Good work! Is he still there?" She searched in her drawer for her corporate hotel directory.

"I think so."

She quickly dialed the Four Seasons, hoping he would be in his room.

"Pronto?" His salutation was all business.

"Franco, it's Christina!"

"My darling," his voice softened. "Where have you been? I called you last night to tell you I wasn't going to be able to make it to San Francisco, but you never called me back."

"Oh, Franco, it's so good to hear your voice. You'll never believe what happened. Someone broke into my apartment and completely destroyed it. They also took the tape from my answering machine."

"You poor girl. Are you all right?"

"I'm fine; I ended up staying at Susan's. I really wish I could've talked to you. Why didn't you try calling me at work?"

"I am sorry, but I lost your card and I forgot the name of your firm. I've been in meetings all day, and didn't have a chance to call Stephano until this morning. Fortunately, he managed to hold onto Susan's card."

"I thought you never wanted to see me again because I had dinner with the Senator." Christina saw that Susan was ready to leave. She held up her finger.

"Christina, I'm not that insecure."

"I know you're not." She lowered her voice. "But I guess I am."

"I got held up in Toronto. It looks like I'm here through the week, then I must fly to Hong Kong."

"When can we see each other?"

"Maybe next weekend."

That would be wonderful. Please try to stop over for at least one day. I really miss you."

"I miss you too, dolcina. Also, it would be nice to see where you live."

"I don't think that will be possible this trip," she said. "I'm moving out of my place until this case gets solved. I'm staying at the Fairmont Hotel, under an assumed name—Margaret Smith. I don't have the room number yet, but you can reach me there all week."

"I'll call you there. Are you sure you'll be safe at this hotel?"

"I've been assured the security is top notch."

"That makes me feel better. I must run now, I'm late for a meeting. Ciao, darling—I will see you soon." The phone clicked silent.

"Ciao darling," she repeated to herself. His accent killed her every time. She felt a burst of energy at the thought of seeing him again.

Susan, who was still waiting by the door, popped her head back in. "How about if I go home with you after work and help you throw some things together for next week?"

"Thanks, Susan," Christina said. "I would really appreciate that. To tell the truth, I'm a little scared to go back to my place by myself."

-

Reentering her condo after the break-in was more frightening than she had anticipated. She had prided herself on decorating her home with light, fresh colors. The white pillows from her couch were still strewn all over the living room. Her sage and cream wool carpet was littered with broken glass and dead flowers. The silk curtains blew in the wind and the moon cast an eerie, gray shadow.

"It's not that bad, Christina," Susan said, trying to add some levity to the moment. "I've seen your place look worse than this.

Remember, last year when you were going through your 'I don't want to see anyone, or leave my house' phase? You didn't let Rosa in for over two weeks!"

"Very funny," she said, "I was depressed. It happens to everyone once in a while. But thanks for reminding me about Rosa. I'll remind her to bring some extra help."

They started in her bedroom, picking up a few business suits that had been thrown from her closet and onto the floor. Christina attempted to straighten out the wrinkles before putting them back into her hanging bag. Many of her things were still in her suitcase, which she had still not unpacked. She found her lovely Valentino dress, rumpled at the bottom of her hanging bag. As she put it back on the hanger and placed it in her closet a flood of warm memories began rushing back to her—she would never forget that incredibly romantic night she shared with Franco.

"Remember this?" Christina held up the string bikini she'd bought in Nice. "It seems like at least a year since we were lounging at the beach without a care in the world." She brushed the sand off and threw it into her laundry basket. "Too bad those days are long gone."

In just one short month, like the drawers and furniture, her life had been turned upside down.

"This place is giving me the creeps." Susan shivered from the cold, damp air that blew through the broken window. "Let's pack up and get out of here!"

"I agree." Christina picked up one of her lamps from the floor and set it back on her dresser. "It's useless trying to organize this mess now. I'll have everything cleaned and pressed at the hotel." She picked up her suitcase, still filled with dirty clothes from her trip, and threw the few clean things she could find on top of them.

By the time they got to the Fairmont, Christina was exhausted. All she could think about was checking into her room and going to sleep. When they arrived at the front desk, the clerk told her that a room in The Presidential Suite had been reserved for her. The bell captain escorted them to the elevator bank that took them to the private suite on the eighth floor. He opened the thick, carved mahogany doors to the foyer. They stepped onto the black and white marble floors. On the hall table were a dozen long stem, red roses, and a dozen white ones. Christina tipped the valet and opened the card attached to the red roses, which were addressed to Margaret Smith. It was from Franco. She read out loud. "I miss you and look forward to seeing you soon. And please, stay out of trouble."

She turned to Susan. "Isn't this so sweet of Franco? But why do you think he sent me both red and white roses?"

Susan had already pulled the small envelope from the white dozen. "We'll find out," she smiled.

Susan opened the card and began reading: "'Christina, I'm glad you're here.' She held the card to her chest and yelled. "It's signed, 'Richard!'"

"What!?!" Christina said, "Let me see that!"

She yanked the card from Susan's hand. "You're right. This is quite unexpected."

"Christina," Susan said, "you've got a predicament on your hands. Not the worst kind, but nonetheless—I wouldn't want to be in your shoes."

"Let's bring them back to my room." She picked up the vase of red roses with one hand and her suitcase with the other.

Susan carried the other vase as she walked into the corridor where the bedrooms were located. She tried opening one of the doors, but it was locked.

"This must be where the Senator is staying," Susan said. "But the room next to it is empty."

"There are supposed to be three bedrooms." Christina frowned. "I don't particularly want to stay in the room next to his. Let's keep looking."

133

They walked out of the empty bedroom into an enormous living room, furnished with a baby grand piano, two round oak tables, and chintz covered couches. Next to the marble fireplace sat an oversized writing desk, equipped with a fax machine, computer and telephone. This must be the room where Richard had been conducting his meetings.

She and Susan walked back into the foyer and into the next room, the most spectacular of all: the library. Speechless, they entered the magnificent two-story, circular library. Row upon row of books lined the walls behind an antique desk. On the other side of the room sat a cordovan, leather sofa tufted with small, brass buttons. Plush, hunter green carpet covered the floor. In the back of the room, they noticed a delicate winding staircase. Unable to resist seeing where the staircase led, they followed the stairs up to the second story, which led to a narrow walkway in front of more book-lined shelves. Above them was a midnight, blue domed ceiling accented with drawings of the heavenly constellations, painted in gold leaf. Christina felt as though she was standing in a planetarium.

"This is spectacular!" Christina stared in awe at the workmanship that must have gone into painting the ceiling. They wound their way back downstairs.

In the lower portion of the library, on the other side of the book-lined walls, French doors opened outside to a rooftop terrace. From the balcony, they marveled at the stunning views of downtown San Francisco and The Bay. They could also see the glittering lights of Treasure Island, which is connected to the city of Oakland by the Bay Bridge.

"This is incredible!" Susan walked to the end of the terrace to savor the breathtaking view and to inhale the crisp, fresh air.

Christina stepped through another set of French doors. These led to a formal dining room. An impressive Chippendale dining table-nearly 50 feet in length, with 20 matching chairs-stood in the middle of the room, underneath an enormous crystal chandelier. Adjacent to the dining room was a gourmet kitchen with all the amenities: a Jenn Air barbecue, a SubZero refrigerator and a six burner, Wolf range.

"Great set-up," she told Susan, "although I wasn't planning on doing much cooking." She ran her fingers along the cool, granite countertops. "But what the hell, maybe I'll throw a party one night."

"Now, that's an idea. We need to take full advantage of this place!" Susan said.

They left the kitchen and continued looking for the third bedroom. Finally, they noticed another door, across from the dining room. Christina opened it up and was delighted at what she saw. She would definitely feel at home here! The third 'guest' room was comfortably furnished with a lovely four-poster bed, fluffy pillows, and a small couch for reading. The walls were covered with a hand painted map of the world; the French windows opened to a view of the many hills of San Francisco. She noticed that it had a separate deadbolt, the key still in the lock. She appreciated that it was a comfortable distance—clear at the other end of the suite—from the Senator's room.

"Let's get my flowers and luggage," Christina said as she sunk into the bed. "I can hardly wait to go to sleep."

Chapter Twenty

It was a gorgeous, sunny Saturday morning. Christina awoke early with an urge to run. As she looked for her running gear, she realized that she had never completely unpacked from her trip to Italy, nor had she done any laundry. She dumped her entire suitcase onto the floor. A pile of junk fell onto the carpet: sand-coated Bain de Soliel sunscreen, a tin of Altoids, a matchbook from Il Castello, an open travel size packet of tissues, a small, square piece of metal that looked like it may have broken off from her suitcase, and a wrinkled map of Forte dei Marmi that had nearly disintegrated from moisture. She placed the dirty clothes in a bag for the hotel laundry service, swept up the mess from the floor and tossed everything into the waste paper basket, except the map, which she wanted to save as a souvenir. She laced up her running shoes and waited for the elevator to take her downstairs.

On the top of Nob Hill, she ran past the Pacific Union Club and Grace Cathedral before heading down the steep hill to the Bay. Once her stride became uniform and nearly effortless, she found it impossible not to think about work. She had not officially resigned the Symex account, and was waiting to see what events were to unfold this coming week. Since she had not heard from Special Agent Peters, she guessed that meant good news. He would have called if the designs had been sold off to a foreign power or if Seike had been found.

Suddenly, Christina stopped dead in her tracks. She remembered that Agent Peters had told her that the plans were useless without the code chip. The brief conversation with him came back to her. *"The master is in the safe, but several prototypes were manufactured."* Something else clicked: what would someone want so badly that they'd break into her apartment.

That piece of scrap metal that had fallen out of her suitcase with the rest of her garbage somewhat resembled a microchip, although it was smaller than the chips she was accustomed to seeing. Could by some remote chance it be one of the prototypes?? Logically it could be, especially if it had been accidentally placed in the file that Ralph gave her last month, and then had fallen out during her travels. She sprinted back to the hotel. She'd thrown that chip away, and needed to get back to her room before housekeeping arrived! It was not yet 9:00 in the morning, and she hoped that the maids were not overly prompt on Saturdays.

She raced into the lobby, and waited impatiently for the elevator. After several seconds, which seemed like hours, the elevator arrived and whisked her up to the eighth floor. She struggled with the key, pushed the front door open and sprinted to her room. Unlocking her door, she found the room still a complete mess. *Thank God!!* She walked over to the wastepaper basket and scooped everything out from the bottom. She found the piece of scrap metal, but only found herself more confused: it was a tiny, square, piece of metal that was no more than an eighth of an inch thick and a half inch wide.

She dialed Agent Peters' office.

"FBI, Northern California," answered the receptionist.

"Agent Peters, please." Christina paced the floor.

"I'm sorry, he is out of town until next week. I'll put you through to his secretary."

"Thank you."

"May I help you?" His secretary's raspy voice made her sound like she had worked there at least 30 years and had been smoking for 50.

"Yes, my name is Christina Caldwell. I understand that Agent Peters is out of town. Will he be picking up his messages?"

"That is unlikely. He's on a special assignment. If this is an emergency we can place a call to him."

"That's not necessary," Christina said. "If by chance he calls in, will you please tell him that I called. I have a question that I think he can answer."

"Will he know what this is regarding, dear?"

"He'll know, thank you." She hung up and wondered if she really sounded young enough for someone to call her 'dear'.

She needed to keep the chip safe; after all, if the chip was as valuable as she thought it was this was probably the reason her condo had been broken into.

She thought about where she would hide it: she didn't want to keep it in her purse or in her hotel room. Her office wasn't safe either. It should be kept close to her at all times. Occasionally, she wore an antique, round, gold locket that had been given to her by her mother. Perhaps the chip would fit in the compartment that her mom had used to place school photos of herself and her brother. Unfortunately, most of her jewelry was still back at her apartment, which meant that she would have to go there alone. She showered and changed, then reluctantly drove back to the Marina.

As she approached her top floor condo, she found the door ajar. She was ready to turn around and run back down the stairs, but the logical, rational side of Christina Caldwell checked in. She and Susan had been in such a rush to get out of there yesterday that perhaps they hadn't shut the door properly—or maybe the police had to come back and found a way to get in. She touched the door and pushed it open. Her heart was beating rapidly. She listened carefully for strange sounds. The surroundings felt still. She didn't see anything suspicious so she tiptoed to her bedroom where she took her jewelry box off her dresser, and then bolted back down the stairs.

In her car, she took her locket from her jewelry box and inserted the chip into the compartment. It fit perfectly. She clasped the necklace around her neck, and tapped the locket. She knew it would be safe. On the way back to the Fairmont, Christina decided to grab a quick lunch on Chestnut Street, the bustling shopping area in the heart of the Marina District where active professionals lingered at the trendy cafes after mountain biking, windsurfing or running. While waiting in line at Jamba Juice, she thought she saw Ralph Stinson walking on the other side of the street. She paid for her fruit smoothie and darted across the street. She called out his name. He turned around, clearly startled to see her.

"Hi Ralph," she said. He looked out of place in his beige windbreaker and 'blue jeans' made of some strange synthetic fiber. "Good to see you. I didn't know you lived here."

"Ha! That's a joke." His eyes did not smile. "I live in the Sunset."

"What's so funny about the Sunset District?"

"Nothing." He looked down at the sidewalk. "Let's just put it this way: these places are a bit out of my league. I'm not as good at managing my money as you probably are."

"I'd be happy to help you." Christina sipped the thick strawberry, banana and yogurt drink through her straw. "That's what I used to do at Kingstone."

"No need." Ralph shoved his hands in his pockets. "I'll be out from under my pile of debt in a few months."

"Time to sell your stock options?"

"Something like that." His glasses slid down his nose.

"Anyway, Ralph, I'm glad I ran into you. I was going to give you a call first thing Monday morning."

"Discovered something new?" He pushed his glasses up.

"I was wondering if you've heard from Agent Peters recently?" She instinctively looked behind her, fearing she may have been followed.

"Why do you ask?"

"I'm curious about a prototype code chip he mentioned to me during our interrogation. He said they needed to track all of them down to make sure none were missing. I was wondering whether or not he'd talked to you about this."

Ralph put his hands in his pockets and rattled his change. "Uh-yes, in fact, I just spoke to him. He told me that they were able to account for all of them. It's nothing you need to worry about."

"That's good to hear—one less thing I won't have to do tomorrow. I better get going. Nice seeing you."

Chapter Twenty-One

The next day, Christina spent most of her Sunday afternoon at the office. When she returned to the Fairmont, she kicked off her shoes and looked forward to a quiet evening watching *60 Minutes*. She jumped when she heard the phone—her nerves were on edge and not many people had known she was staying there.

"Hello Christina," Richard said, "I just got back from Washington and wondered if you would like to join me for dinner."

"Oh, hi, Richard." She sat on the sofa and curled her bare feet underneath her. "Any other night, that would sound great, but not tonight. I'm pretty well situated, but thanks for calling. Also, thank you for the flowers. That was a nice surprise."

"I'm glad you liked them, but I'm not going to take 'no' for an answer so easily. I wasn't planning on going out either. We'll have Fleur de Lys deliver dinner to our dining room."

This was beginning to sound more appealing. Fleur de Lys was one of her favorite restaurants and *60 Minutes* would probably be a rerun.

"Sure I'll join you," she conceded. "At least I won't have a problem getting home."

"Very well then," he said, "why don't you come over as soon as you can so we can have a drink before our dinner gets here."

"How 'bout in a half hour? I have a few things to organize for tomorrow. And Richard, thanks."

Christina sorted through the paperwork she'd brought home from her office and finally put her clothes in the closet. She'd been living out of her suitcase all weekend, and the room was starting to look like her condo without the help of Rosa. Considering she was a guest, she had thought she better straighten up a bit. She picked up the map of Forte dei Marmi and thought of Franco. She wished he didn't have to stay an extra day in Toronto and felt a void in her heart from not seeing him. She smoothed out the map and pressed it into her leather day planner.

She decided not to change out of her faded Levi's and a soft, cashmere v-neck sweater. She slipped on a pair of worn, leather loafers and walked into the next room.

The dining room was lit with candles. Fresh flowers and two place settings were intimately arranged at the end of the long mahogany table. She found Richard in the library. He was seated on the leather couch drinking a glass of red wine and reading *The Economist.*

"Good evening, Richard. This sure is cozy."

"Please join me." He gestured for her to sit down on the couch and poured her a glass of wine. "I'm enjoying a fabulous bottle of 82 Bordeaux, Chateau Lafite. They have an incredible wine cellar here."

She took a sip of wine. "I'd say." It tasted rich, like a combination of blackberries and sweet peppers.

"Do you know any of the history behind this suite?"

"No, not at all," she smiled. "But I'd love to hear it."

"This library, for example, was where Secretary of State Stettinius, in 1945, drafted The Charter of The United Nations. In fact, it was signed right there on that desk." He pointed to the antique desk that sat in front of the book-lined walls.

"The most infamous story I heard was about John F. Kennedy," he continued. "When he visited San Francisco, he and Mrs. Kennedy would stay in the room where I'm sleeping, and it was rumored that Angie Dickinson would stay in your room."

"What great gossip!" Christina said. "I bet the tabloids were thrilled when he came to town."

"I'm sure they were never at a loss for a good story." He replenished her glass. "Rumor has it that she was escorted up a rarely used stairway off the kitchen, and then she and President

Kennedy would meet in the middle of the night, right here in this library."

"Wouldn't we have liked to have been a fly on the wall?" she laughed.

"You and I, and a million others!" Richard said. "Dinner should be here any minute. I hope you don't mind, but I took the liberty of ordering for both of us. Do you like lobster?"

"Yes, I love it." She appreciated the effort Richard was making and she admitted to herself that it felt nice to be taken care of by someone.

"I thought we should celebrate your move to your new home—even if it's only temporary."

"Thanks, Richard." They touched their wine glasses. "I do feel safer here, and it is just up the hill from my office."

At the subtle ring at the front door, Richard let the room service staff in. They set up the dinner in the dining room. From where Christina and Richard sat they could both enjoy the spectacular view of the twinkling lights of the Berkeley Hills and of the Bay Bridge. Strands of white lights connected the peaks and slopes of the seven-mile span of steel. Streams of red taillights and white headlights flowed like molten metal across the engineering masterpiece.

Christina watched the waiters lift the silver, serving tops from the plates. "This sure beats what I was planning to have for dinner. At most, I was going to order a burger from room service and call it a night."

"Well, I hope you enjoy it," Richard said. "Even though you strike me as a woman who has probably seen the insides of some incredible homes, I thought you would find this suite, especially with all the history, a nice change of pace."

They enjoyed their succulent lobster and nearly another bottle of wine, before the waiters came back into the dining room with their dessert: a flambé of cherries.

Over dessert Christina presented Richard with a question she'd been dying to ask.

"Richard," she said, "I know you're planning to run for President. I was just wondering how you're going to address the issue of your divorce."

"You're not the first person to bring that up." He wiped his lips with a linen napkin and leaned back in his chair. "Did you read about the affairs and escapades of my wife in Hollywood?"

Christina nodded.

"Frankly, that was too much for me to handle." Richard shook his head. "And, as we both know, over 50% of all first marriages end in divorce. My feeling is that at least 25% of the people who are still married are unhappy, and that they're only sticking it out for the sake of the children or how they appear to others. It happens all the time in Washington, and I feel that is dishonest. I would rather be forthright with the American people, admit my past mistakes and move on with my life."

"I like that answer," Christina smiled.

He held up his wine glass. "I'm glad to hear I passed the first round of interrogations."

After the waiters left, Richard leaned across the table. "Christina, why don't we think about spending more time together? I feel so comfortable around you. You're such a nice change from all the stodginess back in Washington." He paused for a moment and stared into her eyes. "And I must admit, I've found myself looking forward to seeing you when I'm in San Francisco, and you're on my mind when I'm back in D.C."

She hesitated. "That's kind of you to say, Richard. I also enjoy spending time with you, but I met a man in Italy, and I'm actually quite fond of him. In fact, he's coming out to visit me this weekend."

"Oh-I see," Richard said, backing away. "I didn't realize you were involved with someone."

"I can't say that we're 'involved', but for now things are just perfect, and I don't want to interfere with what we have."

"I can respect that." He reached over and touched her hand. "But, remember— long distance relationships rarely last."

144

She gently pulled her hand away. "Yes, but I'll see how things progress. Anyway, we'll still spend time together. Remember we have your reception on Tuesday."

"Why are you always so logical?" He smiled warmly. "You look tired. How about if I walk you home?"

She laughed and looked toward her bedroom door. "Thanks, but I think this time I'll make it home safely by myself."

Nevertheless, he stood up, pulled her chair back, and walked her over to the door that led to her room.

She unlocked it, and opened it slightly. Richard kissed her lightly on the cheek and said 'goodnight'. As she swung open the door to enter into her room, Richard saw the two bouquets of roses on the dresser against the wall.

"Are the red ones from your Italian boyfriend?"

"Yes they are," she whispered. "Goodnight, Richard."

She watched him walk back to the other wing. Although memories of herself and Franco were still vivid, she could feel herself softening up to the Senator. She turned the deadbolt to lock the door and got ready for bed, feeling safe and secure.

-

The next morning, Christina had left earlier than usual for the office. She had wanted to get in before seven to make some phone calls back East before everyone there went to lunch. The Symex 'road show' had started in New York and she was curious how the presentations to the institutional investors were received. Most of Kingstone's IPO's were over subscribed, and she'd hoped that this one would not be an exception. It was always a good sign when more people wanted to invest in the offering than the amount of shares that were available. The good old law of supply and demand, she thought.

-

Although it was still not yet 8:00 a.m. California time, Franco thought he would be able to catch Christina at the hotel before she left for the office. The front desk operator dialed Christina's room, and after several rings, came back on the line and told Franco that she was not answering. The operator suggested that she might be in one of the other rooms, and tried those extensions.

When Senator Cartwright heard the telephone ring in the living room, he excused himself from the meeting he was conducting.

Franco was startled when he heard a man's voice, but nonetheless, he said in his thick Italian accent: "Is Christina Caldwell available?"

"She's not here right now," the Senator said. "Shall I give her a message?"

"Yes, please tell her that Franco Garibaldi called."

"I'll make sure she gets the message."

The Senator hung up the phone, and returned to his meeting with a smug smile on his face.

Chapter Twenty-Two

"Christina," Margie called through the intercom, "Brandy's on the phone. Can you take the call?"

"Yes, thank you." She picked up the receiver. "Hi, Brandy!"

"Hi Christina, how are you? I just got my pictures back. How 'bout if the three of us get together tonight?"

"That would be great. I'd love to see them. I'm sorry I've been so out of touch—a lot has happened since we got back. In fact, I'm not even living in my apartment anymore."

"What are you talking about?!?"

"It's kind of complicated, but I'll give you the scoop tonight. I'm staying in the Presidential Suite at The Fairmont, under the assumed name of Margaret Smith. The place is amazing!! I can hardly wait for you to see it. I told the man who invited me to stay there that I'd cook dinner for him and a few of his friends. Do you want to join us tonight?"

"Sounds great! What time should I come over?"

"I'll check with Susan, but plan on around 7:00."

"O.K., see you then."

-

Christina left the office just in time to run to one of the local markets, and get back to the hotel before 7:00. As she walked into the kitchen, struggling with several bags of groceries, she almost collided with Richard who had also just stepped in.

"May I give you a hand?" Richard asked as Christina nearly dropped some fresh fruit on his foot.

"Thanks," she answered breathlessly, "I never seem to have enough hands to carry everything."

"It looks like you're planning a party for 20 of your closest friends tonight." He laughed at her as she tried to keep the tomatoes, fresh basil and a bottle of olive oil from spilling onto the floor. "I thought we talked about a small dinner party."

"I only invited two people, but I thought I should buy extra in case you invited sixteen of your friends."

"Actually, only one other man is coming tonight," Richard said.

"That's O.K." She gestured at the kitchen counter, covered with grocery bags. "We'll have leftovers for a week." She pulled out several loaves of Italian bread from the bag. "So, who's your friend?"

"Curtis Saunders. You may have heard of him—the founder and President of Silicon Valley Electronics."

Without question, she knew who he was. And, if she remembered what she had read recently, his company was experiencing a serious amount of trouble. Susan, who stayed on top of all the gossip in The Valley, would know more about him.

"The more the merrier." Christina began chopping tomatoes. "By the way, how do you know him?"

"We met at Stanford Business School 20 years ago and have been close friends ever since. I told him to come by around eight. Is that okay?"

"Sure. I should have everything under control by then." Christina scraped the tomatoes off the cutting board and slid them into a skillet that was sizzling in olive oil.

"I'll change clothes," he said. "Then, I'll help with dinner."

"Thanks," Christina smiled. "That would be great."

Christina heard the doorbell. She rinsed her hands and went to the foyer.

"Hi guys!" Christina said to Susan and Brandy. "Susan, why don't you show Brandy around while Richard and I get everything organized?"

"Who's Richard?" Brandy asked as Susan led her down the hallway.

"Long story," Susan said. "I'll fill you in while I'm giving you the tour."

Richard returned to the kitchen. He wore a long sleeve, light blue Polo shirt and khaki pants. Christina and Richard finished unloading the groceries, opened a few bottles of Barolo, played some Puccini on the THX CD home theater system and began to cook an easily prepared Italian meal: pasta, green salad, grilled vegetables and garlic bread. Eventually Susan and Brandy made their way over to the kitchen. Christina poured them a glass of wine.

"Can we help?" Brandy couldn't seem to take her eyes off of Richard.

"Oh, Brandy," Christina took the lid off of the large pot and checked to see if the water was boiling. "I'd like to introduce you to Senator Richard Cartwright."

Richard wiped the marinara sauce off his hands with the blue and whitecheckered towel he'd attached to his belt. "Pleased to meet you, Brandy."

"The pleasure is mine, Senator." She let the rim of her wineglass rest against her lips for a full minute before sipping and continued staring at him. She looked as though she may faint any minute.

Susan extended her hand. "Hi, I'm Susan."

"Nice to meet you, Susan." He shook her hand. "I've heard a lot about you."

"Why don't you two sit down in the library and have a glass of wine." Christina rinsed a head of lettuce. "We have everything under control. If you hear the doorbell ring, go ahead and answer it. One of Richard's friends will be joining us."

As they walked over to the library, Brandy turned to Susan. "So that's *Richard?* **Senator Cartwright?** One of the most eligible men in the country!?! When did this start?"

Susan and Brandy sat down on the leather couch in the library. "Christina claims it's not a big deal, and that they're just friends," Susan said. "But he sure has gone out of his way to make sure she ended up staying here after her apartment was broken into."

"I don't believe for a minute there isn't anything romantic between them," Brandy said. "Did you see them in the kitchen cooking together? They look like a happy, newlywed couple!"

"I see what you mean," Susan said, "but she's really fallen for Franco. In fact, he's supposed to come out here to visit her this weekend."

A ring at the front door interrupted their gossiping. Susan jumped up to answer it. She opened the door and saw a large, bulky man filling the doorway. His face was ruddy and his hair was sandy. Red stubble, prickly like a cactus, adorned his chin. Susan thought he looked familiar, but couldn't place how she knew him.

"Hi," he said in a hoarse voice, "I'm Curtis Saunders."

Susan flinched when she heard the name.

"Are you Christina?"

"No, I'm Susan. Christina's in the kitchen. Follow me."

"Nice pad." He looked around, swaggered through the library, and nodded 'hello' to Brandy as he walked into the kitchen.

"Hello, C.J.," Richard said. "I see you've met Susan." He put his hand on Christina's shoulder. "And this is Christina, our hostess tonight."

"Gee," C.J. grunted, "I guess I should have brought flowers or something." He flung a six-pack of Miller on the counter.

"Nice to meet you, C.J." Christina stared at his hulking frame. "Glad you could join us tonight."

C.J. pulled a tin of snuff out of his back pocket and opened the can. He pinched some Skoal tobacco and began chewing. His mouth filled with brown saliva. "Can I have a glass or somethin'?"

Christina found a crystal bar glass and handed it to him before he drooled tobacco onto his chin.

C.J. spit the brown glob into the glass. Christina cringed.

"Christina," Susan popped her head into the kitchen, "May I pull you away from this masterpiece of a dinner you're a creating for a moment?"

"Sure." Christina had just finished chopping some garlic and fresh basil. She scooped the ingredients up with her knife and placed them into the simmering tomato sauce. "I'll be right back," she said to Richard. "Will you watch the sauce?"

Susan led Christina by the elbow out to the terrace. "Curtis Saunders is a *friend* of Richard's?"

"That's what he told me. They met at Stanford Business School."

"Christina, I don't want to make you think any less of Richard, but let me tell you—this guy is bad news!!"

"What do you mean?"

"I have a friend who works with one of C.J.'s accountants. He told me that the SEC is currently investigating Saunders and his company. The feds have reason to believe he may have 'cooked the books' to make the stock price higher than what it actually should be."

"How'd he do that?" Christina asked.

"Apparently Saunders set up a bogus company to buy his custom chips—you know, those gate arrays that have been keeping the company alive."

Christina nodded. Actually, Silicon Valley Electronics manufactured semi-custom chips. Gate array chips are put together from the company's design library in order to optimize each chip for a specific application. The application, such as an airplane auto pilot device or a missile guidance control system will depend on what the particular customer's engineering department needs.

Susan glanced into the dining room. No one was at the door, but she lowered her voice anyway. "Invoices revealed that the company delivered the chips, but nothing's legitimate. A bill is sent, but it just sits in a P.O. Box and is never paid. Meanwhile, the earnings look great because the product has been 'shipped', and therefore the stock price goes up. By the time the auditors catch up with them, most of the insiders have sold their stock, and have fled the country to a tax-friendly island in the Caribbean or the Netherlands Antilles. According to my friend, Saunders' accountants are really sweating it. This has gone unchecked for over a year, and the stock price has more than tripled!"

"Sounds like a good 'short-sell' to me."

"You're probably right." Susan rested her hand on the iron railing and stared out toward Treasure Island. "Not only that, but there's a rumor— and I'm not saying it is substantiated— but there's a rumor that he may have been involved with bribing government officials."

"You don't think Richard would be involved with this, do you?"

"Richard's name never came up. Only lower level officials were implicated. But, I wouldn't trust C.J. as far as I could throw him!"

Brandy poked her head out the terrace door. "Dinner's ready." It was nearly 8:30 p.m. and the bright lights on the East Bay hills flickered against the darkening sky. The massive military building on Treasure Island was lit like the White House. "This reminds me," Brandy said while gazing at Treasure Island, "I've got to call Rob. They've probably started filming their movie. Would you two like to go over next week?"

"I can hardly wait!" Susan said.

"Yeah, me too," Christina said, still stunned by what Susan just told her. "Let's go back inside, it's getting chilly out here."

-

After the dinner, they all retired to the library to look at Brandy's pictures while the hotel staff cleaned up the colossal mess they'd made in the kitchen. Listening to Curtis Saunders incessantly name-drop and boast about how profitable his company had become since he'd founded it 10 years ago started to get tiresome for Christina.

"Nice meeting you C.J.," she said, "and I'm sorry to have to miss the rest of these fascinating stories, but I have an early morning meeting tomorrow and should probably get some sleep."

By now he was slurring his words. In a Southern drawl that was undetectable when he was sober, he said: "Yeah—likewise. Thanks for cookin'."

Susan who was also anxious to leave, and disgusted by C.J., excused herself after Christina made the move to break up the evening. Richard stood up to shake hands with Susan. Brandy remained in the library, clinging to every word uttered from C.J.'s mouth.

"We must clue Brandy in about her new friend," Christina whispered to Susan as they walked to the foyer. "I can't believe that she's actually impressed by that guy!"

"I'll give her a call tomorrow." Susan said.

"Thanks, I'll barely have time to brush my hair." Christina gave Susan a friendly hug goodnight. "Thanks for your help tonight. Will you please tell Margie that I won't be in until ten thirty or eleven? I have a meeting in the East Bay at eight."

"No problem. See you tomorrow."

Chapter Twenty-Three

It was nearly 12:30 p.m. when Christina opened the door to the office foyer. She collided with Margie, who was leaving for lunch.

"I'm sorry, Margie." Christina picked up Margie's purse, which had fallen to the floor. "Are you O.K.?"

"Yes, I'm fine. Are you all right? You look like you just ran a marathon. What happened? I've been telling people who have been calling for you that you were expected back mid-morning."

"Traffic could not have been worse!" Christina put down her stack of papers on the receptionist's desk and smoothed her skirt. "There was an accident on the Bay Bridge. We were backed up for nearly two hours. I would've called, but I forgot to charge my cell phone last night. I'll never make that mistake again!"

"I left your messages on your desk. Also, Susan's been looking for you. I think she's in her office."

"Thanks, Margie. Have a nice lunch."

She scooped up her papers and walked back to Susan's office where she collapsed into a chair.

Susan looked up from her computer screen. "Good thing you're sitting down."

"Why? What happened?"

Susan twirled her hair around her index finger. "I started calling Brandy at seven a.m. No answer— so I just figured she turned the phone off. I then called an hour later—still no answer, but this time I left a message for her to call me."

Christina leaned forward. "Don't tell me—"

"You got it." Susan pounded her desk. "She didn't get home until ten this morning."

Christina let out a low whistle. "I hope you set her straight."

"I was honest with her." Susan leaned back in her chair. "After all, she's a friend of mine and I don't want her to be fed a pack of lies."

"Did you tell her that C.J. might be the subject of a criminal investigation?"

"Not initially. I first asked her what in God's name attracted her to him."

"Susan!"

"Well, the guy's disgusting. Anyway, I think his 'supposed' success and alleged connections impressed her."

Christina shook her head.

"I told her what I knew, but she defended him." Susan imitated a defensive Brandy's voice: "Nothing's been proven."

"Which is true." Christina attempted to straighten the pile of papers in her lap. "Is she going to see him again?"

"They'll be at Richard's reception tonight." Susan leaned back in her chair and propped her feet on the desk. "How do you like that one?"

"I don't. I'll try to get hold of her."

"She said she'd be out all day, showing property."

"Oh well, she's a big girl." Christina gathered her papers and stood.

Susan held up her hand. "I just got word from Symex that they let Ralph go."

"Oh no, that's terrible." Christina slumped back into her chair. "Why'd they do that?"

"I don't know. But what I do know is that the company is giving the pink slip to a lot of its middle managers. After a billion dollar robbery it's difficult for any company to bounce back. And, as we both know, a lay-off will help the stock price."

"It just seems strange that they would let him go. It seemed like his job was his life."

"Well, as I said, I don't know the full story." Susan focused on her computer monitor. "But I did hear that he's been acting rather reclusive since the robbery."

As usual, Susan was already one step ahead of the Silicon Valley rumor mill.

Jill St. Anne

"I hope he'll be O.K," Christina said. "I should probably give him a call just to make sure. I'll do it tomorrow when I have time to chat."

Chapter Twenty-Four

In his room at The Fairmont, Richard struggled with his bow tie. He had been trying to tie the perfect knot for several minutes when he heard the telephone ring.

"Richard Cartwright," he answered, irritated to be interrupted just as he almost finished the last loop.

"So what have you done for me lately," Curtis Saunders slurred into the phone.

"What's that supposed to mean, C.J?"

"You know exactly what I'm talking about."

Richard heard ice cubes clink in a glass and then heard C.J take a big gulp. "Listen, C.J. I've got to play this one carefully. But mark my words, by the end of tonight I'll have something for you."

"You'd better. I'm getting impatient."

Richard was ready to hang up, when C.J. added some painful last words. "I hope you haven't forgotten who funneled all that money into your last campaign."

"Tell me something I haven't already heard." Richard slammed down the phone, wishing he'd never met Curtis Saunders.

-

Christina rushed back to the hotel from her meeting, with only a few minutes to spare before she was supposed to meet Richard. She stepped into a floor-length, black, strapless velvet dress that clung to her figure like a glove. As she stood in front of the full-length mirror, she turned sideways and ran her hands along her waist to smooth out the wrinkles. She sucked in her stomach as much as she could.

Good thing I didn't have time to eat lunch today, she thought as she scanned the mirror one more time.

She clipped on a delicate pair of crystal and black onyx drop earrings and pulled her blonde mane back into a French twist, a style she knew accentuated her long neck and prominent collarbones. She touched her locket, questioning whether or not she should wear this rather familiar piece of jewelry to such a formal affair. Looking again in the mirror, it was clear that she was committing a fashion 'faux pas'; however, the practical side of Christina decided to keep the locket close to her. She doubled the chain so it resembled a vintage choker and took off the earrings, which didn't match, and replaced them with diamond studs. Satisfied with what she saw, she reached for a pair of long black gloves and slipped them over her hands and past her elbows. She took a few deep breaths to calm her nerves, picked up a small, evening bag and walked into the library to meet Richard.

Instead of the library, she found him on the terrace gazing out at the Bay. He turned around as she opened the French doors that led to the terrace. "Christina," he said in a slow, trance-like voice, "you're breathtaking."

"Why thank you Senator." She curtsied playfully. He wore a traditional Savile Row black dinner jacket. "I must say, you look quite dignified yourself."

He extended his hand. "Please, come over here and share this incredible view with me."

She reached for his hand and he led her over to the balcony. Standing side-by-side, they soaked in the tranquil sight of white sailboats gliding across the Bay at dusk. She wished Franco could share this with her. She knew he would love it here.

She and Richard did not talk, but she felt warm and comfortable standing next to him. After a few moments, he wrapped his arm around her waist and pulled her closer to him. The gesture seemed natural, and she did not pull away, but when he placed his other arm around her, she began to feel torn as to what to do. She wanted to keep their relationship platonic, but he was becoming difficult to resist.

As he pressed himself against her, she could feel his excitement. "Please Christina," he whispered, "allow me to kiss you. I think I'm falling in love with you. I can't help myself."

She relented and placed her warm lips on his. They kissed passionately for a few seconds before Christina backed away.

"What am I doing?" Christina covered her mouth with the back of her hand. "We can't do this. Franco—my boyfriend from Italy—is coming to visit me this weekend." She stepped several feet away from him. "Let's just forget this ever happened."

"I should apologize, Christina. You made it very clear to me that you were involved with someone else." He moved closer to her. "But don't tell me you didn't have the same feelings I did."

Christina turned away and reapplied her lipstick.

-

The ride in the long, white limousine to the Sheraton Palace was quiet, yet not uncomfortable. He placed his hand on her knee and again apologized for putting her in such a compromising position.

Putting her hand over his, she whispered, "Thank you, I'll be fine. It wasn't a big deal, and it's not necessary to apologize again."

As they pulled into the front entrance area, white-gloved attendants opened their door and escorted them out of the car. They stepped onto the red carpet that covered the marble steps leading to the hotel lobby. Flash bulbs from the cameras of a herd of paparazzi exploded as they entered the building. Reporters from all the major newspapers and television stations struggled to get the Senator's attention.

One aggressive female reporter from KGO shoved her microphone to his mouth. "Senator," she yelled, "what do you think about the recently uncovered irregularities linked with certain defense contracts?"

Before he had a chance to comment, a brash, bearded photographer plowed the woman over and flashed a picture. "Who's the babe? Another Hollywood starlet?" he shouted.

Richard turned to Christina. "Don't let any of this bother you. They'll do anything to sell a story."

He held her hand and pulled her through the crowd.

"What a mob scene!" Christina said just as they made it safely into the lobby of the hotel. "Does this happen every time you attend a cocktail party?"

"Not at all." He took a deep breath, and Christina could tell that he was relieved to have made it into the hotel without another character attack. "Normally, I don't get crushed by reporters and photographers, but because of all the celebrities expected to attend tonight, they're out in full force."

Hundreds of elegantly dressed supporters of Senator Cartwright filled the massive hotel lobby. Above them soared a five-story atrium, with its original plated glass ceiling. She'd forgotten how incredible this renovated 100-year hotel was. Three-foot high Ming Dynasty vases, filled with willow branches, orchids, and cherry blossoms, sat on marble pedestals placed through out the room. All fifty tables in the Garden Court Restaurant, where the reception was held, were decorated with gold candles and tropical flowers. Two ice sculptures, one of a unicorn and one of an elephant, stood on either end of a 50-foot long banquet table. Silver platters filled with fresh lobster, caviar and many other delicacies covered the white tablecloth. She thought that this was certainly an upgrade from the last benefit she attended.

As Christina surveyed the room, Richard squeezed her hand. "Are you ready?"

She nodded and let go of his hand. They walked into a swarm of black tuxedos and sequined dresses. Christina couldn't keep track of everyone she recognized. In particular she noticed ex-President Ford with his wife, Betty, talking with a few patients—people Christina knew have been in and out of the

Betty Ford Clinic several times. Christina looked around the crowded dining area to see if she could spot anyone she knew well. As her eyes focused on the individuals in the room, she saw Ralph Stinson. She was glad to see him out at a social event and was about to walk over to him when she saw Curtis Saunders and Brandy approach him. She didn't realize that Curtis and Ralph knew each other. She also wondered when Brandy would try to sell Ralph a house. She watched for a few moments and then saw Curtis put his hand on Brandy's shoulder. Brandy shot him a dirty look and stomped away.

Susan entered the room, wearing a gorgeous camel colored, lace dress with a pair of matching leather pumps. That's Susan, Christina thought, leather and lace. Her long brown hair, with its natural curl, fell to the mid section of her back. She normally straightened the curl or wore her hair up for work, but tonight she looked playful and sexy. Christina found herself hoping that someday she would find a man who could keep up with her.

Susan spotted Christina, waved and walked over to her. "Aren't you Miss Glamorous tonight!" Susan said.

"You also look stunning, Susan. In fact, you should wear your hair down more often. The men couldn't keep their eyes off of you when you made your grand entrance."

"Enough of the mutual admiration stuff." Susan pulled Christina away from the Senator and the small gathering of people he was talking to. "Just after you left work this evening, Stephano called me. He told me that Franco has changed his mind. He's not planning to come out here as he told you. Instead, he's hooking up with his ex-girlfriend—some coquette from France—at a beach resort in Kuala Lumpur."

"What are you talking about?" Christina swiped a flute of champagne from a gentleman in a white jacket and black bow tie. "Why would he do that?"

"Who knows? But he did tell Stephano that since you were seeing other people, he was going to do the same."

"Does he mean Richard?" Christina sipped the champagne.

Susan put her hand on her hip. "Well, apparently he has reason to believe that you two are an item."

"Now I understand why he's been so elusive," Christina tapped her champagne glass with her fingernail. "Between this French tart and Alessandra, no wonder he hasn't had time to call. I guess Richard was right. Long distance relationships never work."

"What do you mean, 'you guess Richard was right'?" Susan accepted a stuffed mushroom that was offered to her on a silver platter from one of the roving waiters.

"Oh, nothing important." Christina fumbled with her locket.

"Stephano didn't mention Alessandra; we had our own things to talk about. In fact, Stephano might be able to come out to see *me*. He has a flight to L.A. scheduled next week." Susan popped the mushroom in her mouth.

"Susan, that's great!! I'm so glad you two are staying in touch. It seemed that you had a lot of fun together in Italy."

"We'll see if it amounts to anything. I wish I knew more to tell you about Franco. Stephano said that he's been so busy with all of his business trips, that the two of them have barely had a chance to talk."

"Well, to be honest with you Susan, if Franco's attitude is to so quickly run off with his ex-girlfriend, I'm glad I found out now."

She looked over at the Senator and admired his strong profile. "In fact, maybe it's time that I caved into some of Richard's advances."

"I'd be careful." Susan left Christina with Richard and his well-wishers and walked over to the bar to get herself something to drink. She bumped into Brandy who was ordering a scotch from the bartender.

"Hi Brandy," Susan said. "Are you and C.J. having a good time?"

"Hardly," Brandy settled onto a barstool. "You were right. The guy's a real jerk. He ordered me to fetch him a double-shot of whisky without even introducing me to the man he was talking to. When I dutifully returned with his drink, he was squeezing some other women's ass. Anyway, I gave him his drink and told him not to bother looking for me at the end of the evening. I'm leaving without him!!"

"Good for you! I'm glad you found out yourself what a first class loser he is."

"Me too," she swirled her drink with her finger. "But here I am, back at the bar, drowning my sorrows in a scotch and water."

Susan looked for C.J. She saw him talking to Ralph.

"So, you met Ralph Stinson?" Susan asked Brandy.

"That's Ralph Stinson?" Brandy took her finger out of her drink and looked at Susan. "*The* Ralph Stinson, from that Symex company of yours?"

"Yeah, that's him."

"He didn't strike me as someone who would be working on your Symex deal."

"What do you mean?"

"I don't know." Brandy gulped down some scotch. "It seemed to me that Ralph worked for C.J."

"Why would you think that?" Susan took Brandy's drink away from her.

"I wasn't really part of the conversation." Brandy tugged her glass back. "C.J. demanded that I get him a drink and I didn't hear much. But it almost sounded like C.J. was bossing him around."

"Could you catch anything they were saying to each other?"

"I told you," Brandy guzzled down the last drop of her drink, "I could hear their tone of voice, but I couldn't hear what they were saying."

"Brandy," Susan pleaded, "this may be really important. Think hard. Did you pick up anything?"

"I don't know," Brandy whined. "I heard a few words, but they didn't make any sense."

"What did you hear?" Susan probed, "Do your best, and repeat everything you can remember."

Brandy held up her hand to the bartender. "I heard him say something about 'Chinks', and no deal without a ship."

Susan looked puzzled. She repeated what Brandy said to her. "Chinks, no deal without a ship."

Brandy nodded. "'Chinks' probably means 'Chinese'."

"Right—that sounds like the kind of a disgusting racial slur that would spill from C.J.'s mouth. But why would he be talking about ships with Ralph?"

Brandy turned to Susan. "Hey, maybe that Chinese guy, Seike, is a spy working for his government."

"Brandy," Susan placed her hand on Brandy's shoulder and took a long breath. "Seike's Japanese. His last name is Yamashuta." She removed her hand. "But you're right, I have a feeling there may be a connection."

Susan pondered the phrase Brandy heard a little longer. "Do you think he could have said 'chip' instead of 'ship'?"

The bartender brought over Brandy's drink. "Yeah, he could have." Brandy took a quick swig. "As I said, it was difficult to hear."

"If he said 'chip', I better tell Christina right away."

As she turned away from the bar, Brandy grabbed Susan's elbow. "You better not interrupt them now. Look who's walking toward them."

A reporter from ABC and her camera crew were setting up in front of the Senator. When the bright studio light went on, the reporter began asking the Senator questions, while Christina stood graciously by his side.

"You're right," Susan said. "I don't want to inadvertently end up on the 10:00 news. I'll catch her before she leaves tonight."

Chapter Twenty-Five

The T.V. crew broke down their equipment. Still standing in the atrium, Richard whispered into Christina's ear. "How about if we escape as soon as possible?"

"I'd love to." Christina's eyes danced. "But you're the guest of honor. We can't be the first ones to leave."

"You're right, we won't be the first ones to leave, but as soon as I make my obligatory toast, and thank everyone for coming, the reception will start to break up."

"Sounds like a plan to me." Christina smiled and held out her hand. "Start talking!"

Richard picked up a silver coffee spoon and clinked his crystal champagne glass several times. The low roar silenced and the crowd turned toward the front of the room.

He held his glass high in the air. "Thank you all for coming tonight. I am overwhelmed by the success of this evening, and flattered by all your support. Exciting and challenging times lay ahead for this country, and I am honored to represent the State of California."

Listening to him talk, Christina began to feel a surge of excitement and power. Her skin tingled. Her date for the evening—and someone who had just confessed that he was falling in love with her—could possibly be the next President of the United States.

Richard answered a few questions that were relevant to politics and his campaign. Flashbulbs ignited around the room as he posed for pictures with several of his supporters, friends and colleagues. He motioned for Christina to stand next to him. He wrapped his arm around her waist and pulled her close to him. More flash bulbs exploded, blinding them both.

They dashed out of the grand atrium to their waiting limousine and slipped into the back seat of the car. Richard shut the window between them and the driver and pulled Christina onto his lap. They kissed vigorously for several seconds. Christina began to unravel his bow tie and unclasped his gold and onyx studs. As she unbuttoned his shirt, Richard started unzipping the back of her dress. His cufflink got caught on her necklace. The chain broke. Christina felt the locket come loose. She pulled the chain from her neck and clutched it tightly in her fist.

The limousine stopped in front of the Fairmont. They hastily reassembled their clothing and rushed to the elevator bank. Inside the elevator they picked up where they'd left off. Richard ran his hand up her leg to the top of her stockings, which were attached to a garter belt. He slid his fingers into her silk panties, but before he could go further, the elevator stopped. The door opened and they stumbled into the foyer of their suite. He picked her up and sat her on the hall table, pulled off her panties and tossed them onto the black and white marble floor. Lost in the moment, Christina loosened her grip. The locket she was holding crashed to the floor. As it hit the ground, the locket broke open. The chip skidded across the slick marble.

Christina heard the impact and pulled away from Richard in order to see where the chip had landed. She eased off the hall table, trying to gracefully reach for the chip while simultaneously resisting Richard, who was pulling her back. Richard looked down. He let go and exclaimed, "So you **do** have the chip!" He then whispered under his breath, "C.J. was right all along."

She was aghast at what she was hearing and was almost too stunned to speak. "What do you mean, I have *the chip*." Christina remembered her self-defense classes and pushed Richard away with the heel of her hand. How could she be so betrayed? She was actually falling for this man. This had always been a major fear of hers. Whenever she let herself open up and become vulnerable, that's when everything took a turn for the worse. She tried to stay calm and rational, but she was too hurt and upset. "What do you know about this chip?!? Is this the only reason I'm here? Because you—of all people—also want your hands on this chip?!?"

Richard put his hands on her shoulders. "Christina, stop shouting. Please give me a chance to explain."

She scrambled away from him and snatched her panties and the chip from the floor. "No," she shot back. "I don't need an explanation."

"Christina!" He threw his bow tie on the floor. "Please listen to me."

"I don't feel like listening right now." She put the chip in her evening bag. "In fact, I'm getting my things and leaving!"

As she marched down the hall, Richard shouted after her. "I won't let you leave. I'm going to stand in front of the door until you hear me out!"

"What a joke!" she huffed to herself as she threw her toothbrush, contact case and glasses into a duffel bag. She would come back later, after he'd returned to Washington and retrieve the rest of her things. Knowing that he was blocking the front doorway, she tiptoed across the hall floor to the side door off the kitchen. She would use the secret hallway that Angie Dickinson supposedly used during the Kennedy years. The door creaked a little when she opened it, but Christina made it safely to the seventh floor, without Richard knowing she had left the suite.

Chapter Twenty-Six

Downstairs, she walked with as much dignity as she could muster outside to the circular driveway, where cabs line up and wait for guests. But since it was after midnight, the doorman had to call for a cab. Still clad in her long evening gown, she stood under the brightly colored flags that whipped in the wind and shivered in the cold, foggy weather for several minutes. She contemplated waiting in the lobby, but she was too frightened that Senator Cartwright would come downstairs any minute.

Finally a cab pulled up, and Christina slid into it.

"Where to, lady?" the driver asked.

She remained silent for a moment. She had not given any thought as to where she would go. Her first thought was Susan's place. She muttered to the driver Susan's address and hoped that she would be home.

As the cab pulled away from the hotel, she stared out the window. The muted glow of a street lamp in the fog cast a dim light on two lovers huddled together. At least they had each other, she thought. She felt like such a fool for falling for Richard's affections. Not only that, but by accepting Richard's invitation to stay at The Fairmont, she had pushed Franco away.

She had hoped that he would understand the circumstances. And now, because of her stupidity and flirtatious ways, he was enjoying a sun-drenched furlough from his busy work schedule with his ex-girlfriend. Her heart ached. At the same time she felt incredible pangs of guilt. She'd come within seconds of having sex with Richard.

The cab pulled up to Susan's apartment building. Christina asked the driver to wait. She pressed Susan's buzzer and kept her finger on it for several seconds.

"Damn!" She waited for over a minute, but there was no answer. She pressed the button again. She knew that Susan's buzzer was loud enough to wake the dead, but after several more minutes, there was still no answer.

"Hey lady!" The driver yelled from the cab. "Do you want me to sit out here all night?"

She trudged out to the cab and crawled into the back seat. Her body felt like lead—she was so tired; all she wanted to do was crawl into a warm bed.

The driver turned his head around. "O.K. lady, where to?"

"Honestly, I don't know." She felt incredibly alone and frightened. "Take me back to Italy," she mumbled.

"What did you say? Speak up! My shift was over a half hour ago," he said impatiently. "Where to!?!"

As she sat slumped in the back seat, she saw the bright headlights of a long, black BMW pull up next to the building. It looked like Brandy's car. She saw Susan hop out of the passenger side and blow Brandy a kiss.

"I'm staying here," she said to the driver, elated that she would have a safe place to sleep tonight. "What do I owe you?"

Stumped by her sudden change of mood, the cabbie shook his head. "Eighteen-fifty."

She handed him two, twenty-dollar bills. "Keep the change."

-

Christina took off her high heels and ran toward Susan's entryway.

Susan jumped when she heard her name and whirled around.

"Christina, my god," Susan said. "You nearly scared me to death. What happened?"

"It's a long story."

Susan put her hand on Christina's bare shoulder. "Come upstairs, girlfriend."

When they got into Susan's apartment, Christina said, "I can't wait to get out of this dress. Do you have an old sweatshirt I could put on?"

"Sure." Susan scurried into her bedroom where she put on a flannel shirt and gray, baggy sweatpants. Christina fell onto the couch in the living room. "You look awful." Susan brought out a pair of leggings and an extra large blue sweatshirt with 'NAVY' printed on it. Christina figured that the sweatshirt was one of Susan's ex-boyfriend's. "Come into the kitchen," Susan said. "I'll make some hot chocolate."

Christina peeled off her dress and stockings. The sweatshirt came down to her knees. "I didn't tell you, but a week ago I found a strange looking metal object in my suitcase. At first, I didn't think it was anything important; in fact, I thought it was just something that broke off from my luggage."

The kettle began to steam. Susan poured the hot water into two ceramic mugs that were filled with cocoa.

Christina stirred the hot chocolate with a spoon. "Thanks Susan." She wrapped her hands around the warm cup. "Remember how Agent Peters said that the stolen plans were useless without a code chip? That the master was in the safe, but that several prototypes had been manufactured?" She took a sip of cocoa. "I thought I'd better keep this piece of metal safe until I found out if all the chips were accounted for, so I went back to my apartment to retrieve a locket that my mother had given me."

Christina told Susan how she'd run into Ralph Stinson in the Marina. "There was something strange about the way Ralph answered me," Christina said, "so I didn't fully believe him when he said all the chips were accounted for. You know— women's intuition."

Christina sat on Susan's kitchen counter. "The next morning I phoned the FBI, but Agent Peters was on a special assignment. I didn't think it was an emergency at the time, so I didn't leave a message."

Susan opened a box of biscotti and dipped one in her hot chocolate. "I would've done the same thing, but you still haven't told me why you ended up on my doorstep looking like a lost cat."

She told Susan about her encounter with Richard and how he reacted when he saw the chip fall out of her locket.

"I obviously couldn't trust Richard, and I was scared to be alone with him," Christina took another sip of the warm cocoa. "Knowing he was blocking the front entryway, I sneaked out the back stairway. And *voila*," Christina held her arms in the air, "here I am!"

"Wow—I bet that threw you for a loop. I was beginning to like Richard. But, I'm glad you're here—and in one piece! Let's adjourn to the living room." The hardwood floors were covered with brightly colored, Indian carpets. Dark, African masks hung on the wall above her leather couch. Susan lit a small candle that was positioned under a clay pot. After a few minutes the room smelled of the soothing herb, lavender. "Now, I have to tell you what I learned about Ralph and C.J. tonight!"

Susan sat on the floor, crossed legged. She wrapped her hair into a loose bun on the top of her head. "For one, Brandy's never going to see C.J. again, and secondly, Brandy overheard C.J. talking to Ralph about some deal that would fall through without a chip. The chip they were talking about must have been the chip you've been carrying around for the past week. C.J. and Ralph probably used the Senator to get to you. And that means that Ralph must have somehow been in contact with Seike."

"Or C.J. may be involved with Seike, and they coerced Ralph into their scheme in order to get the chip," Christina added. "They probably offered him a huge cut—at least enough for Ralph to move out of the Sunset District, live in luxury, and never have to work again." Christina pulled the bobby pins that secured her French twist and shook her hair. "When Ralph realized that he no longer had the chip, he probably assumed that he must have accidentally given it to me before we left for Italy."

"How could he have 'accidentally' given it to you?"

"I'm not certain. But, every time I've been to his office, his desk has been cluttered with a million different things. The chip

171

is so small; it could've easily found it's way into the papers or the envelope he gave me before we left for our trip. Plus, he was adamant about getting back the original file. I guess when he figured he couldn't do it himself without causing too much attention, he had Seike and his thugs take it from me."

"That seems logical."

"Yeah, but I still don't understand how the Senator became such a crucial part in all of this." Christina furrowed her brow.

"C.J. probably assumed since Richard is now 'Mr. Eligible Bachelor' you'd be interested in him." Susan put her mug down and wiped her lips with her sleeve. "C.J. probably used Richard to get information from you."

Christina buried her hands in her face. "It's hard to believe that something so innocent has escalated into such chaos." She got up and moved to the couch. "I better get in touch with Agent Peters tomorrow morning, and let him know I have the chip. Also, I should tell him about what Brandy overheard."

"Don't worry about that tonight," Susan said, "you better get some sleep."

"You're right, I'm exhausted." She stretched out on the leather sofa, without even bothering to get a pillow. The African masks, with their contorted facial expressions, appeared to be jeering down upon her. "I don't know what I would do without you, Susan."

She fell into a deep sleep. She would take this uncomfortable couch over the Fairmont any day.

Once again, Christina woke up well after Susan had already left for work. Feeling stiff, she eased her way off the couch and stumbled into the kitchen to get some coffee. On the kitchen counter, Susan had left the paper opened to the 'Bay Area' section. It took a moment for Christina to realize that the smiling blonde on the arm of Senator Cartwright was herself.

"Oh my god." She picked up the paper and read the caption: "Senator Cartwright with his new friend, Miss Christina Caldwell, at his $2500 per plate fundraiser."

"Great, this is just what I need." She crumpled up the paper and threw it in the trash.

It was almost eight o'clock, and assuming that no one would be at a government office before then, she took a shower. The hot, steaming water soothed and comforted her muscles that ached from the combination of tension and the night on the couch.

She poured some water into the coffee maker and dialed the FBI headquarters.

"Special Agent Peters," he barked into the phone.

"Oh—hello, this is Christina Caldwell. I wasn't expecting you to answer."

"No one's here yet, and I have a lot of catching up to do. I just got back from Russia last night. I noticed you called last week."

"I called because I had something I *thought* you might be interested in. Now, I know, you'll be interested."

"What's that?"

"I think I have one of the prototype chips."

"You're shittin'! How did you end up with that?"

"I think Ralph Stinson may have accidentally enclosed it with some information he gave me over a month ago."

He shouted into the phone. "You've been carrying it around with you ever since!?!"

"I didn't know what it was at first." She poured herself a cup of coffee, opened the refrigerator and pulled out a carton of milk. "That's why I called you last week. But when your secretary said you were away on a special assignment, I felt it could wait until you returned." She dripped some milk into her coffee. "Anyway, over the course of last week, several events have taken place which lead me to believe that Ralph Stinson, as well as a man by the name of Curtis Saunders, may be involved with Seike Yamashuta."

"Curtis Saunders? That fits with a lead we've been working on for the past several years."

"Really?" Christina looked for sugar but couldn't find any.

"He's tried to obtain defense contracts by bribing government officials. We haven't been able to nail him yet, but this could do it."

So—Susan was right, Christina thought.

"Well, young lady," Peters exhaled a deep breath into the phone, "you better get in here right away. We need a statement from you, and we also need to get that chip back. Does anyone know you have it?"

"I'm afraid a few people do."

"Listen, Christina, you're not safe if anyone knows you have that chip." She heard Peters clear his throat. "We received some unfortunate news this morning. The night watchman at Symex didn't make it. He died last night."

Christina let out a slow, deep breath. She could not speak for a moment. "That's awful. I'm so sorry to hear that."

"We need to talk. When can you come in?"

"I'll call my office and tell them I'm taking a personal day. I'll be over within the hour."

"I'll see you then."

"Oh, I just remembered!" she said just before Agent Peters hung up. "I don't have my car here."

"We'll send a government vehicle over for you. Where are you?"

"I'm at my girlfriend's apartment." She gave him the address and then called her office to tell them she wouldn't be coming in today. She asked to be transferred to Susan.

"Hi Christina," she answered. "How did you like that picture of yourself in *The Chronicle*?"

"If things had turned out differently last night, I would've thought it was great." She'd been so attracted to him at the moment that picture was taken, and then only an hour later, she'd felt totally betrayed.

"You two look like the perfect couple. Too bad the rest of the San Francisco Bay Area doesn't know the real story."

"Tell me about it." Christina's memory flashed back to the moment their smiles were captured on film. "Anyway, I'm not coming in today. The FBI is sending a car for me."

"Good. I don't think you should go anywhere without a bodyguard until Stinson and Saunders are in custody. And for that matter, Seike Yamashuta. I read in the paper that the night watchman died last night."

"I know." Christina rinsed out her coffee cup and dumped the coffee grounds down the sink. "Agent Peters just told me. I can't believe how tragic this whole thing has become. I feel just horrible for his family."

"I do too. But Christina, this is not our fault," Susan said.

"I still feel responsible." She felt the coffee turning in her stomach. "At least the plans are useless without this chip."

"You're right," Susan said, "but you're not out of danger yet. Seike and his cohorts have killed once for that warehouse full of chips. And from what Agent Peters told us, it sounds like they'll stop at nothing if they know how valuable those designs are. It wouldn't mean a great deal for them to kill again."

Christina agreed, but was too overwhelmed to say anything.

"Be careful," Susan added, "and call me if you need me."

Chapter Twenty-Seven

The same highly definable, yet unmarked car that had met Christina at the airport two weeks ago was at Susan's apartment in less that an hour. She walked downstairs to also find the same type of driver: a no-nonsense 'suit' with dark sunglasses and short brown hair. She didn't have anything else to wear besides her long, black evening gown, so she kept on Susan's sweatshirt and leggings. As far as shoes went, all she could find in Susan's closet were a pair of beat-up hiking boots that were several sizes too large for her.

The agent said, "hello", showed her his badge and opened the back seat door for her. She slid in and suddenly felt ill again; the vinyl seats and the 'new car' smell didn't help her already troubled stomach.

After they had driven only a few blocks, Christina tapped her driver on the shoulder. "Excuse me, but do you mind if I sit up front? I'm feeling a little queasy, and sitting in the back seat doesn't help."

"Sure, Miss Caldwell. I'll pull right over."

"Please call me Christina." She noticed that this man wasn't a day over 30. "By the way, what's your name? I didn't quite catch it when you flashed your badge for that full half-second."

He laughed and shrugged his shoulders. "Sorry about that. I tend to get so caught up in procedure that I forget the personal side of things."

He pulled the car to the curb and Christina got into the front seat. He took off his aviator-style Ray Bans and extended his hand. "My name's Dan Stevenson."

She was startled when she noticed his deep blue eyes. What a shame he always wore those dark glasses!

"Pleased to meet you Dan, and thanks for driving me over to your office."

"Sure no problem. It's a nice change from pushing papers back at my desk."

When they reached the FBI headquarters, Dan escorted her to Agent Peter's office.

"Nice sweatshirt." Peters stood up from behind his desk.

"Thanks, but it's not mine."

He smiled. "They generally aren't." He motioned for her to sit down, as he sat down himself. "Let's get right down to business. Show me the chip."

She reached into her small evening bag, which she still had from last night, and handed the chip to Agent Peters.

He turned the piece of metal between his thumb and index finger. "This sure looks like what we've been looking for."

"Is this enough evidence to arrest anyone?" She hoped that it would be, and that this ordeal would finally come to an end.

"I'm afraid not." He placed the chip in a plastic, zip lock bag and attached a red and white evidence tag. "We're thankful we have it, but we have no proof as to how it got into your hands."

"I'm sure Ralph inadvertently gave it to me when he delivered the IPO documents before we left for Italy."

"You're probably right, but we can't arrest Ralph Stinson based on this information. We need something more solid."

"What do you have so far?"

Agent Peters pushed up his shirtsleeves. "We have telephone records that indicate that Stinson made several phone calls, after hours, to Saunders' company, Silicon Valley Electronics."

Christina interrupted him. "But since they're both in the same industry, that means nothing. Right?"

Agent Peters pointed his finger at her. "You didn't let me finish. We also noticed that several calls were made to his home in Saratoga, but we can't arrest anyone based on phone calls."

Christina stretched the sleeves of her sweatshirt over her hands. "It's just hard to believe that Ralph would get messed up in something like this."

"Not really." Peters pulled out a cigar from his desk drawer and clipped the end. "His credit report revealed that he has debts going back for ten years."

"But how did Ralph get involved with Seike?"

"We're working under the assumption that Yamashuta couldn't decipher the plans without the help of someone in the industry. And, of course, they couldn't do anything without the chip from Symex. Enter Ralph Stinson." He lit his cigar and took a hefty puff. "And, given Saunders' track record, we're also assuming that Saunders was the person Yamashuta chose to either build the missile or finish the plans to a point where they would be complete enough to sell to a foreign power." He leaned forward and lowered his voice. "Or use themselves."

Christina asked, "Use themselves?"

"We can't rule anything out at this point. There are quacks all over the world who work for terrorists." He took another puff and shook off a clump of ashes into a tin tray. "My bet is that Yamashuta, Saunders and Stinson are all in it for the money. I don't think they plan to blow up the world. But our fear is that whomever they sell the plans to will do just that."

"This is really frightening." Christina took off her glasses and cleaned the lenses with the bottom of her sweatshirt. "And the more I think about it, the more sense it makes to me."

"Why's that?" Peters asked.

Christina put her glasses back on. "Ralph mentioned to me that his financial situation would be changing soon. I just assumed that he had planned to exercise some stock options."

"Nothing quite so honest, I'm afraid." Peters rested his cigar on the edge of the tin tray. He stared at her for a few seconds. "Christina, I'd like to ask your help on this matter."

She frowned. "How could I help the FBI?"

"It's highly unusual to bring a private citizen into our affairs, but you're the perfect person to lure Stinson into a situation where he may implicate himself."

"Isn't that called entrapment?" Christina asked. She remembered that term from a recent insider trading scandal.

"Not exactly," Agent Peters said. "The FBI has to be concerned with crossing the lines of entrapment and in order to accomplish this mission, we first need to consult the U.S. Attorney's office and have them approve every last detail. If we don't follow procedure and anything goes wrong, they could all walk."

Christina sat back in her chair and pondered what Agent Peters was proposing. She desperately wanted to help. She felt responsible for what had happened. On the other hand, this was unknown territory and could be extremely dangerous. Was it worth it to get involved?

Peters was waiting for her answer. It looked like he was holding his breath. "Let's hear what you have in mind," she said.

Peters let out a huge breath and relaxed in his chair. "Okay— listen up." He rested his hands on his desk. "What we want you to do is to call Stinson and arrange for him to meet with us. It's as simple as that. The caveat here is that we don't want you to mention anything to him about what will take place in the meeting. Just tell him that we would like to get together. If he agrees, the authorities might go easy on him. He probably won't be tried as an industrial spy and traitor, and one who has traded the safety of his fellow citizens for monetary gain."

Christina knew it wouldn't be as simple as that. Ralph was involved with some seasoned criminals. Serious money was involved. Ralph wouldn't surrender that easily. She also knew that if she stuck her neck out that far, she could become a target. If she was going to get involved, she wanted to be better informed and in more control of the situation.

She wanted to be there when he was apprehended.

"I understand what you are getting at, sir, but I've gotten to know Ralph pretty well, and from what I've learned, he wouldn't agree to a meeting without wanting to know what it's all about. There's no way he'll go in blind."

Agent Peters raised his eyebrows. "Well then, Miss Caldwell, what do you have in mind?"

"From what I've heard, it sounds like you need me to lure Ralph to a place where you can apprehend him red-handed."

"May I ask what you mean by 'apprehend him red-handed'?" He folded his arms and leaned back in his chair.

"As far as he knows, he thinks I still have the chip." She pushed her hair behind her ears. "I could fabricate some story saying that I want a cut of whatever he's getting."

"Now calm down, Nancy Drew," Agent Peters said. "This is a very serious and dangerous operation you're proposing."

"I understand that," she said, brushing off the reference to her favorite childhood, fictional heroine. "But we both know that those plans are useless without the chip I just gave you. You can't prove anything until he admits that this chip is the only means to getting his payoff."

Peters uncrossed his arms. "O.K., you have a point."

"Thank you," she said, feeling much more sure of herself. "Now, please, hear me out." She stood and paced in front of Peter's desk.

"First, I call Ralph at home and tell him I was sorry to hear about Symex firing him. Of course I won't be so blunt, but you get the idea. Then, maybe we'll small talk for a few minutes."

"Uh hum," he nodded.

"Then I'll go for the jugular." She picked up a pencil from Peter's desk and clenched her fist around it. "I'll just come right out and say it. I'll tell him I have what he wants, and I want half of whatever he's been promised by the ultimate buyer."

She sat back down, but remained perched on the edge of her chair.

"He'll know exactly what I'm talking about. I won't mention the chip over the phone in case all the lines are tapped." She pointed her pencil at the wall behind Peters. "Next, I'll set a place for us to meet. It won't be some dark alley or anything like that. It will be somewhere light and safe. You and the U.S.

Attorney's office will arrange for a full backup unit and we'll go in for the kill."

Agent Peters interrupted. "Christina, you're getting carried away. I appreciate your willingness to help, but it doesn't work that easily in real life."

Her shoulders fell and she folded her hands in her lap. "What's wrong with it? It seems plausible to me."

"Parts of it, yes, but many of the elements need work."

"Such as?"

"Well, first of all, a 'real' extortionist wouldn't offer to hand over such a valuable piece of information without truly expecting to be paid. How do you think Ralph could afford to pay you?"

"I'm sure he's been in touch with the ultimate buyer. If it's Seike or someone involved with Seike, they probably have a few extra million lying around from the proceeds of the warehouse heist."

He pounded his fist on his desk. "That's not a sure thing." He was clearly irritated. "In fact nothing's a sure thing!"

Christina stood up. "I'll tell you what is a sure thing. These guys aren't gonna stop at anything until they get what they want! I'd rather set them up on our own turf, and have us call the shots. They still think I have the chip, and for all I know, they'll kill me for it. Remember, the guard is dead."

Christina could feel her face and neck becoming red, and she knew that she had better calm down. Losing her cool was a sure way to lose credibility. She settled back in her chair, took a deep breath and continued.

"Now, back to your concern about how they are going to come up with the money to pay me. How about if we just throw it out there and see what they do. After all, who cares whether they cough up the money or not? It's not like I'm going to give him the real code chip. If it's important enough to Ralph, and it sounds like it is, he'll think of something."

He cracked a faint smile. "Christina, you're incorrigible."

-

Leaving the FBI, Christina asked Dan if he could drop her off at the Fairmont instead of at Susan's apartment. This way she could retrieve the remainder of her personal belongings while he accompanied her.

When they arrived at the all-to-familiar entryway to the Presidential Suite, everything looked the same as it had when she and Richard first stumbled into the room Tuesday night. The hall table was returned to its position against the wall. The vase of fresh flowers that had been knocked over was once again standing upright.

She was thankful that she'd remembered to pick her underwear off the floor. She led Dan through the library and back to her room.

"Wow—this is some place," Dan whistled.

"Yeah, it was great while it lasted, but I'm not safe here anymore." She unlocked her bedroom door. "This will just take a minute."

Dan took off his blue blazer and waited on the leather couch in the library.

She emerged from the room with her duffel bag, overflowing with rumpled clothes. "Let's get out of here."

They left through the back entrance. She didn't want to take a chance of running into Richard.

Dan gave the parking attendant his ticket. "Where do you plan to go?" He put his coat and Ray Bans back on. "It's still not safe to return to your apartment."

"I know. I guess I'll just keep staying at my girlfriend's house until everything is cleared up."

"Is there any security there?"

"No, none. She doesn't even have a doorman."

"Well, in that case, I'll arrange for around-the-clock protection. You shouldn't be staying anywhere without it. How about if I go back to your friend's apartment and check it out for you?"

"That would be great." Christina smiled. "Did Agent Peters tell you what we have in store for Ralph Stinson?"

"A little bit, but he plans to fill me in tomorrow when we formulate the details. In the meantime, why don't you give your friend a call and ask her if it's O.K. if I do a cursory check at her place while she's still at work."

She walked back into the lobby where it was less noisy and pulled out her cell phone. She dialed Susan's direct line and got right through.

"Hi, Susan! Listen, there's this adorable FBI Agent that wants to check out your place."

"What are you talking about?"

"He just wants to make sure no one has planted any bugs or tapped the phones. Is it okay if he looks around? Also he wants to arrange around-the-clock protection for us. What do you think?"

"Well, uh… I don't know."

"Susan, he's gorgeous! I thought you'd be dying to meet him."

Susan lowered her voice into the phone. "What about the pot?"

So that's why she was flailing, Christina thought. "Where do you have it stashed?"

"In my bathroom. Top drawer on the left. An old diaphragm holder."

"I'll make sure he doesn't find it. But don't worry. It's not like he's bringing drug sniffing beagles."

"Okay. Let him in."

"I'll stall him until you get home. Get home early!"

"I'll hurry!"

-

Christina led Dan up to Susan's apartment.

Dan took off his coat and threw it over a stool in the kitchen. "This will take about a half hour."

"I'll make some coffee," Christina said.

Dan pulled from his pocket a small, metal device. When he turned it on, static crackled. He got down on his hands and knees and dragged the device across the floorboards in Susan's front hallway. After several minutes on all fours, he got up, and did the same along the crown molding on the ceiling. He walked into the living room, where he felt the mud in each of the plants, pointed the metal sensor under the couch, the chairs and the coffee table. Christina ran into the bathroom before Dan began his search in that room. She found what she was looking for and slipped it into her pocket.

Christina smelled the coffee brewing. She retreated to the kitchen and fetched two mugs from the cabinets.

Dan came back into the kitchen and swiped his hands together. "Everything's come up clean."

Christina was about to hand him his coffee when she noticed it was almost 6:00.

"Since it's after hours, would you like something a little stiffer to drink?" She held the coffee pot over the sink in a tipped position, ready to spill it down the drain.

"Sure, I'll have a little chocolate in that coffee."

"Not quite what I had in mind," Christina smiled. "But I know she has some cocoa around here."

Susan blew into her kitchen shortly after 6:30. The first glimpse she got of Dan was of his solid back. His suit jacket was still off and there was something sexy and powerful about seeing his gun harnessed around his shoulders and waist in its leather holster. Susan raised her eyebrows and smiled. She indicated to Christina that she approved.

Christina introduced them to each other and poured Dan some more coffee and Susan a glass of Chardonnay.

"May we please get out of my kitchen," Susan said. "If I'd known I would be having a party in here, I would have at least swept the floor."

As they were walking back to the living room, Susan's front doorbell rang. Susan reached for the button to answer it, but Dan put his hand over hers and answered it himself. The security officers were downstairs. Dan buzzed them in. They all walked downstairs to meet them in the lobby.

"Dan—is upstairs secure?" one of them asked.

"Tight as a drum. She has a middle unit, with a window that opens to a small courtyard. The only access is through an inside stairwell."

"All right then, we'll plant ourselves here in the lobby."

The two agents properly introduced themselves to Susan and Christina, then they told them to forget they were there.

Dan stayed downstairs for a few moments to talk with the security officers.

"You're right!" Susan said as they walked back upstairs. "What a doll! Too bad he's not the one providing our round-the-clock protection."

When Dan returned to the living room, Susan and Christina were sitting on the floor. Susan had lit some candles. The fragrance of the aromatic plant, myrrh, smoldered from an incense stick on her bamboo end table.

"This all sounds so exciting," Susan said to Dan.

"I don't know if I would use the word 'exciting'," Dan said. "Serious would be more appropriate. This is one of the biggest cases the agency has worked on in a decade. We're going to be up all night finalizing the security arrangements. We have a full day ahead of us tomorrow, collaborating with the U.S. Attorney." He looked at Christina. "Christina, you know what you have to do tomorrow, but just keep it at that. Make the

185

initial contact, set your time and place, but don't say anything else."

"Don't worry, I'll play by the rules." Christina finished her glass of wine.

"Good. Now I'd better be leaving." He stood up and patted his gun and then turned to Susan. "It was nice to meet you." His voice was firm. "I'm sure I'll be seeing you again soon."

"Nice to meet you too. I hope you don't mind if I don't get up." She extended her hand upward to his.

"No, not at all, I'll find my way out. Goodnight."

Susan watched Dan's backside disappear down her hallway. "What a straight arrow," she said. "I can't believe that after spending an hour with us he still remained the consummate professional."

"I know. He is kind of stiff. But, as he said, it sounds like he's going to have a rough night."

"Maybe there's some rule in their operations manual that prevents them from getting too close to those they protect."

"I don't know about that," Christina said, "but I sure wouldn't be in the mood to drink and chit-chat with two giddy women if I knew that I had to work all night. I'd bet he's a lot different on the weekend."

Christina poured Susan another glass of wine. The sweet smelling incense filled the room. "Now tell me more about Stephano coming out this weekend."

"Oh geez! I can't believe I forgot to tell you." She covered her face with her hands and peeked through her fingers at Christina. "He's not coming this weekend. He thought that maybe next weekend would work out better, but that's not what's important. He told me that Franco returned from his jaunt to Kuala Lumpur early. He's back in Italy, and if you stay up late enough, you should try to call him. I'm sure he'll be in his office first thing."

"Hmm—I wonder if there was some trouble in tropical paradise?" She brought her glass to her lips. "Thanks for telling me. I better call him. We need to iron out some things between us." Her eyes started to water. "I really miss him, and I can't believe I almost had a fling with a guy who was trying to use me."

Susan placed her wineglass on the wicker trunk that sat in front of her couch. "We've all made mistakes in the relationship department before. Chalk it up to a learning experience."

"You're probably right, but at this point I don't even care. I better put this wine down and start drinking coffee if I want to stay up until midnight to call Franco."

"How about if we go out and get a double espresso on Chestnut Street?" Susan blew out the candle. "That should do the trick."

When they reached the lobby of Susan's building, one of the FBI men stood up. "Where are you two ladies going?"

"We're just gonna run out and grab an espresso," Susan said.

"Sorry, not tonight," he said. "It's too dangerous, even if we accompany you."

"All right," Susan said. "I guess I'll go upstairs and make some in the kitchen."

"May we offer you any?" Christina asked, feeling sorry for them having to sit there all night.

"We'd love some."

-

Buzzing from the caffeine, Christina had no trouble staying up well past midnight.

In Italy it was now past 9:00 in the morning. Franco was probably sitting in his office catching up on his messages.

"There's no time like the present." She took a deep breath and punched the fifteen-digit number to his office in Massa Carrara.

His secretary answered in the delicate tones of an Italian Countessa.

Christina asked in her rudimentary Italian if she could please speak with Franco. She held her breath as she was put on hold.

The secretary came back on the line and asked in perfect English, "Franco would like me to ask you 'Christina who'?"

Christina laughed, grateful Franco hadn't lost his sense of humor.

"Christina the Clown," she said to his secretary.

"Buon Giorno, Christina." Franco promptly took her call. "How's the traveling circus?"

"We've been very busy." She smiled into the phone. "Too bad I missed you when the troupe stopped in Kuala Lumpur."

"It's amazing how news of my personal vacation schedule travels across the continents. I trust you have been in touch with Stephano?"

"Not directly. The grapevine also includes Susan."

"I see. Now I know how to send an emergency message."

"Anyway Franco, before you tell me about your trip, I really need to apologize about any misunderstanding you may have had about me and Senator Cartwright." She settled into a leather chair in Susan's living room. "Nothing happened between us, and I only considered a relationship with him after I heard you ran off to the beach with your ex-girlfriend."

"Well, I must say, when I called you at the Fairmont and he answered the phone, I figured I was ancient Roman history by that point."

"Nothing could be further from the truth! He's extremely devious. I can assure you that was an innocent mistake. And if you left a message, I never got it."

"It doesn't matter anymore, Christina. After spending a few miserable days with my ex-girlfriend, Celine, I knew that she was only interested in me for my family's money, our jet, the houses—you know what I mean. I forgot how spoiled she was. She nearly forced me to land in Hong Kong because she forgot her Patek-Philippe and needed to buy a new watch. Once in Kuala Lumpur, I arranged for us to stay at a primitive resort on the beach. You would have loved it. The accommodations were simple grass huts that opened up to the vast ocean. It was beautiful, and so relaxing—just like sleeping on the beach."

Christina thought back to their last night together, when they'd slept on the beach, and back further, to the first time they'd made love. She could still see the bright moon, hear the lapping waves and feel his warm body.

Franco continued. "She despised it and flew over to Singapore the next day where I'm sure she spent the next several days ordering room service at the Shangri La."

"I'm sorry to hear you had such a lousy time, but to be honest, I'm glad things turned out that way." She slung her legs over the arm of the chair. "I'd go there any day with you. It sounds lovely."

"It was. I thought about you the entire time. It took an experience like that to realize how much you mean to me."

Her heart was warming and her stomach fluttered. She felt so lonely without him. She curled up in the chair and pulled one of the brightly colored, Indian pillows to her chest.

"Christina," he said, "I need to spend more time with you. You are all I think about. In fact it's *distracting*. I'm finding it difficult to concentrate on work."

"I can't tell you how wonderful that is to hear. I also can't stop thinking about you." She squeezed the pillow tighter. "When I thought I'd lost you to Celine, or for that matter Alessandra, I didn't know what I would do. I need to spend more time with you also, but how is that possible? You have your hectic life in Italy and the constant pressure for you to marry Alessandra." She let the pillow fall to her lap. "Besides, I'm in the middle of a crisis here in San Francisco."

"Has that situation with your client worsened?"

"To say the least," she swung her feet back onto the ground. "But I really can't talk about it until everything is resolved. You won't believe it when I tell you."

"Please be careful, Christina. I am very concerned about you, and I can not understand why you are still involved in this."

"Don't worry about me. Everything should be over within the next few days. I'm just as worried about our relationship. It's so precarious. There are so many variables out of my control. I hate that feeling."

"We'll work something out, my darling. In the meantime, I'm going to finish the painting I've been working on for you. I think I could have it delivered to the Port of Oakland by next Friday. I'll include it in a special shipment of marble that we're sending by air that is supposed to meet up with one of our container ships. Also, I'll mail a pass over to you so they won't give you any problems at the Port."

"Thank you! I can hardly wait to see it!" Once again, she was feeling full of life.

"I must go now. Ciao, dolcina."

"Ciao, Franco." She paused and then said the words she had never told him before, "I love you."

She knew that by the mere utterance of those words, she was setting herself up for a disappointment.

But he said: "I love you too."

Elated, she hung up the phone. She felt light and free again, like she was in Italy. But something stronger stuck with her: she knew that she could spend the rest of her life with Franco. Yet she had to stop thinking like this. His parents would never allow it.

Chapter Twenty-Eight

"What's gotten into you?" Margie asked as she saw Christina skip through the doors at 7:30 am. "You look like you just came back from a day at the spa. I haven't seen you look so refreshed in days."

"I'm in love, Margie. It's as simple as that." Christina set down Margie's muffin and coffee. "In fact, I didn't go to sleep until after two o'clock this morning and I haven't had a good night's sleep in over a week."

"Well, it's great to see your spirit back. Listen; there are some FBI guys in your office. They said you knew they were coming. Is everything all right?"

"Don't worry, everything is under control."

She walked into her office, grateful that soon this entire ordeal would be over. She caught herself daydreaming of spending a full week in a grass hut with Franco. It would be so romantic. The sun would warm her body, constantly chilled by the San Francisco summers, and she would wake up in Franco's arms every morning to a spectacular sunrise. "Yeah, right," she said to herself.

"Good morning, Miss Caldwell."

"Oh—good morning." She snapped out of her daydream and noticed the two men sitting in her office. One's eyes were covered with tinted glasses and the other was wearing a navy blue blazer that didn't quite cover his rotund belly. "I'm sorry I'm a bit late, I haven't been sleeping much lately."

"Are you ready to make your call to Stinson?"

"Yes, I had planned to do it first thing."

Tinted glasses said, "Good, but we have to go off-site. Given the proprietary information your firm deals with, we're not authorized to tape any conversations within the confines of your company walls."

"I understand." She pushed her glasses onto her head. "So are we going out to some inconspicuous white van, with ACME Plumbing painted on the outside, that's equipped with the latest in surveillance equipment?"

"Very funny," he responded dryly. "No, in fact, we have an office suite here in the city that the department uses on a regular basis for purposes such as this."

"All right then, let's go." She picked up her briefcase and led them out to the lobby. "So much for getting some real work done this morning," she mumbled to herself.

Remarkably, the office they used looked like an executive suite, unlike the stark government vestibules she had become accustomed to seeing recently. Instead of the typical slab flooring, she stepped onto hardwood floors, covered with oriental carpets. There wasn't any metal furniture in sight, only an antique mahogany partners desk that stood in the middle of the room.

They led her into the next room, which was more of what she expected. A large metal table, covered with telephones, cables, and sophisticated recording equipment, stood in the center of the room. There were no oriental rugs. The windows were covered with metal blinds.

"You're free to place the call when you feel you're ready," the agent said.

"Is there a chair or something I could sit on?"

"No problem." They dragged one of the heavy, upholstered chairs in from the reception area.

"Would you like a cup of Darjeeling tea, also?" The one with the large stomach asked as they set the chair in front of the table.

"No, thank you," she responded, not amused.

"O.K., here I go."

She lifted up the cold, metal receiver and asked, "Do I just dial, like a normal phone?"

"Yes. You don't even have to dial nine."

It was before 9:00 in the morning and she prayed Ralph was still at home. She punched the number, and took a deep breath. One ring...two rings...three rings. Damn, she didn't want to leave a message and she certainly didn't want to remain camped out in this makeshift office all morning.

He answered on the fourth ring.

"Hello?" He sounded groggy.

"Hi Ralph, it's Christina." She used her friendliest, perkiest voice.

"Christina?" His voice rose. "You're the last person I expected would call."

"How are you doing, Ralph? I was sorry to hear about the lay-offs at Symex."

"Thanks for the condolences," he mumbled, "but I'm actually enjoying myself. They gave me a great comp package—in other words they're paying me to sleep in for the next several months. I gotta tell ya, it's nice not having to fight the commute everyday."

"Well, I'm glad to hear you're not hurting."

She looked up at the agents who were eyeing her intently. She had better get to the point.

"Anyway, Ralph. I should probably cut through the bullshit. I'm pretty sure I have something that you want."

"And what would that be, may I ask?" His tone changed dramatically.

"Well, how about if we play a little guessing game? What's worth a ton of money, but weighs less than an ounce?" She shook her hand in front of her face. "No—that's too obvious, how about this. What has the power, when used in conjunction with something that was recently stolen, to wipe out the entire population of a large metropolitan area?"

She was enjoying her game; but it was obvious by the way the agents were glaring at her, that they were not.

"O.K., Christina, cut the crap. What do you have?"

193

"You have to guess. I'm sure that engineering degree from MIT is worth something."

"So, you *do* have the chip."

"I'm sorry Ralph, I couldn't quite hear you." Her voice was extremely sarcastic. "Could you please speak more clearly? I thought you said something about a chip, but you need to be more precise."

"You know exactly which chip I'm referring to, you smart ass! You've had the code chip all along haven't you?"

She looked up at the agents and gave them a thumbs-up.

"I guess you're right. I've had it all along, only because *you* gave it to me. Now, I plan to give it back to you, but you're going to have to pay."

She paused and waited for his response.

"How much do you want?"

"I want half of whatever you're getting."

She could hear him take a deep breath. "That's impossible! I don't have anything to give you until I keep my end of the bargain. They need that chip."

"That's obviously not going to work," she curtly responded. "You certainly don't expect me to accept an IOU, do you?"

"Listen, Christina, I couldn't even get a home mortgage. All that shows up on my balance sheet is a measly savings account. After I deliver that chip I'll be set for life, and I'm talkin' the good life. But, I have nothing to give you up front."

"Talk to your source. Ask him to give you a quarter of it now. It sounds like he wants to get paid as badly as you do. And you and he both know the plans are useless without this chip."

Surprisingly, he did not object or ask any more questions. "Fine, where do you want to meet?"

"Are you familiar with the Palace of Fine Arts in the Marina?"

"Isn't everybody?"

"Meet me under the rotunda at 8:00 tomorrow morning. I want to miss the morning joggers, and leave before the tourists arrive."

"Make it Friday, I have some things to take care of before then."

She looked up to the agents to get their approval. They nodded 'yes'.

"Fine."

Ralph slammed down the phone. Christina slumped back into her chair and breathed a huge sigh of relief.

"Well done, Miss Caldwell," the portly one said. "Until Friday we are going to increase your personal security. In addition to the officers in the lobby of your girlfriend's apartment building, we're assigning Dan Stevenson to guard you."

"What do you mean 'guard me'?" she asked.

"Stevenson will drive you to and from work, sit outside your office—basically follow you everywhere."

"And when I'm sleeping?"

"We'll have you moved to a hotel. A female agent will accompany you. And don't worry, it's not going to be the Fairmont."

"I'm getting pretty tired of moving around." She picked up her briefcase. "It would be heaven to sleep in my own bed for a solid week."

"This will be over soon." The agent with the dark glasses put his hand on her briefcase. "Then you'll be able to move back home."

When she returned to her office, Dan Stevenson was waiting in the lobby for her. Instead of his standard blue blazer, he was wearing a brown leather bomber jacket and a pair of Levi's.

"Hello Christina," he said, "I guess you were told we're going to be glued at the hip for the next 24 hours."

Dan followed Christina down the corridor to her office. "Things could be worse," she said.

"I'll try to stay out of your hair."

"I just hope you don't get too bored." Christina put her glasses on and pulled out a stack of papers from her briefcase. "Maybe you, Susan and I could go out to lunch together."

"I'm sorry Christina, but you won't be going outside today. We'll leave the building after work together, then I'll drive you directly to where you'll be staying tonight."

"What do you mean? I'll suffocate in here." She pointed to her large glass windows behind her desk. "These windows don't open. Haven't you heard of office workers getting strange viruses because of stale, recirculated office air?"

"Don't get carried away." He promptly snapped the draperies shut. "It's only for one day. You'll manage."

Within minutes, Susan poked her head into Christina's office. "Hi guys," she said, "how did your morning go with the FBI agents?"

"Pretty well, I guess. Everything is set for Friday morning. I can hardly wait to see the look on Ralph's face when he gets arrested."

Dan looked up at her and gave her a stern look.

"Don't worry Dan, Susan can be trusted."

"Right, Dan," Susan said, "who do you think I am? Some Soviet double agent, posing as a high tech analyst during the day?"

"We never know whom we can trust," Dan said.

"You don't have to worry about me." She sat down in the chair next to him, crossed her legs and started swinging her ankle.

Christina looked up from her desk. "I was going to ask you to join us for lunch, but Dan has informed me that I can't go outside."

"That's O.K.," Susan said. "I just found out that my lunch was canceled. A group of money managers were supposed to fly up from San Diego and we were going to have a working lunch in the conference room, but the fog socked them in at the airport.

Can you believe it? Fog in San Diego. I thought that was only our problem. Anyway, they're coming tomorrow, but the caterers are still coming today. It was too late to cancel."

"How 'bout it Dan?" Christina asked.

"Will it be safe enough for you?" Susan joked.

"It'll be fine," Dan said.

"Bye, Susan. You know where to find us," Christina said. "I need to get to work."

This was probably better, she thought. Unless she was entertaining a client, she always felt guilty about taking more than a few minutes for lunch.

"See you at noon." Susan skipped out the door.

"I hope you have something to occupy yourself," Christina pulled her glasses out of her briefcase. "I'm going to be on the phone nonstop for the next several hours."

It was nearly one when Julie beeped through.

"The caterers just rolled their carts into the conference room."

"Thanks, Julie. Why don't you grab yourself a sandwich. I'd hate to see all that food go to waste."

"Hey thanks. I spent my lunch hour getting a manicure."

"Have you had lunch yet, Margie?" Christina asked as they passed Margie's desk.

"No, I haven't. I was just going to leave and take a nice, long walk along the water. It looks like it's a beautiful day outside."

"Don't remind me," Christina said, wishing she could get outside for some air. "Feel free to help yourself with anything you want in the conference room when you get back."

"Thanks, Christina, but I'm dieting. I want to fit into your clothes when you decide to clean your closet."

"Well, keep up the good work," she smiled. "You're looking great."

The caterers had already set the table in the conference room with china plates, linen napkins and silverware. Susan was uncovering the silver platters of food.

"See." Susan pointed to the food that was neatly spread across the far end of the massive marble table. "This isn't all that bad."

"I'd say." Dan pulled from his coat pocket his metal, bug detector. He walked around the room, the device crackling in his hand.

"What's this I heard about you having to move into another hotel tonight?" Susan piled some pasta salad onto her plate.

"It's only for one night." Christina poured herself some iced tea. "It doesn't sound all that bad. It's also for your protection. We're down to the wire now, and we don't want anything to go wrong before tomorrow."

"Where are you staying?" Susan asked.

"I'm sure it will be somewhere in the Marina, because the sting is—"

Christina noticed Dan whirl around. His face was turning red. "Dan," she said, "you really should loosen up. Susan's not going to say anything to anyone."

Susan walked over to the bar in the conference room, cut a lime in fourths and shoved one of the slices into a bottle of Corona. She held up the bottle. "Want one, Dan?" she asked.

"You should know I don't drink while I'm working." He finished debugging and helped himself to a pile of potato salad.

"Hey, don't worry about peer pressure from this sister!" She sat down on the side of the table. "Anyway, what ever happened to Seike? I can't believe that he's still a fugitive."

Dan cut in, without letting Christina answer. "Neither can we. He's been living on the run for several years now. We questioned his father who told us he hasn't spoken with him since he fired him from Yamushuta Enterprises several years ago." Dan reached over the deli tray and made himself a sandwich. "The only lead we had was that telephone number your friend gave us, but unfortunately it's been disconnected for months. Also, since the robbery, his paper trail has diminished.

He'll screw up soon enough and resurface. His kind always does."

"Didn't you say Stephano is coming out here next weekend? Christina picked a piece of celery out of her salad and nibbled it like a bread stick. "Maybe Seike contacted him since we last spoke."

"That's possible," Susan said. She then leaned over and let her elbow rest on the table and her chin on her hand. "And Dan, if you're really nice to me, I'll arrange for you two to meet."

"I don't need a social secretary to bring someone in for questioning," he answered dryly.

"What is it with you two?" Christina finished her last forkful of salad. "I feel like the mother of two bickering children." She wiped her lips with a linen napkin and got up from the table. "I need to get back to my office and call our lawyers. The reds have been out nearly a month, and we still haven't got the final comments back from the SEC."

"Reds?" Dan asked.

"The red herring," Christina answered. "It's the preliminary prospectus that's sent to institutional and private investors before the deal is given a final okay by the SEC." Dan still had a blank look on his face. "Anyway, you two can stay here and duke it out, or Dan, you can come back to my office with me."

"Nope, duty calls," he said. "Thanks for lunch, Susan."

Chapter Twenty-Nine

Just as the sun was setting after a long day at Christina's office, Dan pulled up to a pink Victorian, bed-and-breakfast inn on Pacific Avenue in Pacific Heights.

"This wasn't at all what I expected," Christina said as Dan walked her up to the front door.

"That's exactly the impression we try to create." Dan opened the door for her. "We don't need to call attention to these matters."

When they entered the lobby a trim woman with short black hair stood up. She did not smile.

"Hello Christina." She extended her hand and shook Christina's firmly. "I'm Agent Cheryl Smith. I'll be staying with you tonight and through tomorrow morning."

Agent Smith turned to Dan. "The room's clean. Powell's upstairs, standing by. I'll take it from here." She looked at Christina. "C'mon Christina, let's go upstairs."

Christina assumed 'clean' didn't mean that the floor was just vacuumed and the sheets were fresh.

Cheryl led her by the elbow up the stairs. Christina turned around to face Dan who was at the bottom of the staircase. "Thanks, Dan. I'll guess I'll see you tomorrow morning. Have a nice night."

"I'll do my best." He smiled slightly. "Susan's meeting me on Chestnut Street for drinks. She's claiming that I owe her a few."

"Hmmm, that sounds interesting." Christina waved goodbye. "Remember, tomorrow morning— 7:00 sharp!"

When Agent Powell saw the two ladies walking toward their room, he motioned for them to stand outside the door, while he did another quick check inside the room.

He returned to the hallway and said to Cheryl: "All yours. Have a good night."

Too nervous to sleep well, Christina was awake by 6:00. The room was decorated with white and yellow wallpaper and lace curtains. Fluffy pillows were piled on the brass bed and on a large, window seat that overlooked a garden. A bowl of scented potpourri and candles were arranged on the pine end tables. This room was meant for romance and she wished that Franco were here to enjoy it with her.

Cheryl was not on the couch where she'd insisted on sleeping the night before. Christina felt nervous and wondered where she might have gone. She got out of bed and went to the bathroom. When she returned Cheryl was unloading a tray of fruit, an assortment of bagels, juice and coffee on the table by the window.

"I just stepped outside to get our breakfast tray," Cheryl said.

"Thank you." Christina poured herself a large glass of orange juice.

"Glad to see you're up early." Cheryl slathered some cream cheese on a bagel. "We have a few things to take care of."

"Like what?" Christina sipped her orange juice.

"For one thing, I'll need to help you put this on." She placed a small recording device and some wires on the bed. "We need to tape these wires to your skin. And this is the antenna." She held up a round metal object, the size of a quarter with a four-inch antenna. "We'll secure this along your backbone. It'll work better if you wear a bulky jacket or sweatshirt. If you don't have one, I brought one."

"That's all right, I packed my trusty gray sweatshirt, just in case I had time to go running this morning."

"Good. Let's get started."

Christina tried to remain motionless while Cheryl applied the wires with white tape. The tape stretched her skin and pulled the small hairs every time the device had to be readjusted. After the wire was secured, Cheryl placed a cold, metal receiver on her protruding backbone. With each prod and poke, Christina felt increasingly uneasy about what was to take place in less than an hour.

At 7:00 am, the telephone rang. It was Dan. He was downstairs waiting for them, wearing his uniform: navy blue blazer, tan slacks and aviator style Ray Ban sunglasses.

"I'll take it from here, Cheryl."

"Good luck, Christina." Cheryl touched her arm. "Don't worry, everything will be fine."

"I hope you're right." Christina watched Cheryl get in her car and drive away. She wished she could do the same.

"Did you have fun last night?" Christina tried to take her mind off of her impending assignment.

"I'll let Susan answer that one," he said with as little emotion as possible. He was still wearing his glasses, but Christina noticed a few faint lines wrinkle on the sides of his eyes and his lips curve into the most minuscule form of a smile.

She knew it! They'd had a great time.

Dan drove over to the Palace of Fine Arts. It had been built in 1915, for the Pan-Pacific games and designed to resemble a Roman ruin. Over the years, it had become a popular, yet not overcrowded tourist attraction. Christina often came here on sunny, Sunday afternoons to picnic with her friends on the banks of the swan-filled lagoon and gaze at the exquisite sand colored structure with hints of the Golden Gate Bridge in the background.

She looked across the lagoon at the octagonal rotunda where she planned to meet Ralph. The dome was surrounded by massive Corinthian columns and sculptured weeping maidens who appeared to be crying for all the men they had lost at war.

At Beach Street, Dan slowed the car down and pointed out a white van. Several ladders, splattered with paint, were secured to the roof of the van. J&J Painting was stenciled onto the door panel.

"Peters and the rest of your back-up are in there. They'll be able to watch and hear everything from inside."

Dan pulled out a microphone and confirmed with the men in the van that everything was in order. He steered the car around and headed back toward one of the side streets.

At the stop sign, he turned to face Christina. "It's all yours now."

Christina felt herself perspire yet at the same time she was shivering. "Dan, I'm frightened."

Dan put his hand on her shoulder. "Don't worry; I'll be stationed only half a block away."

"What if a sniper guns me down before I make it to the rotunda?"

"Christina," Dan squeezed her shoulder. "We have you covered. There are SWAT specialists surrounding this place. If a gun is pulled and poised to shoot, whomever is pointing that gun will get taken out before they even have a chance to pull the trigger. You can't see the sharp shooters, but they're placed strategically around the structure, hidden behind the columns and pillars."

"I guess that's somewhat of a relief," she sighed. "Anyway, I can't picture Ralph as an expert marksman."

Christina checked her wire and recording device and then walked slowly down Beach Street toward the ruins. Unusually, for a San Francisco summer morning, the sun was shining bright and the dew was still glistening on the grass. The sand colored columns and the giant, domed octagonal rotunda reflected brightly in the lagoon. A gaggle of swan, swimming gracefully in the water, painted a peaceful picture.

Christina crept into the giant rotunda, peering behind each column, hoping to spot one of the sharp shooters. She didn't notice anyone so she glanced up, thinking maybe they were hiding somewhere above her, but they seemed to know how to remain invisible.

Suddenly she heard a giant splash in the water. Startled, she jumped nearly a foot backwards.

What happened?!?

Shaking with fear, she looked around her.

Oh God, please don't let anything go wrong.

But it was only the swans. Five or six of them had fluttered their wings and had taken off for a short flight across the pond.

She breathed a huge sigh of relief.

I have got to get a hold of myself. She'd nearly had a heart attack.

An echo sounded with each footstep on the cold, stone floor of the rotunda. She rubbed her arms; she was quite chilled.

Where was Ralph?

She looked at her watch. Ten minutes after eight. She positioned herself directly under the dome of the 13 story stone ceiling and waited patiently. She checked her watch. Twelve minutes past 8:00. It seemed like an hour. The silence, the damp, chilly atmosphere and the musty, dank smell enveloped her.

"Christina!" a booming voice reverberated throughout the rotunda.

She jumped, but didn't see anyone.

Her eyes darted from pillar to pillar, looking for a shadow—or any clue as to where he was hiding.

Everything remained perfectly still. She heard nothing, and saw no one.

"O.K. Ralph, you can come out now." Her voice was stable and clear. "Your game of hide-and-seek is over!"

No answer.

"Listen, Ralph. Don't waste my time, I have what you need."

"It's not Ralph." A deep voice boomed from behind one of the pillars.

The voice was familiar, but Christina could not place it.

"Did Ralph call in sick this morning?"

"You shouldn't try to be funny first thing in the morning, Miss Caldwell. It's not becoming."

Perfect. She wanted him to keep talking so the sharpshooters would be able to place him. She also wanted to nail down whose voice she was hearing.

"Personally, I don't care who Ralph sent, as long as you have my money." She paused for several seconds. "Do NOT play games with me."

"How do I know you brought the chip?" The voice boomed.

"Trust me. The minute I get into work this morning, I'm quitting. My desk is already packed. I want to cash it in, just like Ralph."

She kept looking for some sign as to where he was hiding.

"How do *I* know *you* have the money?" she asked.

"Walk over here, Christina, and I'll show you."

Christina could still not determine from behind which pillar he was hiding, but she walked in the general direction of the voice.

"Wrong way," he shouted. A bone-chilling laugh sounded from the other side of the rotunda.

She snapped her head around and looked in the other direction.

He laughed again. "We're in an echo chamber."

She felt like she was Dorothy, listening to the mysterious Wizard's voice booming from behind a black, velvet curtain.

"It's amazingly simple to throw one's voice." The deep voice bellowed throughout the rotunda. "A smart girl as yourself should know that."

A shadow crept out from behind one of the pillars.

"O.K., here I go," she whispered into the microphone.

As she walked over to the shadow, a large body lurched from behind the pillar.

C.J.!!

She tried to remain calm and in control.

"I should have expected you were behind all of this." Her entire body trembled.

"Let me see the money." She willed her voice not to shake.

He lifted up a black, leather bag, unzipped it and reached in. But instead of grabbing stacks of bills, he pulled out a gun.

Christina stood, frozen in place. She wondered if the agents could hear her heart pounding.

He pointed the black, metal pistol at Christina. "Now, why don't you hand over the chip, and we'll all walk away quietly."

"Oh, a gun." Christina emphasized the word, gun, so that the FBI agents could hear her loud and clear. "How courageous of you, C.J. You didn't think you could overpower me without one?"

"O.K., Caldwell, you've gone far enough." He edged toward her. She would have felt better if she'd seen his hand quiver, but he was holding the gun straight and steady. It was evident that he wasn't afraid to use it.

Why wasn't anyone coming to her defense?

He stopped less than five feet away from her. "Give me the chip."

She stared directly into the black, metal barrel, paralyzed by fear. He reached out a hand. "The chip."

Suddenly a shot rang out. C.J. let out a loud, low scream and fell to the ground. Blood splattered onto Christina's face, neck and clothes. C.J. crumpled to the floor. He covered his bloody shoulder with his hand. At the sight of the thick, scarlet blood, she felt sick to her stomach. Two men in uniform appeared from behind the pillar and held him down to the ground. The high-pitched wail of an ambulance shrieked in the distance.

Christina's knees buckled and she collapsed to the ground.

"You never should've gotten involved, Caldwell! It's not over!!" C.J. shouted as the police officers restrained him and waited for the paramedics.

Christina pulled herself from the ground. "It sure is over for you, C.J."

Dazed, she looked around for Dan, or at least one of the agents from inside the van. *Why wasn't anyone coming to get her?*

Tires screeched from the other side of The Palace. A late model, 1970's American car skidded around the corner, heading for the Golden Gate Bridge.

Ralph?

Dan's sedan and two police cars squealed out after the car. Finally, Agent Peters came out to the middle of the rotunda to escort her back to where the van was parked.

"Well, you did it Miss Caldwell." Peters shook her hand, which was still cold and shaking.

"Thank you. I can't believe it's finally over."

"Well, it's not over yet. We still need to recover the diskette that the plans are encoded on, but we're pretty certain that your friends, Mr. Stinson or Mr. Saunders, will be able to supply us with that. One thing we do know for sure: at least a foreign power won't get control of them."

"One thing I know for sure," she told Agent Peters, "I'm looking forward to moving back into my own house and getting on with my life."

"I'm sure you are." He patted her on the back. "Come on, we'll drive you home."

Chapter Thirty

Christina had never felt better about returning to her home. Miraculously, her plants were still alive. Thank goodness for Rosa. She ripped off her clothes and took a long, hot shower. Watching C.J.'s blood swirl down the drain, she finally felt as though she was able to get on with her own life. She stepped out of the shower and wrapped herself in a thick terry towel. She picked up her cordless phone, sank into her over-sized, down filled sofa and called the office.

Margie answered promptly on the first ring.

"Hi, Margie. I'm pretty beat. Do you have any messages for me."

"Yes, two came through me, but I'm sure you have more on your private line. First, the boys from New York called. They know what's been going on, and they want you to take today and Monday off. Second, Franco called. He's coming to San Francisco tomorrow. He said he left you a message on your home machine."

Her stomach fluttered. *This weekend?!? Tomorrow?!?*

"Thanks, Margie," she managed to say. "See you Tuesday. Have a nice weekend."

"You too, Christina."

"No doubt about that!" She raced for her message machine.

Her messages rambled on: one from Susan, *save*. One from Brandy, *save*, one from her parents, *save*, Finally, Franco's voice. The sound of his delicious accent made her skin tingle.

"Christina, my darling, I miss you terribly. I'm coming to see you. I'll be there Saturday morning and will call again from the plane. Ciao, dolcina."

Thank God New York gave me today off, she thought. She had a lot of pampering to catch up on. Her nails were a wreck, her hair needed a good trim and she hadn't had a facial in over six months.

Instead of making the coffee she had intended to drink, she brewed some herbal tea, and listened to her other messages. Susan, of course wanted to know how things had gone that morning. Her message continued: "Dan and I"—-giggle—"wondered if you wanted to join us tonight." Christina couldn't help but giggle herself when she heard the message.

Next it was Brandy calling to say, "Hi" and that her friend, Rob Carmichael, wanted them to come over to Treasure Island next Saturday. Apparently Brandy didn't know why Christina had been out of touch lately.

Finally, she was able to collapse in her bed for a well-deserved nap. She would return her phone calls later.

A gun was held to Christina's face. She pleaded with the killer not to shoot her. Alarm bells rang in the background. But the sound was not a bell; it was her telephone.

Sweating with fear, she reached for the phone.

"Christina," It was Susan. "You haven't returned my phone call. Dan told me everything that happened this morning!

Congratulations, girlfriend! Anyway, he and his roommates are throwing a party at his place tonight. He wants you to stop by."

"I don't know, Susan," she yawned, "I can't tell you how wiped out I am. I was planning on taking it easy tonight. Franco's flying in tomorrow."

"No excuses. Just join us for a short while. You need to celebrate your victory. You did it Christina! You nailed 'em!"

"I haven't really had a chance to think about it; I'm just glad to be home."

"I'll be over at eight. That will give you an extra hour to nap, and some time to freshen up."

"O.K. see you then."

No chance of going back to sleep, she thought. Instead, she put on her running gear and headed out the door. She knew that this would be the best way to wake herself up.

Her buzzer rang at 8:05 p.m. Susan was illegally parked on the sidewalk and waiting for her outside.

"You sure are a bundle of energy today, Susan." Christina hopped into her vintage '64½ Mustang convertible with its original 289 horsepower engine.

Susan veered onto the street. "Something really clicked when Dan and I went out for drinks last night. He acted like a normal, free spirited young guy." She bounced in her seat. With her long, curly hair blowing in the wind, she looked like a high school student. "In fact, we're going camping this weekend."

"That's great, Susan! But what about Stephano? Wasn't he supposed to come out to visit you? Franco didn't mention anything about it to me when he left his message yesterday."

"Who knows, and who cares." Susan circled Dan's apartment building on Russian Hill for the third time as she looked for a parking place. "I haven't heard from him for nearly a week now, so I'm sure he got held up."

They finally found a place in a 'red zone.' At most it would be a thirty-dollar ticket. Even the illegal places at this time of night were taken.

They trudged up four flights of stairs to Dan's apartment. The door was wide open and music was blasting. The smell of stale beer reminded Christina of a frat party back in college. She didn't really want to be here, but she wanted to see Dan and thank him for all his help. Also, she wondered if he had ever caught up with Ralph.

Dan greeted them at the door. A keg of beer leaked onto the linoleum floor in the kitchen. He offered them each a plastic cup filled to the rim with a thick, sudsy head.

"Hi Dan." Susan kissed him on the cheek.

"Hey, Dan." Christina shook his hand. "Good to see you again. Doesn't it seem like a year has gone by since this morning?"

"All in a day's work for me." He smiled and squeezed Susan's waist.

"So whatever happened to you this morning? I saw you speed off after a car." The music vibrated the apartment.

"Yeah, Ralph Stinson. He barely made it to the Golden Gate Bridge before he spun out of control. I apprehended him within a half mile of the Palace of Fine Arts. We brought him in and asked for the disk. He claimed that he didn't have it, but that Saunders did. Sure enough, when we searched Saunders' house, we found it stashed under a pile of books, sitting idle until he got his hands on your code chip."

"I'm sure glad this is all over." She set her half-finished beer on a milk crate in the hallway. "Thanks again for all your help. You really made it bearable."

"We couldn't have done it without you, Christina. I should be thanking you for your help."

"Well, in that case," she smiled, "you're welcome."

"What's going to happen to those two?" Susan asked.

"Espionage is a very serious offense. Obviously, their sentences are up to the judge, but they could be locked away for a lifetime."

"How deeply involved was Saunders?" Christina asked.

Dan shook his head. "I'm really sorry, but I can't talk about that."

"I understand." Christina could count on Susan to get the real story. "I'm sure you'd rather not talk shop at your party."

"You got that right," he said. "Can I get you another beer?"

"No thanks." She looked down the hallway and saw a young couple making out. "In fact I should get going. I know it's kind of early, but I have a busy weekend. Do you mind driving me home, Susan?"

"Are you kidding," she laughed, "and lose my illegal parking place? Of course, I'll drive you home."

She turned to Dan and blew him a kiss good-bye. "I'll be back in a half-hour."

Susan peeled a parking ticket off her windshield.

"Here, file this in my glove compartment." Susan handed Christina the ticket. "There's some of your mail in there. I picked it up from work. There's one letter in particular I thought you'd want to see."

Curious, Christina rifled through a stack of tickets shoved in Susan's glove compartment. She found her mail smashed in between them. There were quite a few bills, some invitations and an envelope with the official seal of the United States Senate.

"Aren't you going to open it?" Susan asked.

"I can't read it in the car. It's too dark. I'll wait until I get home."

"Aren't you dying to find out?"

"All right, stop under this street light."

Passing cars honked as Susan abruptly pulled over to the curb.

Christina unfolded a neatly hand written letter from the envelope. Her fingers felt heavy, double bond stationary. At most, she was expecting a terse note, typed by his secretary, on cheap paper. Instead, she read aloud:

Dear Christina,

As I fly back to Washington D.C. I am writing you this note. I'm sure, by now, you have figured out my relationship with Curtis Saunders, but I can assure you that all he wanted me to do was to confirm that you were in possession of a chip that was of interest to him.

I did not ask enough questions up front, and I did not realize that I was going to fall in love with you in the process. You can't fault me for that. In fact, I nearly forgot about my original intention after our

212

first dinner together. Please find it in your heart to
forgive me.

Always,
    Richard

Christina didn't know what to think anymore. The Carole King song, *It's Too Late*, played its tune in her mind. All she cared about was seeing Franco and picking him up at the airport tomorrow.

"Wow, that's pretty serious!" Susan cranked the car into first gear and sped away from the curb. "He really fell for you! What Senator, especially one who's running for President, would write something like that in his own handwriting? What are you going to do?"

"Nothing," Christina responded. "I'm not going to do anything with it." She folded the letter and put it back in its envelope. "You're right, though, he knew what he was risking by writing this. I guess he trusted me enough not to sell it to the *National Enquirer*."

Nevertheless, she wanted to keep the letter. She would store it somewhere safe. This was a memory she couldn't bring herself to throw away quite yet.

Susan slowed to a roll in front of Christina's building. Christina hopped out and yelled to Susan as she was nearly halfway down the block. "Thanks for the ride!"

She was going to say, 'have fun camping,' but Susan had already turned the corner. She had places to be, people to see.

Christina fell asleep dreaming of Franco. They would be together in less than twelve hours.

Chapter Thirty-One

The private airfield at San Francisco International was difficult to find. Instead of taking the traditional airport exit off of Highway 101, she had been instructed to turn off at 'North Access Boulevard' and follow the signs to the Executive Aviation Terminal.

Driving in her convertible, she felt free and alive again. Her blonde hair was flying in the wind, and the cool breeze was exhilarating. For the past two weeks, she'd never put her top down, for fear of being shot.

She maneuvered her way through the various exit ramps, and pulled up to the security gate. The guard directed her to the parking lot.

Before getting out of her car, she brushed her hair, put on some lipgloss and adjusted her sunglasses. She looked up as she heard the loud noise of a powerful jet engine. Shading her eyes, she watched the sleek Gulfstream glide into a smooth landing.

After a strong blast of the jet engines, the engines hummed for a short time while cooling off and then abruptly shut down. A heavy door swung open at the front of the plane and the mechanical stairway eased down. Franco was the first to emerge. She had almost forgotten how gorgeous he was! The wind blew his black, wavy hair across his face and his copper, wire rim sunglasses. He wore a knee-length, brown leather coat, faded jeans and leather boots.

She had hoped that he would think that she looked pretty hot herself in her favorite well-worn Levis, torn at the knees, and wearing thin in the seat. A black body suit clung to her chest and the leather belt around her waist was cinched in an extra two rungs.

He raised his hand when he saw her. She ran out to meet him. He dropped his leather duffel bag, grabbed her waist and pulled her into him. They kissed passionately for a full minute, and then walked back to her car with their arms entangled around each other's waist.

"What do you want to see first?" Christina asked.

"The inside of your bedroom, of course."

"Exactly what I was hoping you would say."

She sped back to the city, flying over the hills. They bounded up the stairs to her apartment. Franco took off his coat and affectionately attacked her. They fell onto the couch in her living room and then onto the floor. He ripped off her jeans and unsnapped her body suit. They made love on her carpet for several hours. The bellowing foghorn provided the background music.

They eventually crawled into her bedroom and did not emerge until the following morning.

Chapter Thirty-Two

"I'm starving!" Christina opened her eyes and looked over at Franco, who was lightly snoring in her warm bed.

She shook him gently. "Franco, are you hungry?"

He stretched his arms and rubbed his eyes. "Only for you my darling."

"You're impossible!" She kissed him on his face and then began to work her way downward.

After another hour, Christina threw off the covers and took a shower, relishing the pounding hot water. She wrapped herself in a soft terry robe and walked into the kitchen.

"Damn! I forgot to go shopping!" She stared at the inside of a stark white refrigerator. A bottle of wine, a small container of olives, and a jar of mustard were its only contents. *This is not the way to impress an Italian mama's boy!*

She crawled back into bed, clean and fresh, and whispered, "You stay here. I'll run out and get us something to eat."

The morning air was still brisk and foggy. She buttoned her bulky cotton sweater close to her neck and pulled her Giant's cap low over her forehead. The aroma of freshly roasting coffee beans blew onto the street: the Marina District was just waking up. Only a few markets opened early on Sunday morning: Lucca's Delicatessen on Chestnut Street was one of them.

She chose an assortment of fruit and vegetable salads, dark, plump olives, several varieties of cheese, some Italian pastries, chocolate biscotti and freshly baked bread. She also purchased a quart of whole milk that she would steam for their coffee.

At the checkout counter, she almost dropped the container of milk. The clerk was reading the Sunday paper. Christina caught the picture on the front page: Curtis Saunders being taken away from the Palace of Fine Arts in handcuffs!

She grabbed her own thick, Sunday edition of the *San Francisco Chronicle*, threw the clerk a twenty-dollar bill and ran back to her apartment. Her curiosity was killing her, and she wanted to stop and read it, but she would rather share the excitement with Franco. She could hardly wait to get copies of this article and send them to her parents. At least this would help explain why she'd been incommunicado for the past several weeks.

Franco had just stepped out of the shower when Christina walked through the front door. The white towel, wrapped around his waist, contrasted superbly with his darkly tanned, muscular chest.

"You're right, I'm starving!" He greeted her with outstretched arms.

"Good, me too!" She gave him a quick kiss and handed him a pastry. "Here, while you're eating, I'll read you this article. It will give you some idea of what I've been going through these past few weeks."

They crawled back into bed. Franco chewed the pastry as she read the article to him.

"Christina, darling, please slow down. I can not comprehend everything that quickly."

"I'm sorry, Franco. That was inconsiderate of me." She had a terrible habit of talking a mile-a-minute when she got excited.

"You're forgiven," he smiled, "now please keep reading."

A tourist from Nebraska had snapped the picture and sold it to the *Chronicle*. The article explained that while the FBI could not comment on all points, Saunders and Stinson were clearly implicated. Mention was also made of Seike Yamashuta, who was still a fugitive. The story briefly covered the chip heist and touched on the proprietary designs Symex was developing.

She turned to page A14 for the remainder of the story.

A blown up picture of her face, with her name in bold letters typed underneath it was the first thing she saw. She recognized the photo from the one taken at the Sheraton Palace last week, except Richard Cartwright had been spliced out. Her cheeks grew hot when she saw the picture and thought back to that night with the Senator. Thank goodness Franco could not read her mind.

She continued reading to Franco. The rest of the details were sketchy. Again, the FBI could not comment on everything, but they did confirm that Christina Caldwell had played a crucial role in averting a disaster of global proportion, and in bringing two of the men involved to justice.

"Christina, this is amazing." He pulled her closer to him. "I had no idea how serious this was. No wonder you've been so preoccupied. I only wish I could have been here with you."

"I'm just glad you're here now." She nuzzled her nose and lips to the nape of his neck. "It means the world to me to have you here now."

"I'm so proud of you, dolcina." He kissed her cheek and then started to massage the back of her neck. "You've been through an amazing ordeal. It sounds like you need another vacation."

He wrestled her under the cover and moved on top of her. "Fly back to Italy with me." His breath was warm against her ear.

She desperately wanted to fly away with him, but it was impossible to drop her life and career. "Franco, that's the best offer I've heard in a long time. But——"

He pressed his finger to her lips. "No 'buts' until you take more than two seconds and think about what I said."

Christina noticed the room getting brighter and warmer. The sun was finally breaking through the dense, morning fog.

"Franco, I promise I'll think about it, but now I want to do something for you. You were so kind to show me your beautiful city by the sea, and now I would like you to see mine."

"Where are you taking me?" He plucked some grapes from the bunch.

"You'll see."

Christina found her wicker picnic basket buried under several boxes of old shoes. She carried the basket into the kitchen and arranged everything she had bought this morning into the red and white checkered cloth lining.

With Franco in the passenger seat, they cruised past the Saint Francis Yacht Club and up through the Presidio.

"The Presidio is an abandoned military base," she explained to Franco. "As you can see, it's located on some of the most prime real estate in the country." She pulled over at one of the scenic overlooks so Franco could admire the view of the sailboats on the Bay and the grandeur of the Golden Gate Bridge. They got out of the car, leaned against the hood and breathed in the clean, sea air.

"Next, I'm going to take you to The Palace of Legion Honor." She drove near the cliffs above the Bay. The fresh smell of the eucalyptus trees and the clean ocean air stung their noses. "It's an art museum and I thought you would like seeing the paintings."

She parked near the white, pillared building, designed in French Classical style, which sat on the edge of a golf course and overlooked the Bay and the Golden Gate Bridge.

They strode under the grand archway and through the cobblestone courtyard. Before they reached the building, they paused to touch the Rodin sculpture, <u>The Thinker.</u> Once in the museum, Christina enjoyed watching Franco admire the paintings. He breathed in every detail, and did not speak for nearly an hour. He was a true artist, paying homage to the great masters of his trade.

They left the museum hand in hand, and walked over to Christina's car to get the picnic basket. Her basket of goodies was not as elaborate as the one Franco had surprised her with nearly a month ago—no candles, no fresh flowers, and no chocolate. Nonetheless, they had each other and the spectacular view of the Bay, the ships and sailboats crossing under the

Golden Gate Bridge and the light brown hills of the Marin Headlands in the distance.

"Christina," Franco squeezed her hand, "I've been doing some thinking since you left Italy."

She could feel her heart beating against her chest. She dreaded the moment when he would have to break it to her that he was going to marry Alessandra.

Franco leaned back on his elbows and stretched his legs along the blanket. "Instead of flying back to Italy tomorrow, I'm going to spend some time looking for warehouse space for Garibaldi Marble. We could use an office and some storage space on the West Coast, and I guess San Francisco is just as good as Los Angeles. Even better, you're here—not L.A."

Christina rested her head on his chest. "Franco, that's fabulous. I didn't know how I was going to face the fact that you were flying home tomorrow, and not knowing when you would come back."

"I still must leave tomorrow night, but I'll be back soon." He smiled and wrapped his arms around her. She felt like she could conquer the world, as long as she had Franco to come home to every night.

Chapter Thirty-Three

"Do you want to borrow my car today while you look for office space?" Christina asked as she was brushing her hair.

"Thank you for your offer, but I hired a driver. I don't know my way around this town, and it's better that I not waste time getting lost."

"Will I see you this evening?"

"I'm afraid not, my darling. I have meetings back in Italy tomorrow afternoon that I cannot miss. Remember, I lose nine hours on the trip home."

Her throat choked up, and she could not respond for a few seconds. "I can't believe you have to leave so soon. It seems as though you just arrived."

"It was a rather short trip, but two days is better than nothing."

He pulled her into his chest, kissed the top of her head and hugged her for several minutes. He felt and smelled so wonderful. "Doesn't all this traveling exhaust you? I don't know how you do it."

"It helps to have your own plane. If I'm tired, I sleep. If not, I work. It's a modern convenience I could never do without."

She looked up and flipped her hair. "But of course."

Franco looked at his watch. "Listen, my darling, we must say goodbye now. I'm sure my driver is downstairs by now. Why don't you walk me down?"

She lifted her briefcase and locked the door behind her. She was determined to focus all her energy on work until he returned.

A black, Lincoln Town Car was parked in the driveway, blocking access to her garage. A wave of sadness nearly crippled her when she saw the car. Once he got in, she would never know when she'd see him again. It could be next week or it could be six months from now.

Franco put his fingers under her chin and forced her to look into his eyes. *Those deep, beautiful, dark brown eyes.*

"Dolcina," he said softly, "I don't want to see that sad face."

Her eyes filled with tears.

"And no tears." He wiped a small tear from the corner of her eye.

"Franco, how do you expect me to feel?" She did her best to hold back more tears. "It's hard not knowing when you'll be back."

"I'll be back, dolcina." He picked up his suitcase. "The sooner I get into that car over there, the sooner I'll find myself an office."

"All right then," she said. "I hate long good-byes anyway. Get going and call me before you take off."

They kissed goodbye and he slid into the back seat. She watched the car back down the driveway. A wave of sadness nearly paralyzed her.

Once in the privacy of her own car, she let the tears stream down her face the entire way to work.

Christina moved slowly as she walked into her office.

"Why so glum?" asked Julie. "I thought you were in love."

"I am. That's the irony."

"Makes sense to me." Julie shook her head and answered an incoming call.

Every Monday morning, as usual, Christina took her coffee and went into Susan's office to rehash the weekend's events.

"What's wrong?" Susan's face was flushed and her eyes sparkled.

Christina slumped into her chair across from Susan's desk. "Franco's gone, and I'm not sure when he's coming back."

Susan finished punching some keys on her calculator and jotted down a number. "Did your weekend turn out differently than you thought it would?"

"We had a wonderful weekend together. It couldn't have been better. I just don't know when I'll see him again. Normally I don't care this much—I guess I fell for him pretty hard."

Susan looked up from her pile of paper. "I think it's great that you've finally let yourself fall this hard. For as long as I've known you, you've always kept guys at arm's length. Love hurts—but it's worth it, if it's for the right guy." She leaned forward and rested her forearms on her desk. "Is he the right guy?"

"I think so," Christina took the lid off her coffee. "We're so comfortable together. We talk and laugh about everything—in spite of the language and cultural barrier. The upsetting part is that his parents are pressuring him to marry an Italian girl. If he refuses he's finished at Garibaldi Marble. Also I heard Stephano say that she's a great cook. I can't compete with that. I guess I should say, I don't want to compete with that."

"Well, you have a point there. I know how important Italian families are, especially this one. But I think Franco's more independent than that."

"I hope you're right." Christina drank some of her coffee. "In fact, he's looking for some office space today. He wants to open a West Coast Division of Garibaldi Marble."

Susan threw her hands up in the air. "So there you have it! What are you so worried about? He's talking about spending some serious time out here. You may even see him next week."

"You make it seem so obvious." Christina reached for a tissue. "Everything is going so well, my biggest fear is that it will come to a crashing end."

"I can't believe you, Christina." Susan slapped the top of her desk. "You survived being chased down by criminals, a break-in at your apartment, an FBI sting Friday morning—with a gun pointed at your face, no less—and the burden of knowing you were carrying around a code chip that could jeopardize the national security of the United States. And you're worried about whether you'll see Franco again! Of course he'll be back soon!

For God's sake, he's looking for office space out here. That's quite an investment, both in time and money."

"I guess you're right." Christina blew her nose.

"I think you're sleep deprived and run down. After work, go directly to bed. And here, take these." Susan opened her drawer and tossed her a bottle of echinacea tablets. "Doctor's orders."

"Thanks Susan." Christina wiped her eyes for the last time. "I'm sorry to come in here and dump on you like this. You didn't even have a chance to tell me about your weekend."

"Don't worry about it. That's what friends are for. I only have time for a brief summation, but do you see this nice sunburn?"

She pointed to her sunburnt cheeks.

"Let me just say this— it's a full body tan. We pitched a tent next to a crystal clear, mountain lake. Between skinny dipping and then baking our naked bodies in the sun all day, we managed to enjoy a fantastic weekend together."

"I'm so glad to hear that!" For a moment, Christina forgot how miserable she was. "Does he look as great in the buff as I imagine he does?"

"Better." She flashed a naughty grin. "Anyway, get out of here." She waved her hand toward the door. "We both have a ton of work to do."

A ton of work was right! Christina had almost forgotten what it was like to concentrate on her job for a full ten hours. At least New York wasn't giving her a hard time. The favorable press she'd been getting couldn't hurt as far as business development was concerned.

She returned calls, both personal and business, for five hours straight. It seemed as if everyone had called to hear about what had happened at the Palace of Fine Arts and to ask how the hell she'd become involved. Also, because her picture appeared with Senator Cartwright less than a week ago, everyone was dying to find out about that story. "Is he as handsome in real life as in all the pictures?" "Does his power intimidate you?" "What's he really like?"

Most of her calls resulted in appointments for the current week and next. Business was pouring in; she was back in her element, and again on a natural high.

Around 2:00, she realized she was starving. She ran downstairs to the deli located on the first floor and bought a yogurt and an apple. She would have preferred something more substantial, but her only choice was a soggy tuna fish sandwich with mayonnaise oozing onto the Saran wrap.

She ate the apple on the elevator. When she got into her office she finished the yogurt in less than a minute. This would hold her off until the end of the day—which seemed to be nowhere in sight at this point.

Her phone beeped.

"Franco's on the phone," Margie said through the intercom.

"Thanks Margie."

"Hi Franco," Christina said. "I miss you already. Any luck finding an office?"

"I think so. I've narrowed down my decision to the East Bay, somewhere closer to the Port of Oakland."

"That's probably best. Office space is more reasonable there."

She had forgotten how easily she could slip into her business mode and remove her heart from the situation at hand.

"The Port of Oakland reminded me of something, dolcina. I promised I would send your painting tomorrow with a marble shipment we have going out. I have one small detail I need to add, which I could do when I get home this evening—or I should say early tomorrow morning, Italian time. You'll be able to pick it up this Saturday. Did you receive the pass I mailed?"

"Oh yes, thank you. I got that last week."

"Good, that will help you avoid any security problems."

She heard loud, surging noises in the background.

"We just pulled up next to the plane. I need to confirm the flight plan with my pilot. I better say 'good-bye'."

"Ciao, Franco. Have a safe flight. I love you."

"I love you too, dolcina."

She could hardly wait to see her painting. Her mind raced ahead to Saturday. She had plans. What were they?

Treasure Island. The movie set. Brandy's friend, Rob, would be in town. Perfect! Treasure Island is on the way to Oakland.

She called Brandy's mobile phone. The static was terrible, and Christina assumed that she was in her car.

"Hi Brandy, it's Christina. I'm glad I caught you. What time are we planning on going to Treasure Island next Saturday?"

"Rob asked me to pick him up at nine. He was in a minor accident and his car's going to be in the shop. Unfortunately, I can't pick him up them because I'm showing property in Berkeley that morning."

"I'd be happy to swing by his place. But you'll need to drive him back to the City. Susan and I have to run an errand at the Port of Oakland."

"An errand? At the Port of Oakland?" Brandy's voice rose.

Christina chuckled. "I guess it's not your typical dash-to-the-dry-cleaners errand. Franco's been working on a painting for me. He's shipping it tomorrow and he said it'll be there by Saturday."

"Ooh, that's so romantic," Brandy sighed. "I would love to go over there with you, but I'm scheduled to drive some Hong Kong billionaire around Pacific Heights. He's ready to make an offer."

"We wouldn't want you to miss that." Christina mentally calculated the six-figure commission Brandy would make on the sale. "I know you're busy and I have a million phone calls to return, so how about if we just meet you there at 9:30 Saturday morning?"

"I can hardly wait. Bye doll!"

Chapter Thirty-Four

Christina finally finished with all of her paperwork and phone calls by seven, and ducked out of the office without saying goodbye to anyone. She could hardly wait to get home, put on a soft sweatshirt, and order a pizza. She was exhausted and famished.

As she phoned the local pizzaria, she noticed Richard's letter next to the phone. It had been recently opened. She remembered tucking the envelope under the phone, not next to it.

Had Franco read it? What if he had, and he thinks that there is anything between us?

She lost her appetite thinking about it. This could result in a terrible misunderstanding.

Everything was so perfect. Should she call and explain—or just let it go?

She looked at her watch; it was three o'clock in the morning in Italy.

"Don't be so insecure!" she said to herself as she redialed the pizzaria.

-

Her week flew by with all the meetings and appointments she had scheduled. Andrew Jacobs called from New York to congratulate her on all the business she had brought in that week.

"It's just the beginning," she told him. "I'm back in full force and nothing's going to get in my way now."

"That's what we like to hear, Caldwell. You're a fighter—keep up the good work and enjoy your weekend."

"I will, sir. Thank you very much."

She hung up the phone and walked into Susan's office.

"So, are you seeing Dan tonight?" she asked.

"Of course. How about you?"

"I feel like renting old movies and going to sleep early. I want to get up early and go for a run, and then I'll pick you up. Shall I go to your house or Dan's?" she asked with a big smile.

"Well, you saw his apartment, and since I'm not too keen on sharing a bathroom with three guys, it's safe to say I'll meet you at my house."

"I'll pick you up at quarter to nine, then we'll get Rob."

"See you tomorrow. Enjoy your peaceful evening."

She returned a few more phone calls, set up some presentations and appointments for the following week, and left the office by six.

Her only stop on the way home was at Blockbuster, where she rented "To Catch a Thief" and "Roman Holiday", two of her favorite, classic movies.

There was only one message on her machine when she got home.

"Christina, this is Franco. I have some bad news." Franco's voice sounded somber and slow, and completely different than she had ever heard before. "Alessandra's father died last night. I will be out of touch for the next several days. I'm sorry to have to leave this on your message machine, but there are many things that need to be taken care of here. I will call again soon."

The message shocked her. She hoped he was coping well with this tragedy. She also felt sad for Alessandra. She knew how she would feel if her own father died. Then something else entered her mind and she was struck motionless. This would most certainly clinch any marriage plans that had been uncertain before Alessandra's father's death. For an instant she hated herself for putting thoughts of her relationship ahead of Alessandra's misfortune. That was an extremely unfair and selfish thing to think and she felt guilty for even letting it enter her mind. But she also knew that Alessandra needed Franco, and she was all too familiar with Franco's gallant character. She looked at her watch. It was not yet seven in the morning in Italy, but she had to phone Franco. She wanted to let him know that she was there for him if he needed to talk.

He answered after several rings. She hoped she had not awakened him.

"Franco," she whispered because it sounded like he was sleeping. "It's Christina."

"Hello, Christina." His voice was cool and unemotional. "This is not a good time. I told you I would call you soon. I cannot talk now."

"I'm sorry to hear about Alessandra's father," she said. "Call me when you can. Again, I'm sorry to have disturbed you."

Was Alessandra there? In the same bed with him?

He hung up the phone without saying 'goodbye'. He'd sounded so different. She felt like a complete stranger. I better give him time, she thought. He was probably in the process of making a life altering decision. Nevertheless, she hated the feeling of him slipping away from her.

She slowly placed the phone back in its cradle. Tears welled up. Their relationship was probably over. She'd known this would happen sooner or later. She couldn't control what was happening back in Italy. After several minutes of uncontrollable sobbing, she picked up the phone to call Susan. She knew Dan was with her, but thought she'd try anyway. After a few rings she got her answering machine.

"Susan, i-it's me," her sobbing made her words almost unintelligible.

"Christina, what's wrong?" Susan said picking up the phone.

"Franco left me a 'Dear Christina' message."

"What are you talking about?"

"Alessandra's father died and he told me that he would be out of touch for a while." She wiped her tears on her sleeve. "I told you that everything was too good to be true and it would come to a crashing end."

"You don't know that for sure. It's unfortunate that her father died, but that shouldn't change your relationship. Why don't you wait a week and see what happens?"

"I know what will happen. Alessandra doesn't have any brothers. This is the perfect opportunity for her to play up her misfortune. Don't you see? If they were married, Franco would be the legal and most logical heir to her family's business?"

"Well, yeah, it's logical," Susan said, "but you're assuming things you don't know."

"What I do know is that Alessandra's father wanted him to run the business. I was a summer fling, and that's all! I never should've let myself open up to him. If I hadn't I wouldn't be so miserable now."

"Christina," Susan pleaded, "try to calm down, be patient, and see what happens. You're jumping to conclusions."

"I should have known better." Christina collapsed onto her couch. She felt as if she might break. "Why did I let myself fall for him? I was honestly going to change my life and let him be a part of it. I'll never make that mistake again."

"Christina, all I can say to you at this point, is try to not worry about it. If it is over, it's over. You'll meet other men. Remember, Richard? He'd do anything to hear from you again."

"The man who lied to me and tried to use me? I don't think so."

"OK, OK, OK—but don't drown yourself in tears until you get all the facts straight."

"Easy for you to say." She sniffled and wiped her eyes.

"Why don't you concentrate on something fun, like going to see Rob tomorrow. I can hardly wait, and I know Brandy's really looking forward to it."

"Thanks, Susan, you're right. It'll be fun seeing him again. Plus, I'm still supposed to get that painting. I guess I'll pick it up for old times sake."

"That's the attitude I like to hear. Now, try to get a good night's sleep."

She watched her two movies, sobbing for the full four hours. All they did was remind her of happier times of romance on the Riviera.

Chapter Thirty-Five

She tossed and turned all night. When she finally dragged herself out of bed, the sun was already shining into her bedroom. Even though she wasn't in the mood to do much of anything, she forced herself to go running.

By the time she returned from her six-mile loop, she felt better and enjoyed a leisurely shower and a steaming cup of coffee. She called Susan, just to make sure she was ready. Susan answered the phone giggling—still in bed with Dan.

"Susan, hurry up and get dressed," Christina said. "I'll be over in 15 minutes. Tell Dan to sit tight for a few hours."

"How 'bout a half hour? I still need to take a shower."

"See you then." Christina hung up and flipped on her T.V., which was always tuned to CNN. Baseball scores never interested her, so she walked into the kitchen to pour herself some more coffee. She wasn't really listening, but could still hear the broadcast. "And in international business news," she heard a deep, male newscaster's voice, "Rossi Quarries and Garibaldi Marble plan to merge."

Christina sprinted back to her living room. In the upper right hand corner of her television screen, behind the head of the newscaster, hung a picture of a young, stunning, dark haired woman.

The report continued: "After the death of GianCarlo Rossi, Miss Alessandra Rossi, the sole heir to the Rossi fortune, announced her plan to merge her late father's company with Garibaldi Marble."

The empty coffee cup dropped from her hand. Christina had known this merger would occur, but it was a shock to see a full color picture of Alessandra on her television screen. It didn't help that she was beautiful. She had long, straight black hair, big brown eyes, dark eyebrows, and a perfectly straight, thin nose.

She turned off the T.V. and shuffled into her bedroom. She fell face down on her bed and let the news sink in. She remained there for several minutes. There was nothing she could do now except wish Franco well and hope that they would remain friends.

It's time to move on with my life, she told herself.

She dragged herself off the bed and put on a pair of khaki shorts, white Keds and a Polo T-shirt. She pulled her hair back into a ponytail, placed on a sun visor, grabbed her cell phone and drove to Susan's. The morning was already sunny and hot. Christina put down her convertible top and turned on the radio.

"An unexpected heat wave is passing through Northern California," the radio announcer said. "High temperatures in the 90's are expected later this afternoon."

The hot, still air made her nervous. She remembered perfectly well the conditions before the Northridge earthquake that occurred while she was living in L.A.

She'd spent nearly 12 hours in her car, waiting for the rescue crews to dig her out of the rubble created by a fallen freeway ramp.

She thought back to that early morning when she'd been driving her old Honda to work. She was ready to pass the red Toyota in front of her when a blue van cut her off. She cursed the van for getting in her way— and then her car shook uncontrollably. She thought she had a flat tire, so she slowed down. This time a violent jolt knocked her feet off both the gas pedal and the clutch. Her car lurched to an abrupt halt. Her head hit the steering wheel. Looking up, she watched in horror as the massive concrete freeway ramp collapsed around her.

The Toyota ahead of her was crushed instantly. Nothing more than a one-foot tall pancake of red metal remained.

Despite the heat, her skin turned to goose flesh as she thought of that terrible memory. She reached under her seat to make sure she had a bottle of water and a flashlight.

She pulled up in front of Susan's apartment building, and called her from her cell phone. She realized it was the lazy thing to do, but someone else's car was blocking the driveway and there was no other place to park.

Susan answered the phone on the first ring. "I'll be right down." A minute later she came bouncing down the stairs, holding hands with Dan.

"Bye, sweetie," she said to Dan. "I won't be back until later this afternoon."

"Bye, darlin'." He gave her a big smooch on the cheek.

Christina waved 'goodbye' to Dan as they pulled away from her apartment building.

"You two are so great together." Christina smiled and looked over to Susan. "I'm glad things are working out so well."

"Me too. He's such a doll." Susan pulled the vanity mirror down and dabbed on some sunscreen. "I'm kind of glad Stephano decided not to come out to visit me. It would have been awkward telling him I could only fit him in for a half-hour lunch."

"Well maybe you two could still stay in touch." She maneuvered the car around a corner and onto the freeway. "Maybe Franco and I will manage to remain friends."

"Try to keep your mind off Franco today. O.K?"

"I will." Christina wanted to mention the CNN report, but she'd cried enough; it was better if she just dropped the subject.

They pulled into the circular drive in front of Rob's co-op. The building resembled a French Chateau, with a stone facade, faux turrets and large, plated glass windows. Susan waited in the car while Christina ran in and asked the doorman to ring him. The building appeared to be ten stories high, and sat on one of the highest hills in San Francisco. The views from his penthouse must be spectacular.

Rob emerged from the elevator. He was wearing jeans and a light pink, cotton button down shirt. "Hi Christina, nice to see you again!" he smiled warmly and shook her hand. "You look bright and fresh this morning."

234

"Thanks, Rob." She was grateful that her sunglasses hid her red, swollen eyes. "I'm glad we're finally able to get together after all these months. Brandy couldn't stop talking about you when you left our table at Postrio. She really thinks a lot of you."

"We always have a lot of fun together."

Without opening the door, he jumped into the back seat of Christina's convertible.

"You remember Susan, don't you?" Christina said.

"Yes, of course," Rob said. "I understand you're Christina's partner in crime these days. Brandy's been filling me in, but I'd love to hear the details."

"How much do you know about what's been happening?" Christina asked.

"Well, for one thing, your picture has been plastered all over the paper this week."

"You're kidding. Even in L.A.?"

"Yes, believe me. First we see you on the arm of Senator Cartwright at that fundraiser of his, next we see you hailed as a heroine in an FBI sting. How did all that come about?"

"It's kind of a long story, but what you've been reading in the papers is pretty much the truth. I'll let Susan fill you in on the dirty details while I concentrate on getting us onto the Bay Bridge. This traffic is already crazy!"

Susan turned around and finished explaining to Rob what they—especially Christina—had experienced over the last two months.

"What a great story!" Rob said just as they were slowing down to take the sharp turn off the bridge onto Treasure Island. "It would make a great, action packed movie! After this one's wrapped up, I want to hear more details, and maybe have you talk to a screenwriter."

"Wow, that would be fun!" Christina screeched around the ramp that led to the Island.

"Here, pull over at this security check point." Rob pointed to the small gatehouse.

"There's Brandy." Susan waved to her.

Rob told Brandy to keep her car parked and gestured for her to jump in back with him.

At the gatehouse, Rob showed the guard his identification. The guard scrutinized his credentials, and then waved them through.

Before they got near the set, they passed at least twenty fifty-foot long trailers. Rob told them that they were used for catering, makeup and costumes.

"Can I really get up close and personal with Brad Pitt?" Brandy asked.

"Unfortunately, Brad's stunt double is doing most of the work today. Brad may be lingering around the set, but I can't promise anything."

They got out of the car and walked over to the water where an action scene was being filmed. Stunt men were jumping from speeding jet skis onto a speedboat, driven by Sandra Bullock's stunt double. Christina noticed the name 'Chris Rogers' on the director's chair and recalled that he directed several films that were set in the Bay Area. She'd read somewhere that he lived in Pacific Heights.

"Cut!" the director yelled through a bullhorn. "Cut!!!"

The stuntmen and women heard the second command and killed the engines.

He rubbed his throat and continued yelling. "Remember, the boat has to look like it's spinning out of control. You're driving it in a straight line! Sandra could have done that herself, for God's sake."

He paused and yelled, "Take Four!" As he turned to sit he saw Rob and held up his hand to acknowledge him.

"They should be finished in a minute," Rob said.

This time the boat careened in circles.

"Cut!!" the director yelled again and took a sip of water. "Good job, that's a wrap. Bring the equipment to shore."

He put his bullhorn down and walked over to Rob and the three women.

"Hi Rob, good to see you." His voice sounded hoarse.

They shook hands and slapped each other on the shoulder.

"I brought some of my friends over this morning—we'll stay out of your way."

"Not a problem," he smiled. "Your friends are welcome anytime. Hi, I'm Chris." He shook each of their hands.

"Nice boat," Rob said. The cigarette-style boat had just pulled to the shore and the stunt people were climbing out of it.

"We picked it up at a Treasury auction. It had been confiscated from some drug runners in Panama."

"I always like to hear we're budget minded," Rob laughed.

"Have fun touring the set." Chris looked at the three women. "I'm sure Rob will take care of you just fine. Please excuse me; I've got another scene to finish before the noon sun blows the scene. Nice to meet you, ladies."

He walked back to the waterfront and started shouting through the bullhorn again.

"See that huge building that looks like an airplane hanger?" Rob pointed it out in the distance. "Back in the forties, it used to be a hanger, but now it's a state-of-the-art sound stage."

"May we see it?" Susan asked.

They walked past several mobile homes that were set up for the personal use of movie stars. The caterers had already arranged the mid-morning spread on long tables.

"No one's going to go hungry on this set," remarked Christina.

"Oh my god!" Brandy squealed. "I think I just saw Brad Pitt."

"Where?" Susan whirled around.

"Over there!" Brandy pointed to the large custom built, mobile home on the side of the road.

The back of his faded Levi's disappeared into his comfortably air-conditioned mobile home.

"At least I saw him," Brandy said. "And I was less than 50 feet away! Maybe I could knock on his door and ask him for a glass of ice water."

"Probably not a good idea." Rob picked a small bottle of Evian from of the coolers and handed it to Brandy.

"May I have one, also?" Christina asked.

Rob tossed her a bottle. "Thanks." She took a sip and put the bottle in her purse.

They walked into the sound stage and looked around in awe at all the equipment. The arena was bustling with people fixing wires, checking lights and moving cameras along built-in tracks that resembled a miniature railroad.

"There's not too much action going on right now," Rob said. "Let's check out what's happening on the other side of the building?

"This is amazing!" Christina watched a crew assemble a massive set that looked exactly like the inside of City Hall. "I feel as though I'm really in the building. The detail work is phenomenal!"

"That's the idea," Rob said. "It's too disruptive to film at City Hall day after day, so this is what they do instead. They'll probably spend a day in the actual building, but most of the scene will be shot here."

Christina looked at her watch. "It's almost eleven thirty! We should get going, Rob. Susan and I have to drive over to the Port of Oakland to pick up a package."

"I thought the Port is strictly for commercial use."

Christina explained why they were going there.

"You'd better get on your way," Rob said, and then turned to Brandy. "So, do you have to run off also? If you'd like, you're welcome to hang around for a little longer and stake out Brad's trailer."

Brandy raised her eyebrows. "I'm not due back in The City until two."

"Great, stay here with me."

"Thanks again, Rob," Christina shook his hand. "We really appreciate you taking the time to show us around. It's fun to know what goes on behind the scenes."

"My pleasure." He pulled Christina in and gave her a warm hug. "Bye Susan, hope to see you again."

"You too, Rob," Susan said. "Don't forget to call me before you start filming Christina's story. You're going to need a consultant who's close to the source, and I'm dating one of the FBI agents who helped bust those two guys."

Rob laughed, "You've got a deal!"

They left the cool, air conditioned hanger and walked outside into the blazing hot sun.

Chapter Thirty-Six

"Rob is such a kick," Susan said as they exited Treasure Island and turned onto the Bay Bridge.

"Yeah, I really like him. Hopefully we'll see more of each other."

Susan pointed out her window and across the water. "I didn't realize the Port was so close."

"It looks close from here," Christina said, "but we still have to drive several miles across the bridge and then through Oakland."

They maneuvered their way through the busy streets of Oakland and followed the signs to the Port. Along with the packing slip, Franco had enclosed some typed directions that instructed them to park their car in the visitor's parking lot and find their way to the Customs Office.

Christina pulled into a free space and put up her convertible top. They took their purses and started walking aimlessly. They had no idea where the Customs Office was. They wandered around the Port and looked for a sign to the office or for someone to give them directions. They ended up walking closer toward the water. Since it was cooler there, they stayed by the water for a while and watched the gigantic container ships pull into the Port.

"Christina, look!" shouted Susan.

"What is it?" asked Christina.

Susan pointed to the docking area. "That ship over there. The one that's docked."

An enormous black, steel ship with YAMASHUTA written in large white, block letters was moored to the pier.

"Oh my god." Christina covered her mouth.

"Let's not jump to any conclusions," Susan said. "After all, Yamashuta Enterprises is one of the largest conglomerates in the world. They probably ship cargo through here once a week."

"There's only one way to find out," Christina said.

"Christina, are you out of your mind?"

Christina began to creep toward the ship and Susan followed. About 100 feet from the massive vessel, they crouched down behind some crates to see if they could spot Seike.

"The engines are running," Christina said. "Someone must be on the ship. Let's keep watching."

Two men dressed in black, wearing black baseball caps and dark sunglasses, emerged from the bowels of the ship and onto the deck. They appeared to be carrying assault rifles. Another man, dressed in more traditional street clothes, followed closely behind them.

Susan gasped. "Stephano!"

"Sshhh!" Christina put her hand over Susan's mouth. Susan was right. Stephano stood on the deck, smoking a cigarette. One of the other men took off his cap to wipe his forehead. Short blonde hair! He looked exactly like one of the men who'd been with Seike in Italy last month.

"What are we going to do?" asked Susan.

"Let's find out if Seike is on board."

"Are you crazy? Those two are carrying some serious weapons. And what about Stephano? I wouldn't be surprised if he's packing some heat."

"You're right, it's dangerous," Christina said, "but if we're careful, we won't get caught. Follow me."

She grabbed Susan's hand. They tiptoed closer to the ship and began crawling up the boarding ramp that led to the top deck.

"You really want to climb aboard this ship?" Susan whispered.

"It's the only way we're going to find out what's really going on in there."

Susan reluctantly followed Christina up the ramp and onto the ship. They made it safely to the deck without catching anyone's attention.

Suddenly, the ship rocked. A giant wave knocked against the hull. The women stumbled and were thrown against a railing. Susan let out a loud yelp. All the ships around them in the harbor rocked and swayed; the water slapped in long, slow waves.

Stephano and the two men in black were about 20 yards away from Susan and Christina.

The trio fell onto the deck. "What was that?" one of the men yelled.

"It felt like an earthquake," the other one said.

"Yeah, but I thought I heard someone scream." Stephano stubbed out his cigarette.

"Yeah, me too."

"Have a look around," Stephano ordered. "We don't need any problems now."

-

"Shit!" Brandy yelled as she fell to the ground, covering her head. "Earthquake!"

"Calm down Brandy." Rob placed his hand on her shoulder. "It's a minor one."

"Not that minor." Brandy was still crouched on the ground with her hands over her head.

"No, really, it wasn't that bad. If it had been serious you would have seen all the actors run out of their trailers."

"Well if it wasn't that bad, then why did all the food fly off the tables?"

"O.K. you've got me there."

Brandy noticed nearly twenty people running from the sound stage to where the trailers were parked. She felt better. At least she wasn't the only one who was scared.

She could hear bits and pieces of their conversations. She saw a young woman with blood on her forehead that was being bandaged up by a co-worker.

"I guess it was worse than I thought," Rob said to Brandy.

Finally, one of the actors stuck his head out of his trailer and yelled, "Is everyone okay out here?"

"We have it under control," a man with 'CREW' written on his shirt said. "Go back to sleep. We'll let you know when we're gonna shoot your next scene."

-

"Are you OK," Christina asked Susan as they eased themselves away from the railing.

Susan rubbed her shoulder and nodded.

"They're going to come looking for us," Christina grasped Susan's arm. "Where are we going to hide?"

"Over there." Susan pointed to a pile of thick, coarse ropes wrapped around a steel winch on the port side of the ship. "Behind those ropes."

They crawled over to the pile, trying not to make a sound.

"Who's over there?" a deep voice sounded.

Christina's heart stopped beating for a moment. "Don't say anything," she whispered. "Keep moving. They can't see us. They're just trying to see if we'll respond."

They continued to crawl on their hands and knees.

"Hey!" a gruff voice yelled. "You two, what are you doing?"

Then came Stephano's voice: "Grab 'em!"

A strong hand pulled at Christina's ponytail, nearly ripping her hair from its roots.

"Ouch!" she yelled, "Let go!"

The other goon grabbed one of Susan's arms and twisted it behind her.

As her assailant tugged her up by her hair, Christina kicked him in the knee. "I can get up on my own! Get your hands off of me!"

"Feisty, aren't we?" a raspy voice said. The blunt end of a rifle poked into her back.

One of the blond men pulled Christina's arm behind her with such force she felt her muscles tear. She struggled to break loose, but his grip was too strong. Stephano walked onto the deck followed by another man who was smoking a cigarette. Dark stringy bangs covered his face.

"Seike!" Christina breathed.

"Bring 'em downstairs to the engine room," Seike ordered. "We need to push outta here. Once we're halfway out to sea, we'll dump 'em."

"Stephano," Susan cried, "how can you let him do this to us? I thought we were your friends?"

"Shut up, Susan," Stephano yelled. "How can you be so stupid? You two were convenient friends."

"But why did you offer to fly us back to the United States?"

"To get you out of town! What did you think? Little did I know you and your detective friend, Caldwell, would continue nosing around once you got back to the States. You should've dropped everything the minute the plane touched down in Toronto. If you had, you wouldn't be here today, and you wouldn't be dead tomorrow!"

Christina listened in horror. He was serious. She feared that no one would find their bodies in the middle of the ocean.

"What about Franco?" Christina said in Stephano's direction. "Does he know anything about this?"

"Are you kidding? He's too busy running his marble empire. Anyway, you never had a chance with him," he sneered. "His parents have had him married off to Alessandra since he was ten years old. You know the tradition: keep the royalty in the family."

The two goons dragged the girls across the deck and pushed them down the stairs to the engine room.

"Tie 'em down there," Seike barked.

"With what?" one of his hired guns asked. "There's nothin' down here."

"Hold on," Seike pulled a switchblade from his pocket. "Stephano," he ordered, "go cut some rope from on the deck."

He tossed Stephano the knife and continued to push the girls downstairs to the engine room. The room was dark and hot; the temperature well over 100 degrees. One dim light bulb glowed in the corner. The loud hum of the engine drowned out their voices, making it nearly impossible to hear each other without shouting.

Stephano came down the stairs with ten feet of rope and ordered the two blonde men to tie Christina and Susan to a thick pole next to the rumbling, hot engine. The muscle men pushed the girls' backs together and tied their hands behind them, securing their wrists tightly to the metal pole.

"Make those ropes tight!" Seike yelled. He pulled out his lighter and lit another cigarette. "We wouldn't want them slipping loose."

The men cinched the ropes tighter around the women's wrists. Susan screamed as they tied the last knot. By now everyone in the room was sweating profusely.

"Let's get out of here," Stephano yelled. "This heat is unbearable!"

The four men walked to the stairway, and shut the heavy steel door behind them. Christina heard the clamping of a large metal wheel. The door sealed shut. The women were left alone in the dark, sweltering engine room.

Chapter Thirty-Seven

Brandy guzzled down another bottle of Evian. "I didn't drive all this way to an endure an earthquake, come within 50 feet of Brad Pitt, and then leave without even saying 'hello' to him."

"At least we know he's in there," Rob said, pointing to his trailer. "I guess it can't hurt to knock on his door."

"Here I go." She pulled herself off the ground. "I promise not to say I know you if he gives me a hard time."

Rob laughed and waved her away.

-

"Christina, how are we going to get out of here?" Susan asked. "They're gonna kill us and dump us overboard."

"I realize we're in a bit of a bind," Christina said sarcastically. "Sorry, no pun intended."

"How can you make jokes at a time like this?!?" yelled Susan.

"Blame the heat," answered Christina. "It's making me light-headed."

"Well, conserve your brainpower and help me think of an escape plan. We're going to die of heat prostration before they have a chance to kill us!"

"Try to move your hands," Christina said. She tried moving hers, but they were clamped together by the ropes.

"I can't," Susan said. "These ropes are already cutting into my skin."

"Let's try sitting down," Christina suggested. "Maybe there's some bolts or screws at the bottom of the pole."

They eased down the pole together, until they were both sitting on the floor. Their sweaty hands helped them slide down the pole.

"I just kicked something," Christina said.

"What?"

It was Seike's lighter. The light blue Bic lighter sat about four feet from her foot.

"Seike dropped his lighter," Christina said, stretching her leg as far as possible. She managed to touch the lighter with the tip of her shoe. She dragged it towards her body with her foot.

Christina continued to give Susan the play-by-play, because she knew that Susan couldn't turn her head around far enough to see what was happening.

"I need to get the lighter close enough that I can reach it."

Perspiration dripped into her eyes and made them sting. She blinked several times, hoping that would help eliminate some of the discomfort.

Her knee was almost to her chin, the heel of her shoe next to her hip. She felt like a contortionist and was glad she'd stretched this morning before her run.

"It's so close." Christina extended her fingers as far as possible. "But I can't reach it. I can't get it any closer!"

Christina relaxed her leg muscles; the cramps were making it impossible to move. "Susan, try to feel behind you. The lighter is under the heel of my left foot, so I think it's behind your right hand. First find my shoe, then the heel. We need to be very careful and not knock it any further."

Susan wiggled her fingers. There was silence. The rumble of the ship's engines filled the room.

"I found it!" Susan shouted.

Christina finally felt the pressure of Susan's fingers on the back of her shoe. "Perfect! Now I'm going to lift my heel and I want you to try to find the lighter."

Susan lightly fingered the lighter and breathed a sigh of relief. "I'm on it."

"See if you can grip it, and then pass it over to me."

Susan placed her fingers on it and picked it up. Her hand was sweating so much that it slid from her grip. Luckily, it didn't fall far. She tried again. This time she got a better hold on the lighter. She wedged it between her index and middle finger and dropped it into Christina's hands.

"Good job!" Christina felt it firmly in the palm of her hands. She tried to position her thumb over the flint starter.

Her wet hands made it difficult to get a firm grip. She wiped her hands as best as she could on the back of her shirt, and tried again.

She gripped the lighter with her hand and flicked the starter.

"Ouch!" she yelled.

"What's wrong?" Susan asked.

"I'm burning my thumb, not the rope."

She tried again, this time positioning the flame closer to the rope. This maneuver didn't work. The flame burnt the skin on the inside of her wrist. She moved her hand a few inches, doing her best to ignore the excruciating pain. She needed to place the flame directly beneath the rope.

"I got it!" she told Susan.

A strong flame worked its way through the rope.

"What's that horrible smell?" Susan asked.

"It's my burning flesh," Christina winced. "But at least the rope is finally on fire."

"It's working," Susan yelled. "I can feel the ropes loosening up!"

Christina dropped the lighter and let the fire burn the remainder of the rope.

Their hands finally broke free!

Christina brought her raw hands to her chest and held them against her soft cotton shirt. They stood up, still cramped, but relieved to be free from the cinching ropes.

Relishing in their newly found freedom, they forgot the burning rope at their feet.

"Help me stomp it out!" Christina yelled. Frantically, she jumped on the ends of the rope.

"That's all we need," Susan said, "to bite the big one from smoke inhalation."

"Our troubles aren't over yet," Christina said. "We're still trapped in this furnace."

She walked over to the door, only to confirm her original fear. It was locked from the outside.

"We need another plan," Susan said.

"Obviously," answered Christina.

"If we could get Seike or Stephano to come down here, and open the door, maybe we could startle them, hit them on the head, and then make for the door."

"Good idea, but how are we going to get them to come down here? And what are we going to knock them out with?" Christina looked around the dark room.

"Maybe if we start yelling and screaming, they'll hear us and come down."

"It's too loud down here— no one would ever here us," Christina said. "Besides my throat is killing me just from talking to you. I don't think I could yell loud enough for someone standing 10 feet away to hear me."

She remembered the bottle of water she'd tucked into her purse. She pulled it out with a grin of triumph. She took a sip and handed it to Susan. While Susan was drinking Christina dug back in her purse, hoping to find some chewing gum. Her throat was parched. She could barely talk.

"Hey, my phone." Christina noticed her small flip phone. "Do you think it would work down here?"

"We're buried in ten feet of metal," Susan said, "but it's worth a try."

"We need to think this through carefully," Christina said. "If we are lucky enough to get a connection, it's going to be a bad one. We may only be able to get a few words in, and we probably only have one chance."

"Let's try Dan," Susan said. "No, wait!" She held up her hand. "He told me that after he wrapped up the Stinson case he's off-duty for a few days."

"Okay," said Christina, "we need someone who always carries a mobile phone."

"Brandy!" Susan said. "She doesn't even go to the bathroom without her phone. She'll have it for sure!"

"Perfect!" Christina pulled the phone open. She held her breath and punched the number.

"Here goes."

-

Brandy had finally mustered enough courage to ascend the metal stairs to Brad Pitt's trailer when the cell phone in her purse started to ring.

"Damn," she said, "I can't believe I forgot to turn this thing off."

She backed down the stairs and pulled her phone out of her purse.

"Brandy Jensen."

Static buzzed down the line. She heard a few faint words.

"....tina—......help........port......."

"Christina??? Is that you? I can't understand you!" No answer. The line went dead.

She ran back over to where Rob was catching some rays in the hot, afternoon sun.

"Rob, I think I just got a call for help from Christina. The line wasn't clear, but I'm sure it was her!"

"What did she say?" Rob asked.

"It was nearly impossible to hear, but I know they're in trouble, and I think they're calling from the Port of Oakland!"

She grabbed Rob by the hand and pulled him off the ground.

"Get up, we have to drive over there!!!"

Chapter Thirty-Eight

"Did you get through?" asked Susan.

"I don't know. There was so much static, I'm afraid even if I did, she wouldn't have understood anything."

"Let's try again," Susan said.

Christina re-dialed.

"It's dead." She flipped it shut. "What we need to concentrate on now is getting out of this room before the ship leaves the Port."

"Christina!" Susan said. "We're in the engine room! Let's just shut 'em down. We won't be going anywhere if the engines aren't working."

"Good thinking!"

They walked over to a tangled mess of the pipes, levers and valves.

"I have no clue as to how an engine works," Christina said.

"Neither do I. We just need to do something that will either shut it down properly or break it. We don't care what happens, as long as the engines stop running."

"Maybe there's a 'shut off' button or something."

"I hate to tell you, but I doubt it'll be that easy," Susan said.

"Let's twist and turn everything we can find. Something's bound to happen." Christina spotted a large metal knob, and tried to turn it. "Jesus Christ!" She pulled her hand away. "It's burning hot!" She took off her T-shirt and covered the knob with her shirt. It was too tight to budge. She spotted a large steel wheel, and turned it. Hot steam sprayed out, she ducked so the vapor wouldn't burn her face. She kept searching.

"Christina," Susan yelled. "Help me with this lever.

Christina put her shirt back on. Susan was pushing down on a long, black lever. She was using all her weight as leverage but couldn't move it an inch.

"Let's do this together," Christina said. "On three we'll press down."

The poised themselves above the bar and placed their hands on the end of it.

"One, two, three!"

The ship lurched, and the entire engine room fell silent.

"I think we did it!" Susan clapped her hands together. "I don't hear the engines. They're going to have to come down to see what happened. Once they open the door, we can try and run out behind them."

"We better be more careful than that, remember, they have guns." Christina's mind was racing. "We don't have much to work with, so we need to be resourceful." She spilled the contents of her purse onto the floor.

"What are you doing?"

"Get your backpack. We need to see what we have to work with."

Susan found her bag and dumped everything onto the floor.

Christina went through the contents of her own purse. What do we have here?" Christina held up some lipgloss, ponytail holders, a hairbrush, several pens and pencils. "When they open the door we need to scare them—or at least take them off guard long enough so we can get out of here."

Susan nodded. She rifled through hair clips, a tube of sunscreen, a granola bar, hair spray and vitamin packets.

Christina continued her search. She held up a bottle of perfume. "This might do the trick."

"Perfume?" Susan questioned.

Christina pulled the top off of a bottle and poured the liquid onto the remaining piece of rope that had been used to tie them together.

"We'll put this alcohol saturated rope down here." She placed the rope in front of the door. "When one of them opens the door, I'll ignite the rope with Seike's lighter. It'll burst into flames, and at least make him look at his feet for a few seconds."

"Sounds good, but what if two people come down?" Susan asked.

"Good point." Christina put her burnt hand up to her chin, thought for a moment, and started digging through the small mountain of junk from Susan's bag.

Jackpot! She gripped the travel size container of aerosol hair spray.

"If someone else comes in, I'll spray this can and then flick the lighter underneath the spray. If all goes as planned we'll be armed with a mini blow torch."

"Christina—get real!"

"I tried this when I was a kid with my mom's Aqua Net—it really works."

"What should I do?" Susan asked.

"Run for it, and try to clear a path for me. Once we're out, we'll lock the door behind us. Let's sit tight now, and wait for them to come down."

They sat quietly for several seconds when Susan asked, "What's that noise? It sounds like something's leaking. Do you hear it?"

Christina listened. "I think it's coming from the engines. I'll check it out."

A small pool of liquid was forming on the floor next to one of the pipes. The familiar smell of gasoline filled her nostrils.

-

Rob and Brandy raced off Treasure Island and headed for the Port. When they got to the ramp that led to the bridge, Brandy slammed on the brakes, just missing the truck in front of her. Cars were backed up for nearly a quarter of a mile.

"What the hell!?" she screamed. "There must have been an accident on the bridge. We can't get anywhere near it! What are we going to do?"

"Turn around," instructed Rob in a calm and cool tone of voice.

"What are you talking about?" Brandy pounded her hands against the steering wheel. "This is the only way off the Island."

"Trust me. Drive back to the beach!"

Brandy squealed into a u-turn and floored it back to the beach on Treasure Island.

"Why am I driving toward the beach?"

"Just do it."

Brandy pulled up to the sand. Rob jumped out and ran over to the director, Chris, who was talking with a cameraman.

"Chris, please don't ask any questions. We have an emergency and I need to use the boat."

Chris took off his cap, smoothed his hair and put his cap back on. "Sure Rob, whatever you say. Just bring it back in one piece."

Rob waved Brandy over to the boat.

"Get in," he yelled. "We'll be over there in a few minutes. As the crow flies, we're probably looking at two miles."

Rob started the engine and sped off toward the Port. The combination of Rob piloting the boat at full throttle and the choppy water threw Brandy from the front seat to the back.

"Hold on!" Rob yelled back to her as they sped under the Bay Bridge.

The Port was now in sight. Brandy managed to crawl up to the front.

"I don't know if I'm cut out for this 'Bond girl' stuff." Brandy held her hair out of her face and ducked away from the cold waves of water splashing into the boat.

"You're doing just fine," Rob said. "What are we looking for?"

"I'm not sure," she said as they got closer to the Port. "Try to slow down a bit. I can't see with all the water spraying into my eyes."

Rob pushed the throttle forward while Brandy focused on the group of tankers sitting in the water.

"That's it!" she yelled. "Slow down!!"

Rob slipped the engine into idle.

"See that ship with YAMASHUTA painted on the side?" Brandy pointed toward the Port. "I think that's what Christina was trying to tell me. Try to get as close as you can, without making too much noise."

Rob steered the speedboat over to the side of the ship. The fifty-foot tall steel black wall towered above them.

"We're too close to see anything," Rob said. "Do you want me to back up?"

"No, that won't help. We need to get onto the ship."

"I'm sorry to have to break it to you, but I neglected to bring my repelling gear." He shook his head. "Brandy—that's a sheer steel wall. How in the world are we going to get onto the ship from down here?"

"Obviously, we can't do it from here. Pull over to that pier." She pointed at the long wooden dock adjacent to the ship.

Rob maneuvered the boat over to one of the berths. Huge, algae crusted collision fenders, hanging from thick, weathered sea ropes, swung against the wall.

Rob looked up to the dock above them. "Are you thinking what I'm thinking?"

"You got it," Brandy said. "In order to reach the rope, we're going to have to scale that slimy fender. Once we're able to grip the rope, we have a shot at making it onto the deck."

Rob killed the engine and wiped the water off his sunglasses.

"Here, I'll give you a boost."

He cupped his hands under Brandy's feet and pushed her up toward the rope.

"I'm almost there," Brandy panted. "Can you lift me a little more?" She looked over her shoulder and down at him. "All this slime doesn't help. I can't get a solid grip." She stepped onto his shoulder.

He let out a loud grunt and pressed her up and over the fender.

"I got it! I think I can pull myself onto the deck now."

Brandy gathered all the strength she could find in her rarely used arm muscles and pulled her body up along the rope. Fist over fist, struggling every inch, she managed to reach the top of the pier. Propelling herself with her legs she pushed her way onto firm ground.

Sweating and panting she called down to Rob. "I did it! C'mon Rob, it's your turn."

Rob was over a foot taller, and much stronger than Brandy. He scaled the fender and the rope in minutes.

A dark green, gooey substance coated their faces and clothes.

"I bet you'd never make Sandra Bullock look this bad in that movie of yours." Brandy wiped some of the grime away from her eyes. "Now let's be quiet and find our way over to the ship."

Chapter Thirty-Nine

Susan and Christina crouched alongside the steel door and waited silently in the sauna-like conditions for someone to come down and check the engine problem. After what seemed like nearly an hour they heard footsteps pounding down the stairway.

Christina touched Susan's arm. "Are you ready?"

Susan nodded.

The rope was in place. Christina put her thumb on the lighter. She could barely hold it because her hands hurt so much from the burns. She poised the lighter in a position to ignite the rope the instant the door was opened. The metal wheel screeched as it was turned on the outside of the door, and then a burst of daylight streamed into the room. As soon as she saw the dark silhouette of a face, Christina lit the rope. It burst into flames. The man looked down and Christina kicked him. He tripped over the burning rope. Another man followed the first. Christina's eyes had adjusted to the light and she saw that the second man was Seike. She kicked the first man in the small of his back, causing him to stumble onto the burning rope. Susan fled up the stairs as Christina sprayed Susan's hair spray at Seike's head and lit the lighter under the mist. A stream of fire erupted. Seike screamed and covered his eyes and then fell to the floor.

Christina dropped the can, ran outside, slammed the door and cranked the wheel shut. Relief and exhilaration rushed through her body. *Let **them** suffocate and bake to death.*

Susan crouched on the top stair, peering over the top. She turned and put a finger to her lip. She pointed to the deck. Less than thirty feet away Stephano and one of the blonde men stood smoking a cigarette.

"Now what are we going to do?" whispered Susan. "They're bound to come over here to check what happened to Seike."

"Let's just sit tight for now," Christina said, blowing on her hands to cool the burns. "There's nothing we can do. All of our 'weapons' are back in the engine room."

"At least we're out of that deathtrap." Susan smiled and squeezed Christina's arm.

They sat patiently on the stairs, watching Stephano and his every move. Compared to that furnace where they'd spent the last hour, they actually felt cool in the 90-degree heat and blazing afternoon sun. They were thankful for the small breeze, and for some fresh oxygen to breathe.

Stephano walked away, presumably to talk with the skipper. Christina and Susan snuck onto the deck and ran to the side of the ship.

"We've got to get out of here before the ship starts moving," Christina told Susan. "Run for the ramp, and try not to be seen."

They'd run no more than five feet when the ship shook violently, knocking them both to their knees. This jolt felt much sharper than the one they'd experienced earlier. They got up and started running again. This time they only made it another few feet before a huge blast from the engine room launched them high into the air, causing them to flip before falling to the ground. ·

Brandy and Rob, who were now on the top deck crouched behind the rope pile, saw Christina and Susan fly into the air as a fiery explosion erupted in the background. The ship was rapidly catching on fire. Christina and Susan lay unconscious on the deck.

Rob and Brandy ran through the flying debris, grabbed the two listless bodies and dragged them to the ramp. Brandy was not strong enough to pick up either Susan or Christina, so Rob threw Susan over his shoulder and told Brandy to pull Christina, the smaller of the two, as far down the ramp as she could. After Rob made it down the ramp with Susan, he set her down and ran back to Brandy, where he swept Christina up in his arms. Once they both reached the pier they set the women on their backs, holding their heads in their laps.

The fire on the ship was spreading faster and charred debris was falling all around them.

"We have to get medical help." For the first time Rob sounded panicked. "Do you still have your cell phone?"

"No, I left my purse on the boat."

Loud sirens announced the arrival of police cars, followed by a paramedic's van.

"How did that happen?" Rob asked.

Brandy wiped some grim off her forehead. "Believe it or not, I had the presence of mind to call 911 before I got on the boat."

Rob smiled, slapped her on the back. "Good job! You'd make a great 'Bond girl'."

The paramedics rushed over to Susan and Christina and placed oxygen masks over their faces. They started cleaning their bloody faces, legs and arms. Susan opened her eyes first, then Christina.

One of the paramedics looked up. "They're going to be just fine. They have a lot of cuts, and maybe a few broken bones, but nothing that won't heal. We're taking them to Oakland Summit's ER."

Two fire trucks arrived and the firefighters started attempting to extinguish the blaze.

In the midst of the black smoke, two figures limped down the ramp with their hands up in the air.

"That's Stephano!" Brandy yelled.

Two police officers ran over to them and snapped handcuffs on both of their wrists.

Stephano and one of Seike's bodyguards walked past Christina with their hands cuffed behind them. She assumed Seike, and possibly his other bodyguard, had been blown to pieces in the explosion.

She closed her eyes as the paramedics placed her aching body onto the gurney and lifted her into the back of the van.

It was over.

It was finally over.

Epilogue

The doctors requested that Christina and Susan spend two nights in the hospital. Susan had broken her wrist and Christina had splintered her kneecap when they'd fallen to the deck after the explosion. Other than those injuries, they'd sustained some nasty cuts, but were expected to heal quickly.

While in the hospital, Christina got an unexpected call from Franco.

"Hello, Franco." She knew her voice sounded flat, but she was glad to hear from him.

"How are you, Christina? I've been worried."

"I'm not feeling so great, but it's good to hear your voice. How did you know that I was here?"

"Your office told me. Also, because of Stephano's involvement the news is all over the Italian papers."

"Has he called you?"

"He's still in custody and I've heard that his lawyers aren't letting him talk to anyone."

"That must be upsetting for you. After all, you've known him your whole life."

"Honestly, I wasn't that surprised. Over the past five years, I've seen a big change in him. He started going broke a few years ago after his father refused to give him more money than what he earned from working at the company. His image was extremely important to him, and he could not sustain his lavish lifestyle on his minimal salary. Also, I'm pretty certain that he'd developed an expensive drug habit. But enough of that. I'm just glad you're safe, my darling."

My darling? She wondered why was he calling her my darling?

"You really should stick with investment banking. It's much less life threatening. By the way, did you have a chance to get your painting?"

"Oh, Franco," she sighed, "Given all the chaos, I wasn't able to pick it up. I guess I could've asked the ambulance driver to swing by customs on the way to the hospital, but I was slipping in and out of consciousness. You know how that is."

"I see you haven't lost your sense of humor. In any event, it's important you see it. I'll have it delivered to your house by no later than Monday afternoon, and then I want you to call me."

"Sure, Franco," she said, glad to know that they were still friends. "I'll look forward to receiving it." She swallowed. "By the way, how's Alessandra?"

"She's still mourning, but she'll pull through just fine. It's kind of you to ask about her. I must hang up now, but I'm glad to hear you are feeling better. Ciao, dolcina."

"Ciao, Franco. Thanks for calling."

Dolcina?

-

Christina arrived home Monday morning to find that more damage than she had expected had occurred in the earthquake Saturday morning. Her wine glasses had fallen out of her cabinet and crashed to the kitchen floor; a porcelain vase had been knocked over, and a few pictures had fallen off the wall. Other than that, things just looked disorderly.

She would straighten up later. All she could think about was drawing a warm bath, and reading the Sunday paper that had been waiting for her on the front doorstep.

Besides the obvious follow-up stories of the 6.5 earthquake along the Hayward Fault in the East Bay, Christina had made front page news. A picture of the Yamashuta tanker, burning out of control, filled a quarter of the page. The story recapped what she already knew, but it confirmed that Stephano was in custody and that Seike had perished in the explosion. She also read that Senator Cartwright had been suspended from his chairmanship from the Senate Armed Services Committee pending an investigation into his relationship with Curtis Saunders. The only good news she read was about the fate of the microprocessors. After the heist, Seike had them delivered to Hawaii. His plan was to have the Yamashuta tanker, loaded down with legitimate electronic devices, stop in Hawaii to pick up the chips and smuggle them into Japan. But now the FBI was on their way to retrieve them.

When the bubbles from her bath reached the top of the tub, she popped in a Rossini CD, gathered the rest of the paper and sank into the warm, therapeutic water. She continued to read the reports about the damage created by the earthquake. Over the crescendos of the opera music playing in the background, Christina heard her front doorbell. She eased out of the tub, wrapped a towel around her body, and walked to her intercom.

"Hello," she answered.

"Delivery, for Christina Caldwell."

Her moist skin tingled.

"Please, bring it up," she buzzed the delivery man in, "and leave it by my front door."

"We need a signature, ma'am."

"Yes, of course."

She shuffled into her bedroom, threw on a robe, and opened the door. The deliveryman was holding a large package, nearly six feet tall and four feet wide. She scribbled her name, thanked him and dragged the delivery into her house.

The sturdy packaging made it impossible to open it with her bare hands. She fetched a serrated bread knife from the kitchen and started sawing. The anticipation was killing her.

After several minutes of cutting, she managed to break through the heavy tape and cardboard. She pulled out the enormous painting. She tore off the brown paper that covered the frame and canvas and then stepped back.

A life size portrait of herself, sitting in the courtyard at the Hotel della Luna et Stelli, with the bright magenta bougainvillea in the background, stared back at her. Franco had painted her wearing the green dress that matched her eyes. She examined the painting further, and was amazed at the detail. He'd even remembered to dot on the small freckles that appeared on her arms and hands when she spent too much time in the sun.

Her hands. What was that on her hand? Christina looked closer. Wrapped around the ring finger of her left hand was the exquisite diamond and ruby ring she'd seen his grandmother wearing in the portrait that hung in the hotel.

A rush of emotions swept through her. She continued to stare at the painting. Franco's signature decorated the lower right hand corner. Above it was a small inscription. She looked closer. Tears pooled in her eyes.

He'd painted a small phrase with careful brushstrokes: 'Will you marry me?'

It was signed: 'Love, Franco.'

Printed in the United States
6685